The hard body proved very distracting.
"Do the ladies you know carry weapons, Sheriff?"

"We're fixin' to find out."

His silky voice did things to her insides that she couldn't recall having ever experienced with her late fiancé. "I don't have a gun. I told you I want to learn how to shoot."

His gaze slid down her body, then back up to meet her eyes. "Do you want me to search you?"

She gasped. "You wouldn't dare!"

"I will if you don't show me what you've got hidden."

"What kind of man are you that you would put your hands on me?"

"The kind who wants an answer," he said hotly. "Now, either show me or I'll get it myself."

The thrill that shot through her veins told Josie she did not want this man touching her. She instinctively knew she wouldn't forget it…!

* * *

Whirlwind Groom
Harlequin Historical #738—January 2005

Praise for new Harlequin Historical author Debra Cowan's previous titles

"Penning great emotional depth in her characters, Debra Cowan will warm the coldest of winter nights."
—*Romantic Times* on *Still the One*

"Debra Cowan skillfully brings to vivid life all the complicated feelings of love and guilt when a moment of consolation turns into unexpected passion."
—*Romantic Times* on *One Silent Night*

"The recurrent humor and vivid depiction of small-town Western life make Debra Cowan's story thoroughly pleasurable."
—*Romantic Times* on *The Matchmaker*

Whirlwind Groom

DEBRA COWAN

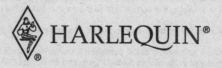

HARLEQUIN®

TORONTO • NEW YORK • LONDON
AMSTERDAM • PARIS • SYDNEY • HAMBURG
STOCKHOLM • ATHENS • TOKYO • MILAN • MADRID
PRAGUE • WARSAW • BUDAPEST • AUCKLAND

ISBN 0-373-29338-0

WHIRLWIND GROOM

Copyright © 2005 by Debra S. Cowan

www.eHarlequin.com

Printed in U.S.A.

To guys in white hats.

Chapter One

West Texas, 1884

Today was the day and Josie Webster's nerves were as twitchy as fat on a hot skillet. In the building September heat, she watched the jail of Whirlwind, Texas, and waited for her chance. Only a minute or so now, and she would have it.

Covered by shadows, she stood across the street from the sheriff's office. The alleyway between the livery stable and saloon was warm, but at least out of the sun. Main Street, wide enough for two wagons to travel at once, bustled as people made their way through town for supplies or business. On the east end of town toward Abilene, a church at the center point of Main and North Street served as the school and had opened its doors to students almost two hours ago. The telegraph and post office as well as the Whirlwind Hotel shared the same side of the street as the jail.

Three doors to her left a thin, older man swept the porch in front of Haskell's General Store. Directly across from her was the blacksmithy. No one paid a lick of attention to her.

Heart hammering in her chest, she patted the scalpel

tucked inside the special sleeve she'd sewn into her bodice. Her doctor father had taught her and her mother how to use the instrument as a weapon after an attack by an old beau had nearly gotten her mother raped. The blade was a reassuring reminder that Josie would never be at the mercy of a killer like the one who sat in the jailhouse across from her.

Nearly two years ago, Ian McDougal had murdered her parents and fiancé in Galveston. Because of a corrupt judge, the outlaw had walked away without spending one night in jail. He and his brothers had resumed their killing spree throughout Texas. When the other three had been killed a few months ago in a shoot-out near Whirlwind, Ian had escaped. He had finally been captured near Austin by a U.S. Marshal. Now he awaited trial in this small town hundreds of miles from Josie's home.

She had arrived the end of August, and in the four days since she had reached this breezy dry town on the other side of the vast state, she constantly felt parched, her throat gravelly. The stark air was quite a contrast to the thick, liquid air of her home on the Gulf.

So far, Whirlwind's sheriff had followed the schedule Josie had observed the past few days. He had already finished his first cup of coffee, taken the prisoner out to relieve himself in the outhouse behind the jail and whittled something. Now it was time for the sheriff to leave his deputy in charge and go over to the Pearl Restaurant for the piece of pie he had every morning at nine-forty-five.

After distracting the deputy, she would be in and out of that jail before the sheriff finished his pie. Then she would finally be able to rest easy for the first time since the cold-blooded murders of her parents and fiancé, William Hill.

As the second hand on her watch clicked into place, the jail door opened and the sheriff stepped out. His fawn-colored cowboy hat didn't hide the rugged lines of his face or the strong profile. He probably wasn't more than eight or nine years older than Josie's own twenty-one years and he looked like a man who could easily talk a girl out of her drawers. He was handsome in a powerful way with a disarming smile that might be able to tempt her to forget serious things and enjoy herself.

Thank goodness she *wasn't* tempted. All she cared about was the lower-than-snake-spit murderer inside Whirlwind's jail. For the past four days, she had seethed as the sheriff took a leisurely stroll after his morning break before going back to his office. Impatience prodded at her, but she wanted to do this right. McDougal was in jail just waiting for her and he wouldn't have to wait much longer.

The lanky sheriff sauntered down the steps, his boots finally touching dirt. A breath eased out of Josie, releasing some of the pressure squeezing her chest. The man paused, one thumb hooked in the waistband of his denims, one resting on the butt end of a gun strapped to his lean hips.

Go. Go on, she urged silently, her pulse spiking. She still had to get past the deputy, but that wouldn't be hard.

The sheriff adjusted his hat, lifted a hand in greeting to the giant black man hammering an anvil at the smithy next door to the jail then turned toward the restaurant at his right.

But he didn't head for the Pearl as she had expected. Instead he went the other way and started across the wide main street…straight for her!

His gaze narrowed on her like a gun sight. Her breath backed up in her throat. She would have run, but he had already seen her. Hightailing it out of there would only make him suspicious. She had no idea what she was about to do, but she had better come up with something.

When had he spotted her? This morning or before? She had thought herself well concealed and inconspicuous in the shadowy alley.

As the sheriff neared, she pasted a smile on her face. Her stomach shriveled into a knot.

"Howdy, ma'am." He stopped inches away.

Her gaze crept up from dusty boots over long, *long* legs, lean hips and a massive chest to blue eyes. She hoped she was still smiling. "Hello."

"I couldn't help but notice you over here." Davis Lee Holt tipped his hat, keeping his tone easy even though his senses were on full alert. That wasn't due strictly to the petite beauty in front of him. Or the stunning green eyes studying him so warily. "Is everything okay?"

"Yes, fine. I'm...new in town."

He recalled seeing her get off the stage four days ago. He had waited and watched to see what she was up to, but he wasn't waiting anymore. Last night, Ian McDougal had tried to escape.

The man had tuberculosis. Davis Lee had known of the condition even before Catherine Donnelly, now his cousin-in-law, had been forced several months ago by the oldest McDougal to use her nursing skills to ease Ian's discomfort. Last night, the outlaw, the only living gang member, had been seized by a coughing fit. When Davis Lee's sometime-deputy, Cody Tillman, had seen blood and gone inside the cell to help him, McDougal tried to overpower the man. The prisoner was too weak and Cody had subdued him soon enough, but the attempt had immediately made Davis Lee's thoughts go to the brunette who had started skulking around town four days ago.

He flicked a glance at the swinging doors of Pete Carter's saloon, which now also served as the stage stop. "Are you waitin' on Pete?"

"Pete?"

Her accent was thick and honey-sweet. "He owns the saloon. Thought you might have business with him."

"Lands, no. I'm a dressmaker."

A dressmaker? That wasn't in the least threatening, so why were his nerves twanging like new barbed wire? Why was she standing next to the saloon for the fourth day in a row?

He couldn't ignore the pinch in his gut that told him the woman had some connection to Ian McDougal. His sweetheart maybe? Sister or some other relative? Davis Lee thumbed back his hat and asked pleasantly, ''You just passin' through, or are you thinkin' about stayin'? Whirlwind could use a dressmaker. We don't have one right now.''

''I suppose you know everyone in town.'' She worried her lower lip.

''Yes, ma'am. And I watch the stage every day so I'll know who might need a hand. I saw you get off the stage four days ago.''

Her eyes widened and he thought he saw a flicker of concern. Why? Had he interfered with something she planned to do?

''You remember seeing me get off the stage? That's quite a memory, Sheriff.''

''It's part of my job.'' The fact was a man didn't forget a face as pretty as hers. Especially a man who'd been made a fool of by a pretty face.

Her figure drew attention, too. She was small and perfectly proportioned. He had always favored a fuller bosom on a woman, but he found himself reconsidering that. Her pale green daydress fit just right, the square-necked bodice smoothing over small, high breasts and sleeking down a taut waist. His palms suddenly itched to touch and he tugged at his hat.

In the two years since he had been run out of Rock River and returned home, Davis Lee had taken to watching every passenger on every stage. He wouldn't be taken unaware again.

Ever since that unfortunate incident in his last town,

Davis Lee erred on the side of caution. He would've noticed this woman anyway because of her slender curves and air of confidence, but now he had a reason to keep an eye on her.

Maybe she had come to break McDougal out of jail or to provide a distraction while one of McDougal's cronies sawed the bars from his cell window and helped him escape.

Davis Lee knew all about distractions, and he wasn't falling for this one, no matter that she looked sweeter than fresh cream and smelled as tempting as rain. Her skin flushed in a way that made him wonder if she turned that delicious shade of pink all over in the right circumstances.

Annoyed at his line of thinking, he removed his hat and offered his hand. "I'm Davis Lee Holt."

"Josie. Webster." Though she accepted his handshake, she seemed to give the information reluctantly.

The name she gave was the same one she used at the Whirlwind Hotel. Davis Lee had already been there and checked the register on the sly so the clerk wouldn't know. The last thing he needed was Penn Wavers blabbing. The near-deaf man was as big a gossip as any old woman. "You stayin' at the Whirlwind?"

"For now. I'm thinking about opening a shop, but I heard about the outlaws around here."

Her lips curved in an innocent, blinding smile and Davis Lee felt like he'd been kicked in the head. He slid his hat back on. "Is your family with you?"

"I'm alone."

Which told him nothing. Her short, light-colored gloves prevented him from seeing if she wore a wedding ring. Was she married? Did she have children? Usually any small prod for information caused people to talk, especially women. Those who didn't have anything to hide anyway.

She gave a small curtsy and stepped around him so that she now stood out in the open.

The mid-morning sun brought out a red tint in her brown hair, which she wore pulled away from her face with a ribbon so that the thick wavy mass tumbled down her back. Her velvety-looking skin had a slight golden cast; a bunch of freckles were scattered across the bridge of her nose.

She was the prettiest baggage he'd seen in a good long while. Since Betsy—or whatever her real name was—in Rock River, truth be told. The memory of the woman who'd stolen Davis Lee's heart and half the townspeople's money squashed the interest sparked by Josie Webster.

She eyed the street. "I thought I should find out for myself if this town is safe."

"I take my job very seriously." He wondered what secrets she hid behind those pretty green eyes, because he was sure she had some. "I can't provide individual protection for everyone, but my deputy and I do a pretty good job. We had some trouble a while back with the McDougals, but that's over now."

Thanks to a U.S. Marshal named Waterson Calhoun, Ian McDougal had been captured near Austin and now sat in jail waiting to get what was coming to him. Since Davis Lee didn't know if Miz Webster had told the truth about why she was in Whirlwind, he saw no reason to tell her that the sole survivor of the outlaw gang was locked up snug across the street.

"Your...diligence is reassuring," she said without meeting his gaze. "I do like what I've seen of the town so far. If I decide to stay, I'd want to feel safe."

"We all do, ma'am. Three of the McDougals are dead, but I heard the last one has been locked up somewhere."

"That makes me feel better."

He carefully searched her face for some sign that she knew the outlaw, that she had more than a passing interest in the man. "You said you were from Austin?"

"No, Galveston," she replied easily.

She hadn't said at all, but Davis Lee knew from the automatic way she'd responded that she was probably telling the truth. He also noticed the irritation that flared in her eyes when she gave the information.

"Thank you, Sheriff. You've put my mind at ease."

Funny, he thought she acted a trifle vexed. "If you need anything, don't hesitate to call on me. Like I said, Whirlwind could use a seamstress. Hope you stay."

She nodded, her gaze flicking past him to the jail for just a moment.

Was she afraid? Or was she trying to figure out how she could get inside to see Ian McDougal? If she were, she'd have to go through Davis Lee first. "I don't think you'll have anything to worry about in Whirlwind."

"Thank you." She bid him good day and stepped up on the saloon's landing, making her way down the walk toward Haskell's General Store.

Watching the inviting sway of her hips, he stroked his chin. Maybe Miz Josie Webster's only concern truly was about moving to Whirlwind. Maybe she *had* been watching the town to reassure herself about its safety.

His eyes narrowed. Yessir, and cows had wings.

Chapter Two

The sheriff was going to be a problem, Josie fumed as she ducked inside Haskell's General Store just to escape the hard gaze boring into her back. A thin man, only about six inches taller than her five-foot-three, was showing a customer to the boots in the far corner of the store. Although she took in the colorful bolts of fabric, barrels of nails and a stack of wooden tubs around her, her mind was on Davis Lee Holt.

She burned to march back to him and demand he give Ian McDougal over to her, but she knew that would be futile. In the past two years, her faith in the law had been shaken. Or perhaps she had simply had her eyes opened.

The fact that Ian McDougal had run out of her house and smack into her after killing her parents and fiancé had been dismissed out of hand. Despite the attorney and sheriff who knew she told the truth, Judge Shelton Horn had declared her testimony wasn't enough to convene a trial for the murderer. But the real reason the judge had let McDougal walk away was because he had never gotten over the fact that Josie's mother had chosen her father over him all those years ago.

The thought of the people Josie had loved and lost tightened her chest. And the prospect of having to deal with Whirlwind's lawman settled a sick feeling in the pit of her stomach. Sheriff Holt threw her off balance. She had never planned on telling him about Galveston and yet she'd been so confounded when he walked right up to her that she had blurted out where she was from the instant he asked.

She certainly couldn't watch the jail from that alley anymore so she had to find another place. And if Holt kept interfering, she would have to stay in Whirlwind a lot longer than she had planned.

She had to be extremely careful next time, but she had every intention of getting access to Ian McDougal.

Then killing him.

Up close Sheriff Holt was rugged and compelling and one of the most handsome men she'd ever seen. It wasn't hard to imagine that his blue eyes would go razor sharp if he were crossed. And the stubborn jaw told her that the man could intimidate if he chose, tin star or no tin star.

Surely the sheriff was gone by now. She edged between a wooden crate full of brooms and a barrel of pickles. The strong smell of brine reached her as she peeked out the wide front window of the general store. When she didn't see the tall, lanky lawman, she left and started across the street for the Whirlwind Hotel. Another hotel, still under construction, stood at the other end of town, but Josie would've chosen the Whirlwind anyway because of its view of the jail.

Halting for a passing wagon, she mentally calculated the money stashed in her hidden skirt pocket. Being as good a seamstress as her mother, Josie had taken on Virginia Webster's customers after her mother's death so she had money to pay for her stay at the hotel. But she didn't know how long she might need to stay. She had to keep back a good part of her money for when she finished with McDougal and fled town.

Sunlight glittered off the windows of the town's businesses. Josie shaded her eyes as she continued across the street, angling away from the jail and toward the hotel three buildings away.

How was she going to keep an eye on the outlaw now that she knew the sheriff was keeping an eye on *her?* Her spot in the alley had been perfect, but thanks to Holt, she couldn't go back there.

She had passed the telegraph and post office when an idea hit her. Stepping back a few feet into the street, she peered up at the hotel then shifted her gaze to the jail.

Smiling, her heels clicking against the planked porch, Josie hurried into the hotel and approached the long waxed wood counter.

Penn Wavers, the elderly clerk, slumped in a chair in the corner, snoring. Josie knew the gangly man was nearly deaf so she stomped on the floor, hoping the vibrations would wake him if her loud voice didn't. "Mr. Wavers!"

"Huh?" His head drooped and he bolted upright, his long white hair flying. He blinked a couple of times as he stepped to the counter. "Oh, hello, miss."

"It looks like I'll be staying longer than I planned. I wonder if I might get a different room? Maybe one on the west side and closer to the front of the hotel?"

"Is there something wrong?" Age filmed his blue eyes, but they were kind. "If so, I'll fix it."

"No, sir. Nothing like that." She smiled. "It's just that I'm a dressmaker and since I have to sit for such long periods, I like to watch the sights. It relieves the tedium."

"I've been told it's louder in those front rooms. Wouldn't you rather have something else?"

"I don't mind the noise. I'm used to it, being from Galveston and all. I'm a little homesick."

"Well, miss, I don't mind moving you, but those rooms cost a little extra."

"Even though they're noisier?"

"They're a mite bigger," he explained apologetically.

More money? She had brought a few pieces of sewing from Galveston to finish up for some of her mother's regular customers, but she wouldn't be paid until she delivered the items. What would she do after that? She stared out the window, finally registering that the curtain hanging there was faded and worn.

"What would you think about making a bargain with me, Mr. Wavers?"

"What kind of barn?"

"No, a bargain," she said louder.

"Oh, a bargain." He eyed her for a moment. "What did you have in mind?"

"A west room closer to the front of the hotel in exchange for new curtains."

He glanced at the faded calico drooping limply at the two large front windows. "If I buy the fabric, would you be willing to make some new tablecloths for the dining hall, too?"

That would be perfect! She pretended to consider.

He leaned in. "You could trade that for room and meals, as well."

Her one meal here, cooked by Mrs. Wavers, had been delicious. "All right, you've got a deal."

They shook on it, both smiling.

Mr. Wavers reached into a pigeonhole beneath the counter and handed her a key to her new room. "When can you start on those curtains?"

"Today if you like. Would you like me to pick out the fabric or would you like to do it?"

"I'll leave that to you. The tablecloths, too."

"Should I ask Mrs. Wavers if she has a preference as to color?"

"She can't tell blue from green." He gestured at Josie's

well-fitted cotton daydress. "Besides, you seem to know what you're doing. I think she'd agree."

"Wonderful! I'll move my things then pick out something at Haskell's."

"I'll go tell Charlie to put whatever you need on the hotel's account. This will work out mighty fine."

"I think so, too."

"You must like Whirlwind if you're planning to stay."

"It seems like a nice place." She glanced out the window, half expecting to find Sheriff Holt staring back at her. "I met the sheriff today. He seems…pleasant. What is he like?"

"Heh." Mr. Wavers peered at her. "You sweet on him?"

"No! Nothing like that." Just because she got a shiver when thinking of those piercing blue eyes did not mean she was sweet on him. She simply wanted to know what she was up against. "I'm…curious."

"He's a fine man. Had his share of troubles, but who hasn't?"

Josie nodded, wondering what troubles the lawman had experienced. He had plainly wanted to know if she were married; she wondered the same about him. Perhaps his coming over to her only meant he was dedicated about doing his job, but Josie knew she couldn't let down her guard around him.

"Thank you for letting me switch rooms, Mr. Wavers," she said in a raised voice. "I'll go move my things."

She patted his hand and headed upstairs, smiling broadly.

Between the sewing she had brought to finish and the new curtains and tablecloths for the hotel, she would be busier than a one-armed bank robber. She needed to work quickly on the hotel's items since she didn't know how soon she would be leaving.

But for now she could watch the jail from her new room without attracting notice. When the time was right, she would make sure Ian McDougal saw justice. And that handsome sheriff wasn't going to get in her way.

It had been two days since Davis Lee had seen Josie Webster's pretty little hide in the alley. Since he'd seen her *anywhere*. So where was she? Was she still watching his jail? In case she was, he had taken the precaution of rearranging his schedule, which had caused him to miss his hot pie. If she had left town using the stage or a rig rented from the livery, he would've known.

Either she had left town by some other means or she was up to something. Intending to find out which, he shackled McDougal to the bars of his cell before going outside and locking the door to his office. He walked a slow but thorough path through town. No sign of her. When she'd left him the other day she had slipped into Haskell's, so Davis Lee made the general store his last stop before the hotel. Maybe Charlie had seen her.

Davis Lee walked into the store, catching the sweet tang of apples as he said hello to Cal Doyle's wife, Lizzie, who was leaving.

Charlie Haskell stood behind the scratched wooden counter, polishing his spectacles. The store owner was small-framed and spare. "Morning, Davis Lee. What can I do for you today?"

Mitchell Orr, Charlie's eighteen-year-old nephew who helped in the store and kept the books, ducked through the faded blue curtain separating the store from the back office. He was dressed just as his uncle in dark trousers and a white shirt with suspenders. His wiry arms held several bolts of white fabric and a red, blue and yellow calico. "Hello, Sheriff."

"Hey, Mitchell." Davis Lee greeted the blond-haired boy before speaking to his uncle. "Just had a question, Charlie.

A woman came in here the other day. She's new to town. Has brown or well, maybe brownish-red hair—''

"You mean that pretty little thing who's staying at the Whirlwind Hotel?'' Charlie peered at him over the top of his glasses, his brown eyes sparking with interest.

Mitchell stopped at the edge of the counter. "Josie Webster?'' he asked eagerly.

Davis Lee figured that a hundred unfamiliar women could have paraded through Haskell's General Store, and Charlie and Mitchell would've known Josie. They weren't likely to forget that heart-shaped face or that creamy skin. Or the graceful curves that made a man crazy to put his hands on her. He sure hadn't been able to forget. "Yeah, that's her.''

"She's been in a couple of times,'' Mitchell offered.

"When was the last time y'all saw her?''

Charlie thought for a minute.

"She was in yesterday for more thread,'' the younger man said.

"And the day before to buy fabric for the hotel,'' Charlie added. "She's making new curtains and tablecloths for Penn and Esther.''

"Is that right?'' So it appeared she had decided to stay, at least for a while. Did that decision have anything to do with Ian McDougal?

Mitchell nodded at his burden. "This is the rest of the fabric Miss Webster ordered. We didn't have all she needed so I had to go over to Abilene. I about cleaned out that store.'' He edged his way out from behind the counter. "I'll take this over to her at the hotel, Uncle. Won't be long.''

"Hold up there, Mitchell.'' Davis Lee stepped in front of him. "I already have to stop by the hotel. I'd be happy to deliver that for you.''

"Oh, I don't mind.''

"Since I'm already going there, it won't put me out.'' He didn't need an excuse to talk to her, but delivering the fabric provided him with a better chance of getting into her room, seeing if he could find anything to confirm his suspicions about her.

Charlie motioned for his nephew to give the cloth to Davis Lee. "She in some kind of trouble?"

"No." She *is* trouble. And he aimed to find out how much. He took the stack from the boy, who looked disappointed. "Just saving you a trip."

"If I were twenty years younger, I'd take it myself." Charlie chuckled. "Can't say as I blame you, Sheriff."

Davis Lee grinned, not bothering to correct the man's assumption that he was romantically interested in Josie Webster.

A few minutes later, Davis Lee stood at the hotel's registration desk, loaded down with four bolts of fabric. "Penn, I've got a delivery here for Miz Webster," he said loudly. "Is she here?"

"I believe so." The man's wizened features creased in a smile. "You working for Charlie now, Sheriff?"

"Just helping out."

"She's in room 214."

"Thanks." Davis Lee started up the scratched pine staircase, his boots scuffing the freshly swept wood.

"No, no, that's not right, Sheriff," Penn said. "She's not in that room anymore."

Halfway up the staircase, Davis Lee turned.

"She's in room 200 now. I forgot she asked to move a couple of days ago."

"Why would she do that?"

"Said she wanted a room at the front of the hotel so she could have a view while she sewed."

Davis Lee's eyes narrowed. That was why he hadn't seen her in the alley since that encounter a couple of days ago. Since he already thought she was hiding something, this news made him even more determined to find out what.

"Thanks, Penn. I'll get this stuff up to her." He reached the top of the second-story landing and turned to the right, going down the hall until he got to the last room. A room he knew had a bird's-eye view of town. And his jail.

She answered his knock right away, her eyes widening when she opened the door. "Sheriff!"

He couldn't tell if it was surprise or dismay he heard in her voice.

Her hair was down, sliding around her shoulders in a silky curtain of rich brown with a shy touch of red. She recovered, her green eyes cool and unreadable. "You have my fabric."

"I told Charlie I'd deliver it since I was coming over anyway." He'd forgotten just how deeply green her eyes were. And how tiny her waist.

She stared at him for a minute. Long enough for her sweet, fresh scent—honeysuckle?—to slide into his lungs. Long enough for him to deduce by the way her lavender skirts clung to her legs that she wasn't wearing petticoats. At least not more than one. A heat he hadn't felt in a long time worked its way under his skin.

He cleared his throat. "You want me to put this down somewhere?"

She blinked. "Yes. Sorry. Come in."

She opened the door wider and he walked inside, noting she left the door open. Which was a good thing seeing as how he had also just determined she wasn't wearing a corset, either.

"I— You can just put them on the bed." Her voice was breathy.

Davis Lee walked over to the neatly made bed that was pushed into the far corner of the room. Two lengths of fabric, one white and one calico, were folded neatly at its foot. He laid the new bolts next to them.

The room was bigger than most of the others in the hotel, but not grand by any means. On the wall beside the bed was a plain dressing table with a wall mirror and washbasin. A waist-high dresser backed against the wall across from the foot of the bed. The middle and right side of the room was empty except for a length of calico spread across the floor. A pair of scissors lay on top as if her cutting had been interrupted. A chair sat at the partially open window facing town.

He didn't have to walk over there to confirm that she had a clear and close view of the jail, but he did. A short lacy curtain hung at the top of the window and he ducked his head to keep it out of his eyes. Yep, sure enough, this window provided a direct view to the jail. And anyone going in or out.

"Uh, thank you for bringing the fabric. You certainly didn't have to do that. I'm sure you have things you need to get back to."

The shimmer of unease in her voice had him leaning one shoulder against the window frame as if he had all day to spend. So far he hadn't seen anything in here except fabric and furniture. And her. "You gettin' settled in?"

"Yes." She offered him a tentative smile, staying over by the door.

Her gaze dropped to his badge and he got the distinct impression she was wishing him gone. "Penn said you changed rooms."

"I— Yes." She gave a stiff laugh. "I wouldn't think that would merit him giving a report to the sheriff."

"He just mentioned it. Any reason why he shouldn't?"

Her gaze searched his, her fingers tangling in the folds of her skirt. "Of course not."

He hooked a thumb into the front pocket of his trousers. "Interesting that you would want to move."

"I don't know why." She shrugged, leaving the door to walk over and snatch a lavender ribbon from the top of the dresser. She pulled her hair back and secured it with jerky movements.

He tried to ignore the way her bodice pulled taut across her breasts. "It's noisier in this part of the hotel."

Her chin angled slightly. He had obviously come for a reason besides delivering her fabric. "I like noise."

"You've got a view of the whole town from here." His gaze slid down her body then back up, his eyes glinting.

Under his hot scrutiny, her pulse hitched. "I—I like to have something to look at while I'm working."

He stroked his chin. "Like me."

"I did not change rooms to watch *you!*"

He grinned and she felt a slow pull in her belly. "I meant I like to have a view while I'm working, too."

"Oh." Heat flushed her face. The man flustered her six ways to Sunday. And he was entirely too amused.

She wanted to get his handsome self out of here. "I hardly see what you find so fascinating about the whole subject."

"Don't you?" he asked softly.

That set off a flurry of panic in her stomach and it wasn't due strictly to the fact that he might know the real reason she had moved into a room overlooking the jail.

Curling her fingers into her damp palms, she asked tartly, "Is changing hotel rooms against the law, Sheriff? Are you planning to haul me to jail?"

His gaze moved slowly, leisurely over her as if he found the prospect appealing. "If I did, I'd have to put you in a cell next to my prisoner. Which wouldn't be good."

"No, it wouldn't." She bit back the temper that threatened, her nerves snapping. She moved to the open door, not caring if she appeared rude. "If that's all, I really have a lot of work to do."

He started toward her, moving with a smooth grace for such a large man. His gaze swept the fabric that lay on the floor, then the bed. "It appears you'll be busy for quite a while."

"Yes," she murmured, her hand tight on the doorknob.

He definitely unsettled her. She told herself it was because of the suspicion in his eyes. Not because they were alone in her room with only a deaf old man downstairs if she needed help.

Davis Lee stopped at the door, close enough that his shirt-sleeve brushed hers. Her fresh scent teased him, bringing to mind the last time he'd purposely gone to a woman's room. It had been over two years, but not long enough to make him forget how a pretty face and sultry eyes could hide betrayal and lies. "If you need anything, Miz Webster, you just holler out that window. I'm sure I'll be able to hear you."

"Yes, all right. Thank you."

Tension bowed her shoulders and he could feel her urging him out the door. Even though he didn't like the way his body tightened at her nearness, he grinned and tipped his hat. "Good day, ma'am."

She mumbled goodbye and nearly closed the door on the heel of his boot.

He gave her door one last look. Yeah, she was definitely up to something.

Three days passed before Josie felt confident enough to make another try at McDougal. Since the sheriff had been to her room, she had been careful to do her spying as discreetly as she could, keeping to the corner of the window.

Holt had changed his schedule, but now that she had this view of the jail, she wasn't concerned. She could usually tell how long he would stay somewhere depending on where he went. He was wont to linger at the Pearl Restaurant and Ef Gerard's blacksmithy.

On Saturday afternoon, she stood at the window's edge,

drumming her sewing-sore fingers on the wall of her hotel room as she waited for the sheriff to leave the jail. She had worked from dawn until dark every day to finish the hotel's curtains and they now hung one story below in the front windows. The length for one tablecloth had been cut, but her mind wasn't on the task.

There! She saw the sheriff leave the jail and go into the restaurant. She hurried downstairs, wondering where he lived. He didn't sleep every night at the jail, and on those nights his deputy stayed there. Once outside, she ducked around to the back of the hotel and made her way behind the telegraph and post office, then the Pearl. Rounding the corner of the restaurant, she sidled up the west wall and peered out at the street.

A few people milled about, but Josie didn't see the sheriff.

She stepped into the open and tried to be casual as she walked to the hitching post in front of the jail where the deputy had left his horse. He had arrived a few minutes before Sheriff Holt left.

The air was pleasantly warm today, but that wasn't the cause of the dampness forming between her breasts. Pausing as if to admire the bay mare who stood placidly, Josie slid her fingers into the looped reins and loosened the leather before she moved away. She passed two older women then ducked into the alley between the jail and the blacksmithy.

Making sure there was no one nearby, Josie threw a stone and hit the horse square on the hock of its left rear leg. The mare nickered and shied away, pulling the reins loose from the hitching post. Dancing into the street, she trotted off.

A second later, Josie heard the jail door open and bang against the wall. Boots thudded down the wooden steps.

"Dad burn it!"

The young, broad-shouldered deputy whom she'd seen with Whirlwind's sheriff thundered past her, putting two fingers in his mouth and letting out a shrill whistle. The mare kept going; the man followed.

Josie checked the opposite direction then hurried up the steps and slipped inside the jail. Sheriff Holt's office smelled faintly of soap and pine. Wood shavings littered the floor around the leg of a wide oak desk.

Her gaze paused on a creased Wanted poster boasting Ian McDougal's face. The paper was tacked onto an otherwise-blank space of wall behind the desk. Three shotguns lined up behind the glass door of a tall gun cabinet. A door in the opposite corner led into a back room. The cells had to be back there.

Her heart hammering in her chest, she reached into her bodice for the scalpel. Knowing McDougal was only feet away had her throat closing up. Doubt slashed through her. Could she really do this?

She closed her eyes and conjured up the last images she had of her parents and William. Their sightless eyes had been trained on the ceiling of her home. Blood spattered the floor and the door. They had died horribly. Her family deserved justice. Yes, she could do this.

Taking a deep breath and sliding her sweaty palm down to a more comfortable position on the thin, ridged handle, she started toward the raspy whistling coming from the back room. It was McDougal. She knew it.

The murdering bastard was finally going to pay for killing everyone she had loved.

She gripped the scalpel so hard the steel gouged into her palm. All she had to do was get close to him.

She reached the door, her steps faltering at the thought of facing the worthless, no-account cur. She reminded herself of the nearly two years she had spent in the Galveston County sheriff's office checking every day to see if McDougal had been captured.

Her heartbeat hammering in her ears, she gripped the doorknob.

"What do you think you're doing?"

The now-familiar voice coming from behind her lashed her already-raw nerves and she nearly dropped the scalpel. No! She quickly slipped the blade into the hidden pocket of her bodice and turned with a bright smile on her face, praying Holt couldn't see her heart banging against her ribs. "Hello, Sheriff. I was looking for you."

"Is that so?" He pushed his hat back and planted his hands on lean hips. His eyes narrowed as he glanced about the empty room. "Where's my deputy?"

"No one was here when I came in." That wasn't a lie, but still her pulse raced.

"There was a commotion outside so I went to check on it." He closed the front door and moved toward her, his boots ominously soft on the pine floor. Worn denim sleeked down his long legs. The chambray shirt he wore looked brand-spanking new. "You must have heard it, too."

"Yes. It sounded like someone was leaving town in a hurry."

"Weren't you just the tiniest bit curious about what was going on?"

Oh, dear. He looked fit to be tied. His eyes had turned a dark stormy blue, suspicious and hard. She refused to panic. She'd dealt with this man—this *big* man—before. And she was prepared this time. "Like I said, I was looking for you."

"There's a prisoner back there, Miz Webster." He inclined his head toward the door behind her. "It's not a good idea for you to be in here alone."

She glanced over her shoulder. "I guess not."

Despite the day's heat, she wished she hadn't forgotten her gloves. Her hands were clammy and shaking awfully.

"You said you were looking for me?" Holt stepped

around her to check the door, once more between her and McDougal.

"Oh, yes." She cleared her throat. "I wonder if you might know someone who can teach me to shoot?"

"To shoot?"

"Yes. You know, a gun."

Irritation crossed his features as he moved to stand in front of her again. "I didn't think you meant a slingshot."

"Well?" She hoped he would believe she had come to the jail only for this reason.

He crossed his arms and studied her. "I just can't figure you, Miz Webster."

"What do you mean?"

"I think your being in my jail has something to do with Ian McDougal."

"Sheriff!" the prisoner yelled. "What's going on out there?"

Josie stiffened. She did not want the outlaw to see her. Or know she was here until *she* chose.

"Just talkin' to a visitor." Sheriff Holt edged closer, causing her to step away. "What do you say, Miz Webster?"

"About what?" She could barely get the words out through her tight throat.

"You seem fascinated with my prisoner," he said softly. "Why is that?"

"I'm not." She clenched one fist in the folds of her skirt and tried to look curious rather than nervous. "Are you saying your prisoner is one of the McDougal gang? You didn't tell me that the other day."

"Don't recall you askin', but I think you already know he is." Holt advanced again, forcing her against the wall. "Are you his sweetheart?"

"No!" The thought made her stomach seize up. She

scooted down the wall in front of him, but he shifted his large body, trapping her against the door.

"A relative? His sister maybe?"

"Absolutely not." How could he think her related to that murdering criminal? "I've heard about the things he and his brothers have done. I don't appreciate being referred to as part of their family."

"Well, I don't appreciate being lied to and I think that's what you're doing."

"I never!"

"What were you hiding when I walked in?"

"Hiding? Nothing. I—"

He leaned in and she pressed her shoulder blades flat against the wood at her back. Holt planted a hand on either side of her. "Something up your sleeve? A derringer maybe? A file? Some kind of weapon?"

She struggled to keep her composure though the hard warmth of his body proved very distracting. "Do the ladies you know carry weapons, Sheriff?"

"We're fixin' to find out."

His silky voice did things to her insides that she couldn't recall having ever experienced with William. "Derringer? I don't have a gun. I told you I want to learn how to shoot."

His gaze slid down her body then back up to meet her eyes. "Do you want me to search you?"

She gasped. "You wouldn't dare!"

"I will if you don't show me what you've got hidden."

"What kind of man are you that you would put your hands on me?"

"The kind who wants an answer," he said hotly. "Now either show me or I'll get it myself."

The thrill that shot through her veins told Josie she did not want this man touching her. She instinctively knew she wouldn't forget it.

A clanging sounded from the other room. "Sheriff, I'm thirsty."

"Shut up." Though Holt spoke to the prisoner, he never took his eyes off Josie.

She realized the noise of metal on metal was the sound of McDougal banging a tin cup or plate against the bars.

The sheriff dipped his head a fraction, his breath soft against her temple. She smelled leather and soap and man. "What's it gonna be?"

Showing him her scalpel proved nothing, Josie told herself. She angled her chin, hoping he couldn't see how she trembled all over. "Very well. I do have a weapon. I'll get it."

She dipped a hand inside her square-necked gingham bodice.

The sheriff drew back, eyes widening. "What are you doin'?"

"Getting my weapon." If she weren't so rattled, she might have laughed at the expression on his face—half anticipation, half stone-cold fear that she might expose herself.

She pulled the blade from between her breasts and saw his eyes darken. Not with curiosity or surprise, but with raw, hot desire. Her stomach did a slow drop to her feet.

"What—" he cleared his throat "—the heck is that?"

The fire in his gaze sent a tingle to her toes and she swallowed hard. "It's a scalpel."

"A doctor's instrument?"

She nodded.

"I thought you said you were a dressmaker."

"I am."

He frowned at the weapon's short silver blade. "You beat all, lady. What are you planning to do with that?"

"Defend myself." She pressed harder against the door, trying to escape the feel of his lean thighs, the warmth from his body. "My father was a doctor and he taught my mother and me how to use this."

"Then why do you need to learn how to shoot?"

"With the scalpel, I have to be really close to someone. Like I am to you."

He eased back slightly, frowning.

She tried not to smile. "But I have no defense if someone were to shoot at me."

"Just what can you do with that thing?"

"Stab it in someone's windpipe or eye. If I go deep enough, I can slice into this big vein here." She touched the side of her neck.

The sheriff eyed the scalpel warily. "You already seem plenty dangerous to me. I'm not sure that you having a gun is a good idea."

If she had known how to use a gun two years ago, her family might still be alive. "Are you saying you won't help me find a teacher?"

"Are you saying you've decided to make a home in Whirlwind?"

"Uh, yes." From the excruciatingly slow way her plan was progressing, she would have to. At this rate, she'd be a year older before she ever got to McDougal. "But Whirlwind seems less…civilized than Galveston. I would just feel safer if I knew how to use a gun."

"And you're going to open a dressmaker shop?"

She laughed lightly. "That's the only skill I have."

Holt stared at her for a long minute, his eyes hooded beneath his hat. "I'll teach you to shoot."

"*You?* But I thought—"

"Change your mind?"

"No." But maybe she should.

"Then I'll teach you. I'm good with guns and I can show you the proper way to handle them."

"Could you give me a lesson every day?" She needed to check on McDougal as often as possible.

"Sure, I can do that."

"Oh, good. Thank you, Sheriff Holt." Why was he so willing to help her? Her smile felt overly bright as she realized exactly what their deal meant.

He finally stepped back a few inches. "If we're going to see each other every day, you should call me Davis Lee."

"All right." She wouldn't. "I'll see you in the morning then, bright and early."

"Tomorrow is Sunday. I'll be in church. Won't you?"

She hesitated. She and her parents had regularly attended church in Galveston. It was the one place she had been able to find a small amount of peace after the murders. But she had come here to kill a man. "Church?"

"It's at the end of Main Street. You can't miss it."

"Oh, yes." She recalled the white frame building with the steeple, and a part of her wanted to be there tomorrow.

"I'll see you here on Monday then. Make it about six-thirty or seven in the evening. I'll have to get my other deputy, Jake, to guard the prisoner."

"All right. Monday." Tarnation!

She would be spending far more time with the sheriff than she wanted. Despite the opportunity she now had to wheedle information about McDougal out of the lawman, she had the uneasy sense that Holt had agreed to teach her to shoot for the very same reason she had asked—so he could keep an eye on her. She didn't like that at all.

Chapter Three

Why in the Sam Hill had Josie Webster been in his jail? Davis Lee was still chewing on that question the next morning during church. He knew exactly how she had managed to wind up in his office the minute he left it. And it was mighty suspicious that Jake's horse just *happened* to spook at the same time.

Davis Lee didn't know what to make of the woman. When she had pulled that scalpel out of her bodice, he'd nearly swallowed his teeth. The last thing he needed was to replay the image of her hand slipping between her breasts. He couldn't seem to stop it though he tried hard to focus instead on the doubts she raised in him.

Maybe he was suspicious because the first time he had seen Josie, desire had hit him hard and fast. He didn't trust such raw instant want. It had gotten him in a passel of trouble before and he wasn't giving in to it again. Still, he spent more time thinking about the intriguing brunette than Reverend Scoggins's sermon.

Catching her in his jail reinforced Davis Lee's certainty that she was up to something. Which was why he had gone straight to Ef and gotten a big padlock for McDougal's cell. One reason—the only reason—he had agreed to teach her to shoot was to see if she was comfortable with guns and knew how to handle them. The woman knew how to use a scalpel, for crying out loud. It was possible she knew how to use a gun, as well.

He had no proof, but he couldn't shake the feeling she had some connection to McDougal. Her request for shooting lessons had seemed too ready. Prepared almost.

After church he turned around and saw her rising from the back pew. The burn of desire he felt didn't surprise him, but the relief that she was here and not slipping inside his jail again did.

She stepped outside and started down the stairs, but the reverend stopped her. Keeping an eye on her, Davis Lee moved into the aisle as his brother, Riley, and his wife, Susannah, gathered up their baby. He greeted Cora Wilkes and her brother, Loren Barnes, who had come to Whirlwind about two months ago to help his widowed sister.

From the corner of his eye, Davis Lee saw Josie move down the steps then stop to speak to Pearl Anderson. This time he walked out on the landing and she glanced up. When their gazes locked, he nodded and met her at the bottom.

He greeted Pearl as she walked past him to speak to someone else, but his attention stayed on Josie.

"Sheriff," she said.

"Davis Lee." He smiled. The peach dress she wore accentuated her breasts and small waist. The color became her, warming her golden skin and deepening the green of her eyes. He couldn't help wondering if the deep-cut bodice filled with white pleating hid her scalpel. "Nice to see you, Miz Webster. Did you enjoy the service?"

"Yes, I did. Did you?"

She was about the same height as Susannah, and she was small. A small brown hat circled by a ribbon matching her dress sat jauntily on her head, crowning the mass of hair she'd worn up today. A tiny mole on her collarbone peeked out at him. "Reverend Scoggins always has something good to say."

A smile curved her lips. "That's the least committed answer I've ever heard, Sheriff."

He grinned, moving his gaze to her face. "I have to say I'm glad to see you here and not in my jail. Did you come to repent?"

She tilted her head, looking more serious than he'd seen before. "You're teasing me."

"Maybe. Are you still interested in your shooting lessons?"

"Oh, yes. I think it's something I should do."

"All right, then."

"You'll still teach me?"

"Yes." Having been hornswoggled before, Davis Lee knew he should keep a distance from her, but he needed to find out whatever he could about this woman.

Judging from his experience with her so far, he wouldn't get far by asking her questions, but he could learn plenty by observing her up close.

"Davis Lee, we're expecting you for lunch."

He turned at the sound of his sister-in-law's voice. "I'm looking forward to it, Susannah. We're not having biscuits, are we?"

Riley laughed as he walked up with his blond-haired daughter resting happily on his shoulder. Lorelai wasn't Riley's blood, but no one could tell him that. Davis Lee had never seen his brother love anyone as much as he loved that little girl and her mother.

"If you two don't behave, I *will* cook biscuits," Susannah said. "And I'll purposely make them hard as rocks."

Davis Lee chuckled. He liked his sister-in-law more every time he was around her. She and Riley had been married only about five months. For a while Davis Lee had wondered if the two hardheaded idiots would ever realize their feelings for one another.

Thanks to her brother, a pregnant Susannah had come to Whirlwind under the impression that Riley wanted to marry her, but he hadn't been the least bit interested. At first.

Davis Lee felt Josie step away and he turned to her. "Y'all need to meet one of our newest citizens. This is Josie Webster. Miz Webster, this is my brother Riley and his wife, Susannah."

"And our daughter, Lorelai." Susannah touched the baby's back with one hand as she shook Josie's hand warmly with the other. "It's nice to meet you."

"Hello." Josie gave a soft smile.

Riley smiled. "Have you just arrived in town?"

"About a week ago."

Davis Lee noticed she told the truth easily on that point. "Miz Webster is a dressmaker. She's going to open a shop here."

"You'd be very welcome," Susannah said.

"Thank you." Josie gave Davis Lee a small frown.

"You'd have no shortage of work if that concerns you." Susannah tucked a stray blond hair into her chignon. "In fact, Riley and Davis Lee's cousin, Jericho, is getting married in about a month and a half. His intended is planning to see a seamstress in Abilene about a new dress."

"I bet Miz Webster would be interested in the job. Wouldn't you?" Davis Lee practically dared her to say no.

Josie's lips flattened, hinting that she was trying hard to remain pleasant. "Perhaps you could refer me to her?"

Susannah pointed to Catherine Donnelly, a raven-haired woman who stood talking to the reverend with a husky young boy at her side.

Before she followed Susannah's gaze, Josie glared at Davis Lee. He could tell by the fire in her green eyes that she didn't like him poking his nose into her affairs.

Too bad. He wanted to get a bead on the woman who had given him the jolt of his life by pulling that weapon from her bodice.

"Let me go get her." Susannah hurried off and returned in a moment with the tall, slender woman. She introduced her to Josie then said, "Josie is a dressmaker."

Davis Lee watched with amusement. Before his little spy left church today, she might have enough work to keep her busy and out of his jail.

As the women agreed upon a time for Catherine to come by Josie's hotel room to discuss her wedding dress, Cora Wilkes and her brother joined them.

"Hello, everyone." The older woman, widowed almost a year ago when the McDougal gang murdered her husband, patted Davis Lee's arm and smiled at him and Riley. "How are you today, boys?"

"Doin' well, Cora." Davis Lee bussed her cheek, wondering if Josie knew that one reason Ian McDougal sat in Whirlwind's jail was for murdering Cora's husband, Ollie, last fall.

"Just fine, Cora." Riley brushed a kiss against her other cheek and shook the hand of the trim, distinguished-looking man next to her.

"Cora Wilkes, this is Josie Webster." Susannah pulled the newcomer forward as the older woman smiled and shook her hand.

"Nice to meet you, Josie." Cora gestured to the man standing at her shoulder. "This is my brother, Loren Barnes."

He shook her hand, his blue eyes warm. "I'm new, too. It's nice that I'm not the only one."

"Where are you from?"

"Fort Smith."

"I've never been there."

Josie spoke warmly, unhurriedly, but Davis Lee felt nervousness ripple off her. Why?

Susannah touched Josie's arm. "I do hope you decide to stay in Whirlwind. You'd like it here."

Josie smiled.

As Susannah and Catherine admired the other woman's dress, Riley edged up next to Davis Lee and said in a low voice, "Why are you lookin' at her like you expect her to pull a gun and hold us up?"

Davis Lee took a gurgling Lorelai from his brother and bounced her on his shoulder as he eyed the seamstress. "Twice I've caught her showing a powerful interest in my jail. She was watching it from the alley between the livery and Pete's saloon until I saw her there. Now she has a room at the Whirlwind that looks right at the jail, and yesterday, I found her inside. I think she's connected to McDougal."

His brother frowned. "How?"

"Sweetheart, maybe, or relative. I don't know yet, but I've got a telegram ready to send to the Galveston County sheriff and see what I can find out. I'd have sent the wire yesterday, but Tony got sick and had to close the telegraph office."

"It sure would be a shame if she's taken up with the likes of a McDougal. She's pretty."

"Which doesn't mean anything. She's probably also a liar."

"Maybe not. Every pretty woman isn't a swindler."

Davis Lee gave him a flat stare. "Just because you found a good woman like Susannah doesn't mean we'll all be so lucky."

"True enough, but maybe Josie will surprise you."

"She will. If she keeps away from my prisoner." Davis Lee watched a shy smile cross her face as Susannah and Catherine spoke to her.

His brother could be fooled if he wanted. Riley wasn't

the one who'd had his heart trampled by a beautiful heartless woman. Davis Lee was harder to dupe and he knew Josie Webster was trying to do just that. First thing tomorrow he would wire Galveston's sheriff.

The next evening Josie paused outside Sheriff Holt's office at six-forty-five. Gray clouds had scudded across the sky all day threatening showers, and the air had been pleasantly cool, but the rain hadn't come. Pressing a hand to her stomach did nothing to calm the flurries there. She had watched the jail today while finishing Gus Simon's work shirts.

Sheriff Holt had reverted to his original schedule and stepped out for his usual pie and coffee at nine-forty-five, then for lunch at twelve-thirty. Josie made a quick trip to the telegraph and post office to send Gus's shirts to Galveston. Midafternoon, Catherine Donnelly had arrived for Josie to take her measurements. As Catherine softly talked about her fiancé, a Texas Ranger who was taking care of some business in Houston, Josie worked up an estimate of the cost and time involved to make a dress for Catherine's upcoming wedding. For that hour, Josie had been unable to watch the jail. As far as she knew, McDougal hadn't been let out other than for a trip to the outhouse.

The sheriff hadn't even allowed McDougal to close the privy door. Whenever Holt escorted his shackled prisoner outside, Josie noted it was with a posture that hinted at quick reflexes and an unstinting alertness. The rugged man caused her tongue to twist on itself, but so far he hadn't shown any inkling of knowing the real reason she was here.

As she lifted her hand to knock on the door of the sheriff's office, it opened and he smiled down at her. His eyes were a piercing blue in the evening light. "Good evening, Miz Webster. How are you?"

"Very well, thank you. I truly appreciate you taking the time to give me these lessons."

"You're welcome." He reached behind him to shut the door. "I'll be back around dark, Jake."

"Take your time," a deep masculine voice answered.

As Josie walked down the steps in front of the sheriff, he asked, "Do you ride or should we take a wagon?"

"I ride. Where are we going?"

"About two miles outside of town."

She nodded, struck by the intense way he studied her. He appeared to be anticipating a reaction from her, but about what?

The sheriff had borrowed a black mare for her from the livery and moved to help her into the saddle, but she had already mounted. She had worn her dark blue split skirt so she could ride astride.

As they left Whirlwind behind, Josie tried to keep her attention on the patches of yellow and purple wildflowers spotting the flat landscape and not the way the muscles in Davis Lee's thighs flexed as he guided his horse.

But the burlap bag full of clanging tin cans that he carried behind his saddle drew her attention to him repeatedly.

She needed to remember that he and these lessons were just her way of trying to find out information about Ian McDougal. Her next attempt on the outlaw wouldn't be hindered.

As they rode leisurely down the dirt road, Davis Lee glanced at her. "I heard this morning that a big hurricane hit Galveston last night."

Concern flared for all the friends she'd left behind. When she was thirteen, a vicious storm had hit Indianola, killing one hundred and seventy-six people in the city down the coast from Galveston and entirely flooding her city. "Was anyone hurt or killed?"

"I haven't heard yet. All of their telegraph wires are down."

Which happened in almost every hurricane. Josie frowned. "So how did you know about the storm?"

"Some folks from Houston spread the word. The sheriff there sent a wire to several counties to the north and west."

"Oh." Josie decided she should keep her mouth shut. Davis Lee wiring the Galveston County sheriff was something she hadn't considered. The very real possibility that he might ask Sheriff Locke about her made her squirm in the saddle.

About ten minutes later, Davis Lee urged his buckskin mare off the wagon-rutted road and into the prairie's short grass. Josie followed, reining up a good distance from the road when he did.

She dismounted, noticing a small stone in a cleared patch of ground just on the other side of her horse. A clump of blue wild verbena grew at the stone's base.

"The McDougals killed our stage driver here," Davis Lee said when his gaze followed hers to the stone. "You met his wife yesterday. Cora Wilkes?"

"Yes." Josie stared at the small memorial the woman had erected, pain flooding her at the similar losses she had suffered. She struggled to keep her face blank as rage grew. How many people would McDougal kill before he was stopped?

"That gang also nearly killed my sister-in-law as well as Catherine Donnelly."

Shocked, Josie spun.

"They nearly ran Susannah to ground with their horses and they kidnapped Catherine." Davis Lee's eyes glinted dangerously. "My cousin is a Texas Ranger who'd been chasing the McDougals for almost two years. The two of us, along with my brother, Riley, and my deputy took care of three of them in a shoot-out several months back. Ian managed to escape, but he's in jail now. He'll pay for what he's done.''

Recognizing the same stern determination in Davis Lee's voice that she often felt, she edged closer to him.

His gaze locked onto hers. ''They killed Jericho's friend, another Ranger and nearly did Jericho in, too. If it hadn't been for Catherine's nursing skills, he would've died.''

Images of her parents' and William's bodies burned in her mind. ''You're lucky they *didn't* kill him.''

The keen interest sharpening his blue gaze made her suddenly nervous and she blurted out, ''What about your parents? Did the McDougals…?''

She fervently hoped not.

''No, they passed away without any help from those polecats.''

Josie nodded.

''The rest of my family is in Whirlwind. You met my brother yesterday. And my sister-in-law and niece.''

''Lorelai. What an angel,'' she said with a soft smile.

''Yes. And Jericho plans to put down roots here with Catherine after their wedding.'' Davis Lee walked through the short prairie grass and stopped several yards away. As he lifted, moved and stacked a few flat rocks, the tin cans in his burlap bag clanged. ''What about your family? Who did you leave behind in Galveston?''

''No one. Have you always lived here?''

''Except for a couple of years I spent up in the Panhandle.'' Curiosity darkened his eyes as he approached with the now-empty bag. ''I was the sheriff in Rock River.''

Just because he blabbed on about his past didn't mean she would. Her hair was pulled back with a ribbon and she brought a thick skein over her shoulder to twist around her finger. ''Did you always want to be a sheriff?''

His eyes narrowed at her nervous gesture. ''As far back as I can remember.''

"Your brother didn't?"

He shrugged. "Riley would rather be with the horses. And, as our pa used to say, I'd rather be with the horses' ass—back ends."

She smiled, her gaze going to the six tin cans perched on mounds of rocks.

"My grandpa was Whirlwind's first sheriff. I wanted to continue the tradition."

"Have the sheriffs of Whirlwind always been Holts?"

"No. For a dozen or so years there was another man here, a good man. When he decided to move farther west, I applied for the job."

Davis Lee had to have noticed her reluctance to talk about her family and the less-than-graceful way she changed the subject. He said nothing yet Josie felt uneasily as if she were being sized up.

Dropping the empty bag to the ground, Davis Lee slid a revolver from the small of his back. His own remained in the holster strapped low on his hips. Keeping the barrel pointed at the ground, he handed her the gun. "This Colt may be a little heavy for you. It's a .45 caliber. What do you think?"

She awkwardly balanced the weapon on her hand, surprised at its weight. "I guess I'll get used to it."

"If you decide to buy one, I can help you. Smith & Wesson makes a .32 caliber that might fit your hand better. They call it a pocket revolver."

She nodded, clasping the butt in both hands and raising it to eye level.

Davis Lee reached out and gently pushed the barrel down so that it was directed at the ground. "Don't point that thing unless you're ready to use it. That's rule number one."

"All right." She was going to learn to shoot really well. Ian McDougal would never have her at a disadvantage again.

Davis Lee moved up beside her, his shoulder barely brushing hers. "Stand with your feet a comfortable distance apart and aim at one of those cans."

"Don't I need to learn how to load it?"

"I want you to get the feel of it first. I don't fancy losing a toe or something more vital if you squeeze that trigger before either one of us is ready."

She glanced at him, noting that the level at which she held the weapon was about the same as his private parts. The realization had heat burning her cheeks. For Davis Lee to lose any part of his lean muscled anatomy would be a real shame. He was one handsome man.

Josie forced her attention back to what he was saying.

"Just practice aiming for a bit."

She lifted the gun, her gaze following the line of the barrel.

He tapped the small piece of raised metal at the barrel's tip. "You can use the sight if you want, but that one is a little off. I learned how to shoot by aiming the gun as if it were my finger. You try it."

She did. "That feels more natural than trying to line up the sight. Can you shoot faster using this method, too?"

He flicked his gaze over her. "How fast do you need to shoot?"

"Just asking." If she were forced to shoot McDougal rather than cut him, she meant to fire as many times as necessary.

The thought of cold-bloodedly killing the outlaw just as he had killed her parents and William bothered her, but she refused to be swayed.

"I'll show you how to load it now." Davis Lee reached over and put his hand on top of hers.

She stiffened, her hand twitching beneath his. Her gaze flew to his face and she saw that his attention wasn't on the gun, but on her breasts.

"Pardon me, Sheriff," she said archly.

"Davis Lee." A wicked grin spread slowly across his face as he held up his hands in mock surrender, his gaze dipping again to her chest. "You're not gonna pull that blade on me, are you?"

"Are you going to give me a reason?" Her heartbeat kicked wildly against her ribs and she found she couldn't look away from the heat of his blue gaze.

"I plan to tell you what I'm doing every step of the way. Don't want to spook you and end up begging for mercy."

She didn't want to find his grin so charming. Or him either for that matter. She turned her attention back to the weapon. "Bullets?"

"Yessirree." He slid six from his gun belt and dropped them into her waiting hand.

Again he covered her hand with his, this time pushing against a rounded part of the gun right above the trigger. A cylinder popped out, revealing six empty slots.

"Those chambers are for your bullets." He plucked one from her hand and slid it in, indicating she should finish.

After she did, he clicked the cylinder back into place. "All right, you're ready. Be smart. Until you're going to use it, keep the gun pointed toward the ground or away from people. Now go ahead and see if you can hit one of those cans."

Knowing that she stood in the same place where the McDougal gang had killed yet another person affected Josie's concentration, but she tried to focus on the targets in front of her.

"When you're ready, squeeze the trigger steadily."

She did and the gun kicked, causing her to flinch. The bullet flew off into who-knew-where. "Oh, fiddle."

He chuckled. "You'll hit the target sooner if you keep your eyes open."

"Oh." She smiled sheepishly. "I didn't realize I'd closed them."

"It's okay. You have to get the feel of it. That's why it's a good idea to practice."

She nodded, biting her lip as she aimed again at the can. The slight breeze cooled her nape. The flutter of grasshoppers in the calf-high grass and the call of a hawk circling overhead shifted to the distant part of her mind.

She fired all six bullets and hit only air.

"Do it again," Davis Lee said.

She loaded the gun as he'd shown her then brought it up and sighted the middle can. She didn't flinch this time. At least she thought she hadn't.

"You gotta stop flinching." He pushed his hat back then resettled it on his head. "It's no wonder you can't see the target."

She tried again. She had to learn to do this. Ian McDougal wasn't getting away from her again. Still, she hit nothing.

Davis Lee patiently watched her reload and fire, over and over. "Don't quit," he said when she dropped her arms to rest them.

Her forearms throbbed. Who knew it took such strength to shoot a gun?

"You'll get it," he murmured. But half an hour later, he looked at her, looked at the cans sitting exactly where he'd placed them. "Can you *see* the targets?"

"Yes." A blush heated her face. Why couldn't she learn this?

He looked genuinely puzzled. "Are you concentrating?"

"Yes."

"I guess this is gonna take a while," he muttered.

She loaded the gun again, anger at herself growing in the place of her earlier determination. Maybe the lanky man beside her was the reason she was doing so poorly.

When he stood so close to her, she could smell the strong

fresh scent of lye soap and a faint whiff of leather and horse. She didn't know why he affected her so, but the man could make a painted lady nervous.

Josie tried to push away the overwhelming sense of his presence and focus. She fired, pausing between each shot to take aim. She hit nothing. "I see why it takes a lot of practice to become good with one of these things."

"I'm assuming you've got better aim with that blade you carry."

He offered more ammunition and she pushed the bullets into the chamber.

"Those are my last bullets," he said.

"I need more!"

"I didn't think it was gonna take this many." He grinned.

She smiled up at him then looked away when she saw the smoldering interest in his eyes. Was he watching her with such fascination because he suspected her real reason for coming to Whirlwind? Or because he felt the same unsettling awareness she felt?

Gripping the revolver with damp hands, she fired until it was empty. She risked a glance at him, catching a pained look on his face.

"That's enough for today." He walked to the rocks and began gathering up the cans. The cans she hadn't come close to hitting.

She waited in a patch of buffalo grass, unwillingly admiring the fluid way he moved, the broad hands that completely covered the cans. "Are you ready to give up on me?"

She held her breath. If he said yes, what would she do? Her skirt caught on a clump of grass and she tugged it loose.

Davis Lee started back toward her, holding the burlap sack full of cans. "It's all in the practice—" He froze midstep. "Don't move."

"What are you—"

"Don't. Move."

She frowned at the hard command in his voice, freezing as he'd ordered.

"Snake. I must've stirred him up by moving those rocks."

"Where?" A sudden crackling noise caused her to involuntarily flinch.

Davis Lee cried out, "No!" The bag fell to the ground, cans clanging together.

She recoiled against a sharp blistering stab above her ankle that felt as if a needle had been jabbed into her flesh. A burning shot up her leg.

He whipped out his own gun and fired twice in rapid succession, aiming between her feet. It happened too fast for Josie to react at all.

She stumbled back a step, hardly able to make herself look down, but she did.

A blackish-brown snake with dark, indistinct-shaped markings protruded from beneath her skirts. Even she could identify the alternating black and white rings on its tail, and the rattle at the end. Nausea rolled over her. "Oh, dear."

She wobbled.

"Are you bit?" Davis Lee rushed up. When he saw that the snake lay unmoving, he holstered his weapon. "Rattlesnake."

Josie stared hard at the reptile as if she could will it to remain motionless.

"Josie, are you bit?"

"Yes." She lifted her gaze to his, feeling detached from her body.

He cursed and scooped her unceremoniously into his arms, carrying her a safe distance away. "I've got to get the venom out of your leg."

He reached their horses and tugged a rolled-up trail blanket from behind his saddle, snapping it open and wrapping it around her before carefully depositing her on the ground. He went to his knees beside her. "Is your vision blurring? Are you nauseous?"

"No." She dragged in air, trying to calm her racing pulse and recall what her father had told her about treating snakebites. "It may be ten minutes or so before that happens. We need to work fast though."

She already felt short of breath, but maybe that was because she was close to panic. A rattler. She had been bitten by a rattler. She had never even seen a snake, but thanks to her father she knew how to treat a bite. She had to stay as calm as possible.

Pulling the blanket around her to keep warm and try to combat the shock she knew would come, she reached for the hem of her skirt the same time Davis Lee did.

"Lie down," he ordered. "You need to be still and quiet."

She knew he was right but needed to do something herself. Pain seared her lower leg as if scalding water had spilled on her.

"Is it burning?"

"Yes." Tears stung her eyes.

"It's starting to swell, too," he muttered.

"Do you know what to do?"

"Yes." He lifted her skirts to her knees, pushing up the hem of her drawers.

She saw several cuts and scratches around a single puncture just above the top of her boot, the bloody blister forming at the bite that was a few inches above her ankle.

Her breathing grew labored and the burning in her leg intensified. Forcing away the panic that clawed at her, she focused on remembering her father's instruction. Her hands moved to her bodice. Any constrictive clothing could increase the swelling and push the flow of venom through her blood faster. She shook so violently she could barely unfasten the buttons, but she managed to spread open the cotton fabric then reach for the fastenings on her corset. Sweat broke across her nape and between her breasts.

Davis Lee stared at her leg, jerking off his hat. "I'm going to cut you and suck out that poison."

"I know," she mumbled. Biting back a whimper at the voracious fire in her lower leg, she fumbled with the hooks down the front of her corset, hoping this would sufficiently loosen her clothing.

He glanced up then froze. "What in the hell are you doin'?"

"Constricts my breathing." She struggled with the last closure just below her waist. "Anything too tight will spread the venom faster."

He frowned, but pulled out his whittling knife with its four-inch blade and reached toward her. The whetted steel sliced easily through the thread securing her corset hook. The loosened garment relaxed, freeing her breasts, her ribs, and she dragged in a deep breath.

He moved back to her leg with the big knife. Josie gasped and lifted herself onto her elbows. "No, not yours. Mine."

"There's no time—"

"Use…mine." Sweat dampened her palms as she reached for her scalpel and handed it to him. "If you butcher me with your knife, you might damage my muscle. Use this."

He took the instrument, pushing her back down before leaning over her leg and aiming intently for the bite.

"Tie your kerchief around my calf about two inches above the puncture, just so it forms a light band. Keep the incision small and in the bite. That will help minimize the damage."

"I know how to do this. How do you—never mind." He applied the bandanna.

She shakily slid two fingers beneath the fabric to make

sure it wasn't too tight then turned her head away as he made small, shallow cuts in her leg. Between the burning agony of the wound and the slices into her flesh, Josie nearly passed out.

She was vaguely cognizant of the fact that a man she barely knew had lifted her skirts.

His lips touched her leg, the heat of his mouth lost under the fever of her skin. She felt the starch seep out of her. Her breathing grew more forced; her pulse raced. The wound throbbed ceaselessly.

"Hang on." Davis Lee sucked at the wound and spit so often that Josie lost track of time.

She curled her fingers into the blanket trying to keep from passing out. The inside of her mouth tasted as rusty as if she'd chewed old nails for breakfast. Fever built in her leg and moved through her body.

After long minutes, she laid an unsteady hand on Davis Lee's knee. "You've done all you can. It's probably all right to start for the fort doctor now."

He dragged the back of his hand across his mouth, studying her face as if deciding whether to stop. "I'll take you to Catherine. She's closer and will know what to do. She's a nurse."

Josie nodded weakly. If they hadn't acted quickly enough, it wouldn't matter what a doctor or a nurse did for her.

Davis Lee dropped her scalpel in his saddlebag then moved to her side. "We'll have to ride double."

She nodded, so drowsy that she was hardly able to control the movement. Another sign of a poisonous snakebite. She tried to remain calm, knew she had to.

Davis Lee reached to button her bodice but her gaping corset prevented him. He cursed, grabbing hold of the stiff undergarment and dragging it off her body. "You don't need this damn thing anyway," he muttered.

Josie didn't even care that he'd removed it; she only cared

about breathing. He clumsily fastened several buttons, half of them in the wrong loop, but her bodice was mostly closed. She found his attempt endearing.

He stood, settling his hat on his head as he stuffed her corset into his saddlebag. "I'm going to lift you into the saddle then climb on behind."

"I can stand." Her tongue tingled.

"That's a damn fool idea."

"The important thing…is to keep the bite below my heart."

"You're fadin' fast. We're doin' this my way." He knelt and gathered her, blanket and all, in his arms, then gently sat her in the saddle.

Wobbly, she curled her fingers into the sleeves of his shirt. He gently pried them off and folded them around the saddle horn.

"Hang on," he said.

"All right."

He slowly released her then climbed up behind her, settling her in the cradle of his thighs. Her vision blurred as the drowsiness leeched her energy. Her head fell against his chest.

"I've got you. Don't worry about trying to hold on."

She snuggled one shoulder under his arm, her fingers closing weakly on the pommel.

"Okay?"

"Yes."

He turned his horse, moved toward hers to pick up the reins and they started for town.

"What about your cans?" she asked sleepily.

He looked down at her, sounding amused. "I can get more."

Agony seared her leg and she felt herself waning, the green grass blurring as they moved. Davis Lee's strong arm circled her waist and she leaned into him. He was hot. And hard.

The pain jumbled the thoughts in her head. Memories of her parents' lifeless bodies. Of the first time William had kissed her. Davis Lee's eyes glittering with suspicion.

With her cheek cradled against his broad chest, she felt safe. And torn. If she survived this, it would be because of him. She didn't want to owe him. It would only complicate matters once she killed his prisoner.

Chapter Four

He talked to her all the way to Whirlwind about everything from shoeing horses to whittling. A couple of times he thought she lost consciousness, and by the time they reached town, she had.

Dusk settled around them as he guided his buckskin up the main street and toward the Whirlwind Hotel. Davis Lee barely paid any mind to the attention he attracted from the few people who were still about. He saw Matt and Russ Baldwin coming out of Pete Carter's saloon and hollered for both of them. The dark-haired brothers, easily the biggest men in Taylor County, hurried out to meet him.

Matt, the youngest by a year, reached Davis Lee first. "What's happened?"

"One of you go for Catherine and one of you come help me!"

Russ, the quieter of the two, turned back and unhitched his bay mare then vaulted into the saddle.

"Tell her I need her for a snakebite." Davis Lee thought he would never reach the other end of town, but he finally reined up in front of the hotel.

Matt met him there, taking the reins of Josie's horse and

flipping them over the hitching post. His gaze skated over her and interest flared in his eyes. "Who is she?"

"Her name's Josie Webster." Davis Lee shrugged off his annoyance at Matt's fascination. The Baldwin brothers were well-known ladies' men. "Here."

When Matt came forward, Davis Lee handed her down carefully then swiftly dismounted.

"Why haven't I seen her before?" The other man stared at her. "She's a beauty—"

Scooping Josie out of Baldwin's arms before Matt could even turn toward the hotel, Davis Lee took the steps at the end of the landing.

Matt hurried behind him. "Why are you bringing her here?"

"Her room is closer than Catherine's house."

"She sure is a little thing. Is it bad?"

"I think so."

The other man opened one side of the double glass-front door. "I'll take care of the horses."

"Thanks." Davis Lee glanced down, concern growing that Josie wasn't waking. Beyond the staircase, three guests sat in the dining room. He stopped at the registration desk and hollered at the man behind it who was slumped and snoring in his chair. "Penn!"

The old man came slowly awake, blinking.

"Get Esther to meet me upstairs!"

Confusion slowly cleared from the clerk's lined features as his gaze went to the woman in Davis Lee's arms. Penn's eyes widened and he pushed himself out of his chair. "That's Miss Josie!"

"Yes." Davis Lee rounded the corner of the desk and started up the staircase.

"What happened?"

"Snakebite," he said tightly.

Penn shuffled toward the dining room. "Esther! Come quick!"

Davis Lee reached the second-story landing, then Josie's room. The door was locked. He stepped back to lean over the wooden stair railing. "Get me a key!"

"Coming, Sheriff." It was Penn's wife, Esther, who answered him.

He heard frantic muttering, then saw her iron-gray hair as she breathlessly mounted the stairs. As round and soft as Penn was narrow and hard, Esther had a sweet disposition and good hearing, for which Davis Lee was thankful.

He stood aside so the older woman could open Josie's door. When she pushed it wide, he strode across the room to the bed in the corner. Josie was still limp in his arms. Her skin was waxy, pale as a cloud and Davis Lee's chest squeezed.

He laid her on the mattress, sitting on the edge of the bed to tuck his trail blanket tightly around her. He wished she would open her eyes or moan or something.

"Should I send Penn for Miss Donnelly?"

"I sent Russ to fetch her." A trained nurse who had come to Whirlwind only a few months ago, Catherine was the first woman Davis Lee had been in danger of falling for since Betsy, but she'd fallen hard for his cousin, Jericho. And he for her.

Esther moved up behind Davis Lee, peering at Josie over his shoulder. "Poor thing. What can I do?"

"Probably ought to get her boots off." What had she said about things constricting her? Maybe he had wrapped her too tightly. He loosened the tight cocoon of blanket.

Esther moved to the foot of the bed and unbuttoned Josie's black boots, slipping them off. Davis Lee lifted the blanket and tugged her skirts up enough to see the wound. Her golden-peach skin was stretched taut and thin. He thought her calf looked more swollen than before but he couldn't be sure.

Aware that Esther stared disapprovingly at his hand on Josie's leg, he pushed her skirts back down. "Josie?"

Her eyes remained closed. He took her hand. Finding it clammy, he tucked it between both of his and rubbed. She was in shock. Maybe he shouldn't have loosened the blanket. Where the hell was Catherine? All he knew to do was keep trying to wake Josie. He kept her small soft hand in one of his and lifted the other to her face, patting her cheek.

"Josie? Wake up."

He cursed under his breath. She was so slight, looked so defenseless lying there. Her lips were barely parted, her lashes dark crescents against her pale cheeks. The rise and fall of her chest was rapid, too rapid.

She opened her eyes.

"Josie?" He leaned over her.

"Sheriff?" she croaked, looking at him through slitted, pain-filled eyes.

"I sent for Catherine. You passed out." He awkwardly patted her shoulder, his stomach dipping like he'd been thrown from a horse. "She'll be here soon." It needed to be now.

"I…can't see you very well. I'm thirsty."

Esther hurried out of the room. "I'll get some water."

Davis Lee squeezed Josie's hand, using his other to tuck the blanket snugly around her once more.

"Hurts." She sounded breathless; her eyes drifted shut.

"Josie, don't go. Stay awake." He tapped her chin gently with a knuckle. "Josie."

Where was Esther? Hell, where was *Catherine?* What if he hadn't sucked out enough venom? For all he knew, that stuff was leeching the life out of Josie. The sound of footsteps rushing up the stairs had him looking over his shoulder. Relief pushed through him as Catherine hurried inside, skirts swishing.

"Russ said there was a snakebite." The raven-haired nurse hurried around him, shoving a small black bag into his chest. She placed a hand on Josie's forehead.

He stood and stepped back to give his friend some room.

"How long has she been like this?"

"She woke up just a minute ago, but before that at least ten minutes."

"Where's the bite?"

"Her left calf, on the inside."

Rolling up the sleeves on her pale blue bodice, Catherine folded back the blanket and reached for Josie's skirts. She glanced at him. "I need to look at the wound."

He nodded, his gaze fixed on the soft crest of Josie's cheekbones, the delicate winged arch of her dark brows, the freckles scattered across her fine-boned nose. Her lips were bloodless. She was still so pale. What if he hadn't gotten help on time?

"Davis Lee?"

"Huh?"

Catherine twirled her finger. "Turn around."

He did, biting back the impulse to tell her that he'd already done more than see her patient's trim, uncovered ankles. He'd ripped the woman's damn corset off.

"Maybe I need to have a look at you, too?" his friend asked in her calm, soothing voice.

"I'm fine, but I'm afraid she's real bad."

She didn't say anything for a long moment. "You cut her."

"I had to. Is it too deep? Will it scar badly?"

"It's hard to say. Did you suck out the venom?"

"Yes."

"How long?"

He massaged the tight muscles across his nape. "I don't

know. It seemed like a long time. She told me when to stop.''

He wanted to turn around, see Josie's face. "Catherine, has she opened her eyes again?''

"No, not yet.''

"She was awake just a minute ago. Said she was thirsty. Esther went to get her some water.''

"Did you clean the wound?''

"No.'' He should've done that. Why hadn't he thought to do that?

His friend stood and reached for her bag, then had to pry it gently from Davis Lee's tight grip. She opened the satchel and removed a thick folded square of linen and a brown bottle marked Carbolic Acid.

Damn this anyway. Josie's ankles were the least of what he'd seen today. He turned around, willing her to open her eyes. "We were out by Ollie's marker. She lost consciousness a couple of times on the way back to town. We weren't more than ten minutes away.''

"Has she been unconscious ever since?''

"Except for that short time a while ago.'' He didn't think Josie looked any better. "She's still shaking.''

"It's shock,'' Catherine told him. "She needs to stay warm.''

Esther walked back into the room carrying a glass of water and an earthen pitcher.

Catherine opened the bottle of carbolic acid and dribbled some of the liquid onto the cloth then gently cleaned the puncture wound and surrounding cuts.

"What do you think, Catherine? Tell me what's going on,'' he demanded. "Is she gonna—''

"Not if I can help it.'' She cleansed the wound again.

"Should I have brought her to you instead of here?'' The thought that his decision might cost Josie her life had his chest pounding so hard it hurt.

"No. The hotel was closer."

That had been his first instinct, but since Betsy, Davis Lee hadn't trusted his instincts about much.

Josie's eyes fluttered open again and her pain-clouded gaze locked with his. "Where am I?" she croaked.

"Your room at the hotel." Relief deepened his voice. "Catherine's here. She's going to help you."

Josie licked her lips and Catherine held her head so she could drink from the glass of water Esther had brought. When she finished, Catherine eased her head back down and handed the glass to Davis Lee. "Esther, help me get her under the sheet. I want to wrap the blanket on top of it. That should keep her warm enough."

Catherine competently rolled Josie toward the wall and Esther struggled to pull the sheet from beneath her split skirt. Davis Lee made an impatient sound and scooped Josie up in his arms. When the sheet was turned down, he laid her back on the mattress.

Esther unwrapped the blanket from around Josie then spread it on top of the sheet. Catherine tucked the covers close to Josie's body, making a cocoon.

Her fevered gaze locked on his. He didn't see blame or fear there. He saw trust. Something hot and sharp grabbed him deep inside.

He cleared his throat. "She's gonna be okay, isn't she?"

"Without knowing how much venom is in her system, we have to wait and see," Catherine said softly.

She gave her patient another sip of water. "I'm going to make a poultice, Josie. And a tea."

Catherine was so composed. Even Josie seemed calm while his insides tangled like rusted barbed wire. He made a frustrated noise and splayed his hands on his hips. Her eyes were closed again. He wanted to do something, wanted her to be all right.

Catherine glanced at him. ''The incision you made is small. It's good you didn't use your big knife on her.''

''She wouldn't let me. She wanted me to use her scalpel.''

''Her scalpel?''

''She carries one with her for protection.''

''All the time?'' Catherine looked bemused.

''Yeah.''

''How strange,'' she murmured.

''Yeah.''

''I think we've done all we can right now. Unfortunately, we'll just have to wait for her symptoms to peak.''

''How long will that take?''

''Probably three or four days. Hard to know how much poison is in there, but from what you've told me about her being unconscious, I think she was bitten pretty good.''

Discomfort flashed across Josie's features and Davis Lee lowered his voice. ''Will it be painful? Worse than now?''

''For a bit,'' Catherine murmured. ''She's clammy right now, but a fever will probably set in soon. Then the sweats. She'll be weak and perhaps disoriented.''

Needing to do something with his hands, Davis Lee jerked off his hat and crushed it, staring at her. ''We were out shooting,'' he said hoarsely.

''Oh?'' Catherine looked up at him, curiosity plain in her eyes. ''Are you and she—?''

''She wants to learn how to handle a gun. I said I'd teach her.'' He shook his head. ''I never thought something like this would happen. I go out there all the time. So does Cora. I've seen snakes there before, but they skedaddle at the first sign of humans.''

''It's not your fault, Davis Lee. You're not thinking it is, are you?''

He shrugged. ''No, just wishing it hadn't happened.''

She lightly squeezed his arm. "You did fine. You kept her calm, got the venom out and got her back here."

"She was calmer than I was."

"You were smart to loosen her bodice."

"She did that. She did everything."

"You sucked out the venom," Catherine said.

Josie nodded weakly, her lashes lifting, her green gaze etched with pain.

But had he done enough? Had he done it in time? His hands closed even more tightly on the brim of his hat. "What can I do? What do you need? Tell me and I'll get it."

"I need some snakeroot."

He frowned. "Snake-*what?*"

"Snakeroot. It's the same as birthwort. I also need some downy plantain. They're herbs. Dr. Butler will have them at Fort Greer. I need enough for four days. Tell him it's for a poultice and a tea."

Davis Lee nodded, the air suddenly stifling. The walls pressed in on him. "Anything else?"

"That's all for now. I'll stay with her tonight."

Davis Lee bit back his own offer to do the same. It wouldn't do for him to be alone in here with her, but he hesitated to leave.

"I need to keep an eye on her symptoms," Catherine said quietly. "Her leg will swell further and I'm very concerned that she may have trouble breathing. I've made her as comfortable as possible."

"I'll fetch what you need."

"Could you also stop by the house and tell my brother Andrew I'll be here overnight? He can stay with one of his friends, either Creed or Miguel."

"Done."

Davis Lee gave Josie one last look before walking out. As reluctant as he was to leave, he was glad to be doing something besides staring at her waxen face. She was in good hands with Catherine, so why didn't the pressure in his chest ease?

Four hours later, Davis Lee had delivered the herbs to Catherine and seen Andrew settled with Miguel Santos, the nephew of the telegraph operator. He had also completed his nightly walk through town. It was a few minutes past eleven and all was quiet.

Jake was at the jail guarding McDougal and Davis Lee was free to head for his small house behind Haskell's that had been provided by the town. Instead, he stood in the street staring at the soft lamp glow in an upstairs window of the Whirlwind Hotel.

When he had returned with the things Catherine wanted, Josie hadn't looked any better. He wanted to check on her one last time, knew he wouldn't sleep until he did.

Using the key Penn had given him so he could keep an eye on the hotel if he heard something after-hours, Davis Lee let himself in, moonlight marking his way to the corner of the registration desk. He lit the candle always kept there by the old man and carried it upstairs to Josie's room.

Mindful of the other guests, he rapped softly with one knuckle. When there was no response, he knocked. Nothing.

He tried the door and found it unlocked, pushing it open to peer into the room. "Catherine?"

But it wasn't Catherine in the chair beside Josie's bed. It was Esther Wavers. The lamp on the bedside table threw a warm blanket of light around the room and Davis Lee stepped over to pinch out the candle on the dresser.

Josie was in bed, the blanket on the floor, the sheet down around her ankles. A splint braced her lower left leg and he saw the white gleam of the bandages Catherine had applied over the poultice. At the same time he registered that Josie wore only her chemise and drawers, his attention moved to the older woman who hadn't reacted to his arrival. "Esther?"

He walked to the bed, his attention snagged on the dark hair spread like sable silk across Josie's pillow. Smoky yellow light slid over her, tucking shadows between her breasts, her legs. Her gossamer-light undergarment fit close to her body, the flush of fever evident even in the muted light.

Davis Lee dragged his gaze to Esther, concerned that something was wrong. The older woman slumped in the chair, head bowed, hands resting loosely on a water-filled basin in her lap. The steady rise and fall of her chest told him that she was asleep. Relief that she wasn't dead or unconscious mixed with a surge of irritation. What good was she doing this way?

Josie made a low, ragged sound, her breath catching in a way that had him turning. He was startled to realize she was crying in her sleep.

"Esther?" He kept his voice quiet and calm, reaching down to take the tilting bowl from her lap.

Moving fitfully, Josie threw a protective arm across her face. He eased down onto the edge of the bed.

Esther snuffled softly and his jaw tightened. He bumped the washbasin into her knee.

"Huh?" She jerked awake, blinking rapidly then squinting at him. "Oh. Sheriff?"

"Where's Catherine?" he asked tightly.

She covered a yawn, her voice scratchy with sleep. "Pearl Anderson's daughter-in-law finally went into labor and there was a problem. Pearl asked Catherine to come so I told her I'd stay with Josie." Her gaze went to the bed, no doubt seeing the distress in Josie's face and body that Davis Lee saw. Guilt darkened the older woman's eyes and she snapped straight in her chair. "I didn't mean to fall asleep. Is she worse?"

"I don't know," he said evenly. "Was she like this the last time you remember?"

"Yes." She nodded, her wilted bun wiggling loosely on top of her head.

"Do you know what time that was?"

"No."

Josie made more of those choppy sobbing noises. A hard-boiled knot lodged in his chest. Was she dreaming or in pain? Catherine had said she might be disoriented, not that she might be delirious. It had to be due to the fever. He placed a hand on her forehead. She was burning up.

"I came by to check on her." A rag floated in the bowl of water and Davis Lee scooped it up, squeezed it. He moved Josie's arm down to her side so he could wipe her face.

"I'm so sorry."

He wanted to reassure the older woman, but all he could think about was Catherine saying that breathing might become difficult for Josie. She might have suffocated before Esther ever woke up.

He forcefully dunked the rag again, wringing it out before moving it gently over Josie's face. "Why don't you go on to bed, Esther? I'll stay with her."

"Oh, Sheriff, I'll be fine now. I really didn't mean to—"

"I insist," he said quietly.

"But someone might find out you're alone in here with her."

And doing what? he thought ruefully. The woman was practically unconscious. He gave her a flat stare. "In light of things, I don't really care."

"*She* might."

"I'm staying. Leave the door open. Hopefully Miz Webster will recover enough to take me to task herself."

Esther hesitated, watching him wet the rag again and repeat the stroking motions on Josie's face. "All right."

She walked to the door. "I'm truly sorry, Sheriff. I don't
know what happened."

He gave a noncommittal grunt, his attention on the slight
figure in the bed.

Esther's footsteps sounded down the stairs then faded
away. The rag warmed with the heat of Josie's flesh. The
nearly transparent garment she wore wasn't a chemise as he
had first thought, but some one-piece thing that looked like
a chemise and drawers combined. Except it wasn't loose
and shapeless like any shift he'd ever seen. This undergarment was fitted. Edged with delicate lace, it curved to her
body like a second skin.

Especially damp as it was from repeated efforts to cool
her down. The thin fabric clung to her breasts, revealing the
darker flesh of her nipples, the dip of her navel, the shadow
between her legs. Her breasts were small but full, and the
perfect size for her petite frame. There was nothing wanting
about them at all.

His mouth went dry and he grabbed the sheet, pulling it
up over her. He dipped the cloth and ran it over her face,
her neck, her chest. The faint tang of kerosene drifted from
the lamp, but it was the scent of soft warm woman and
honeysuckle that filled his lungs. Secluded with her like this,
cornered by the night and the heat, Davis Lee felt his body
harden. He lost track of how many times he wet the cloth,
soothed her skin then repeated the motions.

He lifted her, applying the cool rag to her nape and the
patch of skin on her back not covered by that infernal sheer
piece of nothing. Her sobs quieted, but she twisted on the
bed, kicking off the sheet.

He pulled up the cover and she moved it again. He
couldn't tell if her fever was coming down. High color still
flushed her cheeks and chest. Her hairline was wet, her un-

derwear and the sheets damp. He reached out and stroked a finger lightly against her temple.

She turned into his touch, moaning, "William."

Who was William? Husband? Lover? Brother? She had never answered his questions about her family.

She mumbled incoherently, her arm slanting across her face again.

He murmured soothing words, lifted her arm to draw the wet cloth over her face and chest. She twitched beneath his hand, her head turning from side to side on her pillow. Her hair slid across her face and Davis Lee nudged the wet strands away.

"Blood," she whispered brokenly. "So much blood."

Another sob choked out of her and his heart caught at the deep-reaching agony of it. *Blood?* What was going on in her head? Just another question to add to the others he had about her.

He wished her fever would cool, that Catherine would return. He took her hand and dipped it into the water up to her wrist, spreading the wet rag on her chest for a moment. The tiny mole he'd glimpsed before at the edge of her collarbone teased him. And so did that damn transparent undergarment.

Davis Lee stared at her plump breasts and the dusky nipples that had drawn up like shy buds. Despite the fact that he knew she was lying about something, want pounded through him, low and fierce and hot. He moved his gaze from the flat of her stomach to the dark shadow between her legs. His breath hitched on the same sharp edge of desire he'd felt for another woman with lies in her eyes.

Davis Lee dragged a hand down his face, wishing he could erase this picture of her from his mind. He had no doubt he would carry this image to his grave. What he needed was to focus on getting her fever down, helping her through this. Then finding out her connection to Ian McDougal and why she had really come to Whirlwind.

Chapter Five

The pain woke her, a searing agony that pulsed just below the surface of her skin. Her eyelids were heavy, and when she finally got her eyes open, her vision was slightly blurry. The tight heaviness against her lower left leg confirmed the splint she vaguely remembered Catherine fashioning. A bulky wrap of white cloth kept the poultice in place. The snakeroot must be drawing out the poison because her leg burned like fire.

Pale gray light tinged with the sun crept into the room. Trying to get her bearings, she stared at the dresser at the foot of the bed. She became aware of the damp sheets beneath her, the thick cotton feel of her mouth. The door was open.

Even with her senses dulled by pain and weakness she knew she wasn't alone.

Her head felt too heavy for her neck and it was an effort to look over at the window. Davis Lee. Her mind stalled on that for a moment. She remembered shooting with him, resting against him on the ride here. Catherine Donnelly had put the poultice on her leg then the splint. That was the last thing Josie remembered.

Where was Catherine? How long had the sheriff been

here? His back was to her. One broad shoulder braced against the wall as he stared out the window. He wore the same light blue shirt he'd worn yesterday. At least she thought it was the same.

The lamp's low flame burned beside the bed, giving a golden haze to the watery daylight seeping into the room. Her gaze skimmed involuntarily down the dark trousers that molded his lean hips and long legs entirely too well. She remembered how it felt to be cradled between his hard thighs, held against that brawny chest. Only then did Josie's numbed brain realize that she was nearly naked.

The fine lawn of her combination suit clung to her body like wet tissue. The sweats that she and Catherine expected now slicked her still-fevered flesh, causing the thin cloth to cup her breasts and the tops of her thighs. Who had undressed her? Him?

The fabric was transparent. Josie could see her nipples, her navel, everything she owned. Which meant he had, too.

The heat that flushed her from head to toe had her easing herself up and reaching for the sheet.

"You're awake," he said, turning around.

How had he known that? Startled, she made a desperate grab for the linen and caught the corner, drawing it up to her chest.

"Every time I did that, you kicked it off."

She frowned at the tired rasp of his voice. Dark stubble shadowed his too-strong jaw, sharpening the angles of his face. His eyes burned with blue fire and his coffee-dark hair was furrowed from his fingers. His hat hung on the chair beside her bed.

He moved over to her. She pressed the sheet to her breasts, mortified at the thought that Davis Lee had seen her nearly naked.

He reached for the pitcher on the bedside table. After

pouring water into a glass, he bent down and slid one hard, hot hand under her neck to hold her head.

His touch was gentle, at odds with the no-nonsense line of his lips, the cool knowing in his eyes. She sipped, looking down to escape his intense gaze. The liquid soothed the parched heat of her mouth but didn't quench her thirst.

She drank greedily and he pulled back a little.

"Easy," he murmured.

Trying to slow down, she finished the rest. He lowered her head back to the pillow and returned the glass to the bedside table. Her body still burned with fever, but she could feel the brand of his touch on her nape. His gaze on her body.

Her eyes met his and she was struck by the hard glitter of want in his eyes. Jaw tightening, he stepped away, behind the chair.

She fastened her gaze on her hands. Weakness pulled at her. "I thought Catherine was here."

"She was called away on an emergency."

It took too much effort to nod so Josie just absorbed the information. The mildness of Davis Lee's voice relaxed her unease enough that she glanced at him. No emotion showed now on his handsome face, but his body was taut with a subtle tension. She didn't recall him coming back after he'd fetched the herbs for Catherine.

He gestured to her leg. "Still hurt pretty bad?"

"Yes."

"Do you remember much of what happened after I brought you here?"

"Not really. Catherine, the snakeroot." Somewhere in her mushy brain, she recalled another woman. Older. "Was Mrs. Wavers here?"

"For a bit."

Her body ached. She didn't have the energy of a sun-warmed cat. "I was unconscious."

He nodded.

"How long?"

"Ten or twelve minutes without coming to. Then you were in and out."

She was thirsty and the pain in her leg radiated through her whole body. "I don't remember anything else."

"You were burning up." He felt her forehead, his big, rough hand gentle on her skin. "Still are."

"Yes, I remember the fever...."

And strong hands moving softly over her face, her chest. Her gaze flew to Davis Lee. It had been him. Touching her. Soothing her.

His gaze dipped, skimmed over her body.

She squirmed beneath the sheet. "So...how long have you been here?"

"A while."

She wondered if this dizziness was due to the snakebite or the blue-eyed man standing over her. "Who's watching the jail?"

"Your window has a perfect view of it." His gaze sharpened like a newly whetted blade. "But Jake stayed with the prisoner."

His pointed answer told her he was on to her spying, but she couldn't summon the energy to care or to keep it in her head for more than a fleeting moment. She could barely lift the sheet to blot her damp forehead and neck. For the first time she wondered if Davis Lee could be held responsible for McDougal dying in his custody. She wouldn't want that.

Despite her listlessness and dulled thoughts, she was well aware he had saved her life. He didn't look all that pleased about it. Neither was she. She didn't want to owe him, but she couldn't dance around the fact that she did.

"I...thank you. For saving my life," she said quietly.

His shoulder lifted. "You're the one who knew what to do. I guess that's because your pa's a doctor."

"I could've died out there." She saw a flare of emotion burn through the guarded blue depths of his eyes.

Sober acknowledgment passed between them, and Josie felt a solid connection to another person that she hadn't experienced since the deaths of her parents.

He gave her a crooked grin. "You cured of wanting those shooting lessons?"

"No." She licked her parched lips and tried for a smile. "I might have to save *you* sometime."

He chuckled. "Unless you use something other than a gun, I don't have a prayer."

"My aim will improve," she said weakly.

"I'd say it has to." His eyes crinkled at the corners. He poured more water and held her head to drink. "Feel like you're gonna make it now?"

"I think so."

His fixed attention made Josie think he wanted to say something further, but the moment was lost as Catherine walked into the room.

"Morning," he said. Immediate relief spread across Davis Lee's face. "Doin' all right?"

"Yes." The nurse's gaze met his and it seemed that an unspoken message passed between them. She wore the same blue dress Josie recalled from last night.

He smiled fully at his friend, a smile Josie had seen only one other time. The expression blunted the sharp angles of his face. There was something in his demeanor.... Fondness, respect, something deep and soft.

Josie's gaze shifted to the raven-haired woman then back to Davis Lee. There had been something between them once. When? How serious?

Catherine's beautiful face was exhausted, but her eyes lit up at the sight of Josie. "I'm glad to see you're awake."

"It's only been a few minutes." The lawman scrubbed a hand across his face, stepping back to make room for her.

"I spoke to Dr. Butler about coming in to check you, but he thinks I'm doing everything possible. Still, if you'd rather he examine you, I'd be happy to send for him."

"No. I think you're doing just fine."

"I guess between the two of us we figured it out, didn't we?" Catherine smiled and put a cool hand against Josie's forehead. "I think your fever's down a bit."

Josie blotted her wet face and chest with the sheet. "Now the sweats."

"I'm afraid so. I can give you a sponge bath. That will make you feel a little better."

"Thank you."

"I can bring a bathing tub up here, Catherine," Davis Lee said. "If you want it."

She smiled. "That would be wonderful. I think Josie would appreciate a real bath."

"Consider it done."

Josie wasn't going to complain about getting in the water rather than just getting a wiping-down, but she was a little surprised that the sheriff would volunteer for such a chore when it would be easier if she just took the sponge bath. Josie knew his offer had more to do with his friendship with the nurse than anything about her.

Catherine squeezed Josie's shoulder. "I want to make another poultice and some tea for you."

Davis Lee had remained in his spot away from the bed. "Want me to bring that tub now or wait for you to get what you need?"

"Now, if you don't mind."

He cocked his head toward the door in a silent request and Catherine joined him. Their voices were too low for Josie to make out any words then he left.

As he left, the other woman returned to Josie. "I started the tea before I came up. It's steeping. When he returns, I'll get it."

"I don't look forward to drinking it. Not if it tastes anything like this poultice smells."

"I don't blame you." Catherine made a face. "Since Davis Lee is gone for a bit, let me check your wound."

Pushing the leg of Josie's combination up a little farther, she untied the cloth strips holding the splint in place then gently unwrapped the dressing, peeling it away with the poultice.

"Can you tell anything yet?" Josie tried to see but Catherine hid her view.

"I don't see any signs of infection, but it's still quite swollen. I think the poultice is working but it will take a while."

"How does the cut look?"

"The scar probably won't be too unsightly. Davis Lee was careful."

"Yes, he was." Josie bit the inside of her cheek then asked Catherine what she hadn't been able to ask the man who'd saved her life. "Did you undress me?"

"Yes." She smiled. "And I'm sorry I wasn't here when you woke. I hope you weren't uncomfortable with Davis Lee."

Of course not, she thought testily. She was quite used to being practically naked and alone with men who gave her the shivers. "No," she mumbled.

Catherine pressed a clean dry rag to Josie's perspiring forehead and chest. "The bath will help your fever to come down. Davis Lee said you were a little out of your head."

Josie frowned. "What do you mean?"

"Just that you said some things."

As if her heart weren't already beating too fast. "What things?"

"He didn't say." She grinned. "Are you worried you said something shocking?"

"Of course not," Josie said weakly. But she was. *What*

had she said? "I appreciate you asking him to stay with me during the night while you tended to your other patient."

"Oh, I didn't ask him. Esther agreed to stay with you when I was called away, but when Davis Lee came to check on you, he found her asleep."

He had come to check on her? "He didn't tell me that."

Catherine smiled.

"The two of you are really good friends," Josie ventured, her eyes growing heavy.

"Yes. He was one of the first people I met when I moved here. One of the sweetest men I know."

Sweet? That was a word Josie hadn't put to the sheriff. "Were you...the two of you ever...?"

"Involved? Not seriously."

"I guess that was before you fell in love with his cousin?"

"Yes." At the mention of her betrothed, the same serene pleasure Josie had observed on her mother's face when she spoke about her father suffused Catherine's features.

"Does Davis Lee still care for you that way?"

"Oh, no."

Her tongue felt thick. She fought the drowsiness spreading through her. "He seems to have taken your decision well."

"He knew it before I did."

A loud clambering, interspersed with Davis Lee's husky voice, had Josie's gaze going to the door. In a few seconds, he walked into the room, carrying an oblong tin bathtub. Muscles in his shoulders and arms bunched beneath his shirt as he placed the tub against the far wall. She noticed then that someone had moved her fabric and stacked it neatly in the corner. Catherine? Esther? Or Davis Lee?

He started out the door again and the nurse said over her shoulder, "I can bring the water up with Penn's dumbwaiter."

"I'll do it. Oh, Mitchell Orr was downstairs checking on Josie. I told him she was doing okay, but wasn't up to having visitors right now."

"That's good," Catherine murmured, cleaning the wound again.

Josie didn't much appreciate Davis Lee saying who could and couldn't see her, but she had no energy to protest. Or visit with anyone either, if she were honest. "Thank you," she said breathlessly.

"You're welcome." His narrowed gaze probed hers, and he looked like he wanted to slap her in wrist irons.

Why? Because he knew she was watching the jail? Or maybe because of what she'd said in her fever? Panic flickered. What *had* she said?

Drat this snakebite! And her fever! And him! What if she had blurted out her reason for coming to Whirlwind to the one man who could stop her from getting justice for her family—the man who had saved her life?

It was another three days before Josie could get out of bed, and she was more than ready. Her backside would probably be permanently numb from being pressed into that mattress for so long. On Friday afternoon, she was planted in a chair looking out the window and was working on the same tablecloth hem she'd been working on since after lunch.

The fever and sweats had finally passed and her vision was no longer blurry. But her left calf was still somewhat swollen and she was weak. Catherine said she would be for a while and that she had to rest often.

Even if Josie hadn't given the nurse her word, she would've gone easy. Just having a bath and washing her hair this morning had left her feeling wobbly. It didn't help the boneless feeling in her legs when she put on a clean undergarment and realized her corset was missing. No, not missing. Davis Lee had it. And her scalpel, too.

She wrinkled her nose, watching people move across the street below, go in and out of Haskell's, the Pearl Restaurant. Asking for her weapon would pose no problem, but Josie did not fancy asking for her corset at all. Why couldn't he just discreetly give it to her? She would have to talk to him alone, and considering that Davis Lee had taken pains to *not* be alone with her since that morning he'd seen her nearly naked, it would only make asking for her underwear more awkward.

All morning, she had chewed on that delicate problem as much as she had fretted about Ian McDougal. Had there been any change with him while she was indisposed? Was he still in jail? She wanted to believe he was, but she couldn't assume, not after he'd managed to elude a cell altogether after murdering her parents and William. Not after he'd managed to escape several months ago from Davis Lee and his cousin, the Texas Ranger.

If McDougal were still in jail, she could keep an eye on him from here as she had intended, but if plans had been made for his trial or to move him, Josie would have to do something, and right now she didn't have the strength to do more than lift her hairbrush. Josie could've asked Catherine when the nurse had stopped by this morning, but she didn't want it getting back to Davis Lee. He was already suspicious of her.

When Esther had brought her lunch, Josie tiptoed around the subject by asking the woman if anything exciting had happened in town while she'd been ill. Esther told her about the baby Catherine had delivered the first night of Josie's illness, that Charlie Haskell and his nephew had been over twice to ask about her and that Catherine's little brother, Andrew, had won the county spelling bee.

All things that made Josie feel more a part of Whirlwind,

but didn't do her one whit of good as far as Ian McDougal was concerned. When Josie asked her straight out about the prisoner, the other woman had pursed her lips then said she had no idea if he was here, there or yon.

Frustration swirled inside her. She would be able to find out for herself if she could take a walk in town or sit in the hotel's lobby, but she didn't think her weak-as-powder legs could even manage the stairs.

A dark-haired man coming out of the telegraph office drew her eye. The trim haircut, the wide shoulders molded by a white shirt were familiar and Josie felt a little tug of feminine appreciation in her belly. Davis Lee stepped down into the street, settling his hat on his head as he talked to two of the biggest men she had ever seen.

One had black hair and one had hair just shy of black. They were at least two inches taller than Davis Lee's six-foot-two, with arms so massive they could probably hoist a cow. Her attention stayed on the lanky sheriff. He might not be as big, but he was surely every bit as strong. Josie had felt that for herself.

Davis Lee had been by to check on her every day but he hadn't set foot in her room again. He always came when Catherine was here and he didn't venture inside. Josie dismissed the little pinch of hurt she felt over that. Just because he had saved her life didn't mean she was going soft in the head over him.

She should be glad he was keeping his distance. She *was* glad. If for no other reason than the man had seen far more of her body than he ought and she couldn't look him in the eye.

Davis Lee finished his conversation with the two men and started back toward the jail.

A knock sounded on the door. "Josie?"

She recognized Esther's voice. "Come in."

The door opened a crack and the woman stuck her head

in the room. "You've got a couple of visitors if you're up for it. Cora Wilkes and her brother."

Josie remembered meeting the pair at church. Had that been only five days ago? She felt she had been indisposed for weeks. Loren Barnes had told her he was new to Whirlwind, too. She smiled. "How nice. Tell them to come in."

She braced one hand on the windowsill for balance and as she got to her feet, Esther pushed the door wide. Cora and her brother walked in, smiles wreathing their faces. The older woman was probably six inches taller than Josie, with a slender, straight-spined build. Her warm smile didn't erase the shadow of sadness in her hazel eyes, but her brother's blue eyes twinkled.

Cora adjusted the basket that hung over her arm. "You feel free to tell us if you're too spent for company."

"I'm getting tired of my own." Josie smiled. "I'm sorry I don't have more chairs."

"We won't stay long. Just wanted to come by and see how you were doing." Loren topped his sister by about three inches. His hair was completely white whereas Cora's was a deep brown with a few silver threads.

"It can be hard when you're new somewhere and run into trouble," Cora said. "You go ahead and sit down. Catherine said you'd be weak."

Josie, her knees already wobbling, sank gratefully back into the chair. She stuck her needle into the tablecloth and laid it in her lap.

Loren indicated the window with the tilt of his head. "Got yourself a nice view."

"Yes. I was getting tired of staring at the walls." She bet these two would know if there was any news about McDougal.

"I brought you some marble cake." The other woman took a cloth-covered tin plate from her basket and walked over to the dresser. "I'll just leave it here and you can have it when you want."

"Thank you. It sounds delicious."

Cora moved to stand in front of Josie. "We wanted to come sooner, but Catherine thought we should wait."

"I wouldn't have been good company," she admitted.

"Your color's good." Cora eyed her kindly. "Catherine seems to think you'll recover just fine."

"I think so."

"You're probably getting antsy in here," Loren said. "It's been three or four days, hasn't it?"

"Four." She gave a weak smile. "I think."

"I've never known anybody with a snakebite. I hear it's painful."

Josie nodded. "I certainly don't want to go through it again."

"Where were you when it happened?" Cora asked.

"About ten minutes west of town."

Pain flared in the woman's hazel eyes. "I put a stone for Ollie out that way. A little marker."

Josie hadn't meant to open a wound and saw no reason to reveal that Davis Lee had taken her to that exact spot.

Cora's forehead puckered. "I've seen snakes there before but they've never bothered anyone. I'm glad Davis Lee shot it."

"Too bad he can't shoot the snake in his jail," Loren muttered.

Cora gave him a fond look. "Preachers aren't supposed to say such things."

"Well, somebody should kill that outlaw." He jammed his hands in the pockets of his gray trousers and gave his sister a devilish grin. "Besides, I'm not a preacher anymore."

"I guess that means the prisoner is still in jail?" Josie asked.

"Yes, still waiting on the circuit judge," Cora answered quietly. "I'll be glad to see justice done."

"Let's hope it is." Frustration flashed across her brother's leathery features. "I heard he's escaped trial before, somewhere down by the Gulf."

"That marshal who caught him will be here for the trial." Cora stared past Josie, a distant look in her eyes. "His testimony should be enough to see that McDougal pays for what he's done. And there's Andrew."

"Catherine's brother?" Josie sat forward. "What would he know?"

Cora stared out the window, a distant look in her eyes.

Loren answered. "The kid got tangled up with the gang somehow."

"How old is he?" she asked in surprise.

"Twelve or thereabouts. I don't know the whole story, just that the gang found out Catherine was a nurse and snatched her so she could doctor Ian's tuberculosis. Andrew fetched the Ranger who'd been on their trail—"

"Jericho Blue, Catherine's intended," Cora interjected quietly.

"Yes," he continued. "Andrew fetched Lieutenant Blue. The pair of them took off with Davis Lee and Riley. They managed to get Catherine back safely and dispatch three of the worthless curs. Ian was the only one who escaped, but word is that he had taken Andrew into his confidence about a couple of things. Their shooting Ollie is one of them. The boy can testify to that."

"Oh, my." Davis Lee had told her how he and the Ranger had killed the other McDougals.

She was glad to know there was more than one person who had knowledge of the outlaws' misdeeds and was willing to step forward, but she hated to think about the pain it would rake up. If Ian was indeed tried this time, Josie knew it would be painful for her. Surely for Cora, too. Maybe also

Andrew and Catherine. How many people had the Mc-
Dougals hurt?

"Well, listen to us. It's too nice a day to be so gloomy."
Cora shook her head. "We didn't come here to talk about
that no-good varmint. We came to invite you to dinner."

Cora's brother shot her a look of mild surprise.

"You did?" Josie was warmed by their friendliness but
wondering why Loren looked as if he hadn't known.

"On Tuesday night."

"But Tuesday is—" the man began.

"Do you think you can come?" Cora cut him off, smiling
at Josie.

Her gaze shifted uncertainly between brother and sister.
"Are you sure Tuesday's all right?"

"It's perfect."

"I'd like to, but I'm not sure."

"Why not, hon?" Cora sounded disappointed.

Josie gave a self-conscious laugh. "I don't have the
strength to manage the stairs yet."

"Oh. Well, let's say you're coming, then if you're unable,
you just send word and we'll plan for another time. All
right?"

"All right. I'll look forward to it."

"So will we." Cora patted her hand.

A soft rap sounded on the door frame at the same time a
deep, now-familiar voice said, "Good afternoon."

"Davis Lee." Despite the sadness that lurked in Cora's
eyes, she turned with a fond smile.

The sheriff moved inside, his large body making the room
seem crowded. He hugged the older woman before extend-
ing a hand to her brother. "Loren."

"Hello, Davis Lee."

His shrewd blue gaze met Josie's and she inwardly
squirmed. She thought he had returned to the jail. She
wanted to see him but she didn't. Every time she did, she

was hit with the memory of his hands on her. His gaze. And it sparked an unfamiliar and startling flare of desire. It didn't matter that she had been asleep for most of the time he'd cooled her down with that wet rag. Her body *knew* he had touched her, traitorously going soft whenever she saw him.

She realized that Cora had said something and she forced her attention to the woman.

"Do you need any help with your sewing? I know that snakebite had to slow you down and I'd be happy to help if you're in a pinch."

"It's kind of you to offer, but so far I'm able to manage. I'm working slower but it does give me something to do. I hope to get a little stronger every day."

"If you change your mind, let me know." The other woman patted her hand. "We'll go on now so you can get a little rest."

"Thank you for coming."

Brother and sister said their goodbyes to Davis Lee and walked out. The sheriff followed them to the door. From the hall, she heard Loren's voice, low and urgent, but couldn't understand his words.

Now that she was alone with Davis Lee, she fully expected him to leave, too. Instead he turned, his gaze flicking over her.

He braced both hands on the door frame and leaned in. "Looks like you're coming around, Josie. I see you made it over to your spot by the window today."

"It feels wonderful to get up," she said carefully. She caught the warning tone in his voice. Yes, he definitely knew what she was about.

That shirt fit his broad chest entirely too well. The white fabric shifted with the play of muscle, brought out the deep bronze of his skin and the piercing blue of his eyes. "It's been a long four days."

His intense study had her skin warming. "Catherine's been here?"

"This morning." The top two buttons of his shirt were undone, revealing the strong column of his throat and a hint of dark chest hair.

"Well, I'm glad to see you're up. Just stopped by to check on you."

"Thank you," she murmured. Most likely he had come to see if she was spying on his jail.

He tipped his hat and levered himself away from the door.

"Um, Sheriff?"

"Davis Lee," he reminded in a gravelly voice.

"Davis Lee." She swallowed, fixing her gaze on a spot in the center of his chest. "I wondered if I might get my scalpel."

"Sure. It's still in my saddlebag."

"And my…" She cleared her throat, assailed by the memory of him jerking off her undergarment. "My corset. You have that, too. Don't you?"

"Do I?" His lips quirked. "You saying you lost yours, Miz Webster?"

"No." The banked heat in his eyes flustered her. "Yes."

"What's it worth to you?"

Her eyes widened. "You'd make me bargain for my own clothing?"

One corner of his mouth hitched up in a grin. "Could be interesting."

"And just what are you going to do with it?"

"Well," he said in a voice that sent a jolt of sensation straight to her toes, "I only know one thing to do with a corset."

And the bold sweep of his gaze over her body said he'd done it the day she'd been bitten.

"Oh." She tried to breathe past the lock on her lungs. His gaze was too hot, too raw. She glanced away.

"Any more of your corsets I should be looking for around town?"

Her face burned. "Stop teasing me. It was hard enough to ask you."

He grinned. "I'll be right back with your things."

"Thank you," she said quietly as he walked away.

Davis Lee couldn't miss the blush that colored her peach-tinted skin. Jogging down the stairs, he tried not to think about how tempting she looked sitting in the sunlight with her deep mahogany hair tumbling around her shoulders like gold-touched silk. Or how her modest green-and-white striped dress turned her eyes the color of moss.

He wouldn't allow himself to get waylaid by her pretty face or her sinful curves. The telegram he'd sent three days ago to the sheriff of Galveston County still hadn't been answered. Davis Lee had no choice but to make allowance for the hurricane and any resulting damage, but he was impatient to find out if Sheriff Locke knew anything about Josie Webster.

He reached his horse, which was hitched in front of the jail, and flipped open the saddlebag closest to him. He had the undergarment halfway out before he realized he couldn't go waltzing back to the hotel and up to her room carrying the darn thing in plain sight. Stuffing the corset back inside the leather pouch, he tugged his saddlebags off the buckskin and carried them back to the hotel.

He paused in her doorway. Her full attention was focused out the window. No doubt on his jail. Yes, he really needed to hear from that sheriff. His jaw tightened. "Here you go."

She jerked toward him, flushing guiltily. She was still pale and he noticed a slight trembling in her body, which was what caused him to waver about questioning her. But if she was well enough to resume her spying, she could damn well answer him.

Stopping about a foot away, he flipped open the leather pouch and pulled out her corset, dangling it in front of her.

She flushed deeper, the blush tinting her neck.

He bit back a smile at the shock in her eyes over his familiar handling of her undergarment. He sure did like vexing her. "Where do you want it?"

She snatched it from him, crushing it as small as she could. Josie was used to seeing undergarments, discussing them delicately with men who wanted something new for their wives, but she wasn't used to men handling *hers*. And certainly not in front of her. His hands were big and dark against the lightly boned eggshell fabric. She remembered those hands on her, braced herself against a stirring deep inside.

He didn't act the least bit uncomfortable. He probably handled women's underwear with obscene regularity, she thought irritably.

Reaching back into the saddlebag, he withdrew her scalpel. "I suppose you'll be wanting this—" his gaze dipped to her bosom "—where you can get to it."

"I'd like to get to it right now," she muttered.

At his low chuckle, her fingers curled tighter around the soft edge of her corset. She forced herself to release her grip and hold out her hand. He passed the instrument to her carefully.

"Thank you." His gaze was hot on her breasts and he was probably wondering if she would slip it into the secret pocket of her bodice. But she laid the scalpel on the windowsill.

She expected him to go now. Instead he stayed where he was, filling up the room with his heat and size and purely male scent. His gaze slid over her. "How are you feeling?"

"Still weak, but much better." Unsure of what he was about, she gave him a tentative smile. She was unreasonably glad he wasn't leaving as quickly as he generally did.

"Good. Glad to hear it." His gaze traced the hair that had fallen over her shoulder onto her breasts, moved down her torso and all the way to her black boots. "I've been wanting to ask you something."

She tensed, expecting a question about her interest in the jail. "Yes?"

"Who's William?"

William! Josie's heartbeat stuttered.

Davis Lee folded his big arms and stared expectantly at her.

Pain, loss, anger shot through her. "W-why do you ask?"

"You mentioned him during your fever."

"I did?" What else had she said? McDougal's name, too? Rattled, she pressed her spine into the chair. "He was my fiancé."

"Was?" he probed.

She didn't owe him an explanation, didn't want to give him one, but she found herself saying baldly, "He died."

The sheriff waited a long moment. "What happened?"

As if she would tell him. "I can't talk about it. It's too…upsetting."

"When did it happen?"

"Two years ago." Why did he care? Why didn't he just go?

Impatience flashed across the lawman's strong features and she fully expected he would press but finally he said in a strained voice, "I'm sorry for your loss."

She nodded stiffly, shaken that she had unwittingly mentioned William during her fever, driven to know if there was more. "Did I say anything else?"

"Something about blood."

Her gaze shot to his. The casual ease with which he'd said the words didn't match the intensity in his eyes.

"I reckon I've been wondering about that, too," he said quietly.

Her pulse hitched as her mind hurtled back to the bloody scene where she'd found William and her parents. She should make up something to appease the sheriff, but she couldn't lie. Not after what he'd done for her. Her voice was uneven as she gave him the only truth she could. "As I said, I can't bring myself to talk about it."

He studied her, his blue gaze probing and steady, then before she could blink, he leaned down. His whisker-sanded cheek brushed hers and his warm breath tickled her ear. Sharp sensation shot straight to her core. "Maybe someday you'll trust me enough to tell me."

"Maybe," she murmured, her hands closing tight on the tablecloth in her lap.

Oh, he needed to move away right now because she desperately wanted him to kiss her. He was so close, teasing her senses with an enticing mix of male and leather and the outdoors. All she had to do was turn her head, raise it just a fraction.

It was a struggle to bring her mind back to what he'd said. Trust him? She wouldn't. She couldn't. Why did he have to make it about trust? Guilt nipped at her. She owed him for saving her life, but she didn't owe him every part of herself.

Davis Lee straightened slowly, his breath drifting against her temple, one finger stroking her hair there. The wicked glint in his eyes told her he was well aware of how he unsettled her. He tossed his saddlebags over his right shoulder. "I'll go now. You best rest or Catherine will know."

She forced a smile, determined not to let him see that her spine had gone boneless. "I think she really would."

"I'll check on you tomorrow."

She knew he would. Just as he would check on her every day she was here. For the first time, that warning scared the devil out of her. It had nothing to do with Davis Lee the *sheriff* finding out her connection to McDougal. And everything to do with Davis Lee the *man* sending that delicious shiver through her body.

Chapter Six

Just before six on Tuesday evening, as he did every Tuesday evening, Davis Lee left the jail, this time in Jake's capable hands. Before going to Cora's, he went two doors down to the telegraph office and had Tony Santos send another wire to the sheriff in Galveston. Davis Lee realized it might be too soon after the hurricane for the telegraph wires to be working, but it wouldn't hurt to try and reach Sheriff Locke again.

Lamps from the Pearl behind him and lanterns hanging outside the saloon across the street lit Davis Lee's way as he started for Cora's. Being this close to the edge of town, he had only Ef's smithy to pass before angling down the west side of the big man's barn toward Cora's. The new hotel, which sat behind the livery across the street, was nearly finished. He wondered when the owner would arrive.

The puppy he carried burrowed his nose into the crook of Davis Lee's arm. Cora's house sat at the bottom of a gentle slope behind the shed-size building that had formerly served as the stagecoach stop. Built of unfinished wood, the house was small and homey. Lamps burning in Cora's two front windows put off a warm glow in the cool, still night. Davis Lee's long stride took him from the ground to the porch without touching the two steps. He hoped his friend liked her surprise.

He rapped twice on the door and opened it. "Cora, I brought you something—"

He broke off at the sight of Josie standing on the other side of the table, staring at him. She held a stack of plates, her mouth open in surprise.

His mind flashed the image of her practically naked. It was seared into his brain and had been since he'd tended her during her fever. Knowing exactly what she wore beneath that prim cinnamon-colored dress had his breath backing up in his lungs.

The puppy, black with a white streak across his left eye, wiggled in his hold and snuggled deeper.

Cora straightened from taking a pan out of the squat stove, flicking a satisfied look between him and her other guest before catching sight of the animal. "Well, what's this?"

"He's darling," Josie breathed.

Davis Lee knew she was looking at the dog, not at him, but that didn't stop his skin from going tight. *What* was she doing here?

Cora set the hot pan of biscuits on top of the stove and moved around the table to him.

"You don't have to keep him if you don't want." Davis Lee dragged his gaze to the older woman, but his mind was still on Josie. Her dress skimmed her body like a shadow, molding perfectly to her breasts, tapering to the nip of her waist. The neckline was square and edged with the same buff-colored lace that was on her sleeves. Only the creamy patch of skin above her collarbone showed. "Jake said he'd take the dog back if you're not interested."

"He's such a cute little thing. I'd like to keep him." Cora took the puppy and held him up to eye level, giving him the once-over as he squirmed. "What made you think of it?"

He shrugged. "Just seemed like a good idea when I saw the new litter."

She leaned up and kissed his cheek. "Thank you."

He knew the one-year anniversary of Ollie's death was approaching and he hoped that maybe the company of her brother and the dog might ease it for her a bit.

Josie's gaze shifted from the pup to him. There was a softness in her eyes he hadn't seen before, which started a low throb in his blood. She was a sight. For the first time in a week, a hint of color glowed in her face. Tendrils escaped from her loosely upswept hair and teased the velvety flesh of her neck. His gaze settled on the delicate earlobe he'd been close enough to nip the other day.

She jerked her gaze from his and moved abruptly, setting plates carefully at each chair around the table.

One look at Cora told him he'd correctly read the satisfaction in her hazel eyes.

"Come in, Davis Lee," she said. "Supper's almost ready."

He cleared his throat. "Do I have the wrong night?"

"No." His friend smiled, putting the puppy on the floor and walking to the corner behind the stove to pick up a crate. "I invited Josie, too. I hated the thought of her eating alone."

"Hi, Josie." He nodded, unable to stop his gaze from tracing her curves.

"Hi." Her eyes were wide and wary.

Cora removed some books from the crate and turned to the younger woman, who now looked at her uncertainly. "Davis Lee eats with us on Tuesday nights."

"I don't want to intrude," Josie said quietly.

"Nonsense. This will round out the conversation nicely. Don't you think, Loren?"

"Yes." Smoothing back his thick white hair, her brother walked out of the smaller bedroom. The blue calico curtain that served as a door fell into place behind him. "Now Cora won't feel ganged up on when Davis Lee and I disagree with her."

Davis Lee didn't know what had given Cora the idea to match him up with Josie, but he knew that was what she was doing.

"I'll finish setting the table." Josie wouldn't meet his eyes. She hadn't since he had returned her corset last Friday. He had taken care not to be alone with her for the past few days, stopping by to check on her when he knew Catherine was there.

He didn't fancy being this close to her now. Her light honeysuckle scent already teased him and he wasn't even in the house yet. But he couldn't pass up the opportunity to try and learn more about her. Maybe his little spy would be more talkative if they weren't alone.

He had let lust drown out his instincts with Betsy. He wasn't going to make the same mistake with Josie Webster. He stepped inside and palmed off his hat, hanging it on the nail just inside the door.

Cora made a bed of fabric scraps in the wooden box for the pup. Josie tied a piece of cloth into a knot and teased him until he growled playfully and tugged it away. After washing up, everyone took a place at the table.

As the meal progressed, Loren and Cora had them laughing over stories of sibling rivalry from their younger years. Josie's smile came easier and the stiff set of her shoulders finally relaxed.

"Josie, have you heard about the harvest dance at Eishen's pecan grove?" Cora asked.

"No."

"The Eishens have a dance every year before the start of pecan harvest. You should plan to go."

"It sounds fun."

Davis Lee had never gone. Josie didn't look as if she were too sure of going herself.

"It's coming up," Cora continued. "Not this Friday, but the next. Why don't you go with Loren and I?"

Josie looked at the brother and sister, a smile curving her lips. "All right."

"All the ladies bring pies," the other woman said. "If you want to bake one, you can use my stove."

"Okay, thank you."

"The dance is a good way for you to meet people and let them know you're a dressmaker." She leaned toward Josie and touched the lace at the edge of her sleeve. "I've been admiring this dress. I'm guessing you made it?"

"Yes."

"Your stitch is so fine, I can hardly see it."

"Thank you." Josie flushed becomingly, putting Davis Lee in mind of the rosy tint of her flesh during her fever.

"Who taught you?"

"My mother."

He caught a hint of wistfulness beneath the words.

The older woman patted Josie's hand. "She must be very good."

"Yes." Josie smiled pleasantly, but Davis Lee sensed a stillness come over her.

Loren reached for his coffee. "Did you say you were from Galveston?"

She nodded, dabbing the corners of her mouth with a cloth napkin.

"Do your folks mind you being so far away?"

"They've never said so."

Davis Lee detected a slight crack in her voice.

Cora rose and took a small bowl from the tall pantry behind Josie. "Are they still in Galveston?"

If Davis Lee hadn't been watching so closely, he

would've missed the bright sheen of tears in her eyes before she answered. "Yes."

He noticed she didn't volunteer the information that she'd had a betrothed there, too. He made a mental note to ask about her parents and the fiancé when he heard back from the sheriff down there.

Cora crumbled up a biscuit, added a splash of milk from the pitcher by the sink and set the bowl down in front of the puppy. "Since you've decided to stay in Whirlwind, do you expect your folks to join you?"

"Like Loren did?" Josie smiled warmly at him. "His coming had to be a great help. It must be wonderful to have a brother."

The other woman resumed her seat, nodding. "I don't know what I would've done without him."

"I should've come sooner," he said from his place opposite his sister.

"You had Belle to think about."

The man turned to Josie, a shadow chasing across his face. "Belle was my wife. She passed on several months ago."

"I'm sorry."

"We had a good life. That's what I try to remember, but sometimes it's hard."

"Yes, very," she murmured. After a slight pause, she glanced at Cora. "Any idea what you might name the puppy?"

The other woman pursed her lips. "Not yet."

Davis Lee finished his meal, outwardly showing only mild interest. Inside he took heed of how Josie had deftly steered the conversation away from herself. Even the answers she had given revealed no details.

"Will you be making Catherine a new dress for the wedding?" Cora asked.

"She hired me but now I'll have to see if she wants

someone else since I might not have it ready as early as she would like.''

''I meant what I said about helping you. Let me know if I can.''

''Thank you.'' The smile Josie flashed had a strange tension stretching across Davis Lee's belly.

The older woman stood and began gathering dishes. ''I'm sure glad you were with Davis Lee when that snake bit you. He can handle anything.''

''All I did was follow orders,'' he drawled, grinning when Josie's gaze met his.

She eyed him drolly. ''He's not very good at it, let me tell you.''

He chuckled along with Cora and Loren. Since Cora and Loren's questions had stopped, Josie seemed more at ease.

She rose to help Cora clear the dishes from the table. ''You have a nice home.''

''Susannah lived here with me when she first came to Whirlwind.'' Cora pointed to the doorway covered by a blue curtain. ''In the room Loren has now.''

''My niece was born in that room.'' Davis Lee leaned back in his chair, rubbing a palm over his chest. He wished he could stop thinking about what Josie had on under her dress. It near drove him crazy.

After some of Cora's butter cake and coffee, Josie helped their hostess wash and dry the dishes. Davis Lee brought in water to fill both the kettle and the iron spider hanging in the fireplace then went out back to help Loren check Cora's chickens and her mare, Prissy.

When the men returned to the house, Josie was halfway into her dark wool cloak, the puppy tugging playfully on one end. She was laughing, and the way it lit her whole face had Davis Lee stopping midstep.

For an instant, the shadows were gone from her eyes and they glowed. He couldn't take his eyes off her. The curve of her lips, the golden peach of her skin, the simple pleasure in her eyes when she looked at the pup. Something hot unfurled and spread through his chest.

Loren turned for the door. "I'll hitch up the wagon again. It won't take long."

"No, that's all right." Josie's gaze went past Davis Lee to the older man. "You went to all that trouble to drive me over. I have plenty of energy to walk."

"You sure, hon?" Cora looked her over thoroughly. "It hasn't been all that long since you were snakebit. You're not too spent?"

"I'm fine."

"Davis Lee can walk back with you," the other woman offered.

He sent her a look, letting her know he saw right through her little scheme. Josie opened her mouth, to protest he knew. So he said, "I'm headed there anyway."

"Yes, he's headed there anyway," Cora said enthusiastically.

He mentally shook his head at her blatant matchmaking.

Giving him a panicked look, Josie managed to get her cloak out of the puppy's sharp teeth. "If you're not ready to go yet—"

"I am. Cora, thanks for supper. It was delicious." He covered the few steps between them and leaned down to buss her cheek, saying in a low voice, "You're not very subtle."

"I didn't think you were going to do anything about it," she said under her breath.

If she knew his suspicions about Josie, Cora would have left things alone.

After goodbyes all around, he and Josie started back to the hotel. The sky was icy black, the stars brilliant shards of light against its backdrop. Smoke from the fireplaces of the few nearby homes drifted on the air, mixing with the smells of earth and grass.

Josie's sweet scent curled around him. She kept a careful distance between him, walking slowly as she pulled on her short, dark gloves. He shortened his stride to keep pace with her. "Was the visit too much for you?"

"I'm tired," she admitted with a wan smile. "But Catherine warned me that it would take a while for my energy to return. I might've stayed too long, but I really enjoyed it. Cora and Loren are both so nice."

"Yes."

She moved slowly up the rise beside him, her skirts making a soft swishing noise against the grass. She didn't complain, but she looked wobbly.

He took her gloved hand and tucked it in the crook of his arm. When she resisted, he said quietly, "You look like you're about to fall down."

"I'm sure I'll be fine." She glanced at him, then away. Finally, tentatively, she curved her fingers over his arm.

As they passed the jail, she said, "That puppy is cute. Cora seemed pleased."

"I hope it's some comfort to her."

"You mean because the anniversary of her husband's death is coming up?"

He nodded. "Did she tell you about that?"

"Loren did. He's very solicitous of her."

Davis Lee nodded. "I thought having some company might make at least one of her days easier to bear."

A funny, sad smile quirked her lips. "That's nice."

He watched her carefully, wanting to see what effect his next words had on her. "It's going to give me great pleasure to see Ian McDougal finally pay for killing Ollie Wilkes."

"If he does pay," she said caustically.

Was she doubtful that the law would try the outlaw this

time? Or hinting that he might escape before the trial?
"What do you mean?"

"Just that he's managed to avoid a trial so far."

"He won't avoid it here," Davis Lee said with utter certainty.

"I hope not."

He felt the slight tightening of her fingers on him, sensed her distancing herself again. He about ground his teeth to a nub. Getting anywhere with this woman was like trying to get water from a rock. "There are too many people here that the McDougals have hurt. They won't stand for Ian going free."

She didn't speak for a long moment, the sound of their footsteps lost in the vastness of the night. "What if they have no choice? The judge might be persuaded to say there are no grounds for a trial."

"If that happens and Ian is set free, I can guarantee you Jericho will go after him and he won't stop until the bastard's dead. He'll have all the help he wants, too."

She looked up at him, moonlight skimming over the soft curve of her cheek. "From you?"

"And Riley and just about everybody around these parts. The McDougals have killed a lot of innocent folks and threatened plenty more."

"Like Susannah and Catherine?"

"Yes." He couldn't read the expression on Josie's face, but before she looked away he registered the hollow loss in her eyes.

His heart gave a vicious twist. Was her sadness for her dead fiancé or something more? There had to be more. Davis Lee knew there were layers to her that he might never see.

They reached the Whirlwind Hotel, and when she would've pulled away, he covered her gloved hand with his. "I'll walk you in."

She stared up at him, fatigue plain on her delicate features. He got the distinct sense she wanted to deny him, but after a moment, she said, "Thank you."

They .mounted the steps and he held the door for her. Kerosene lamps on both corners of the registration desk and a small table in the center of the lobby brightened their way to the staircase. A lamp on the second floor sent pale yellow light tripping down the stairs. Penn stood just inside the dining room talking to a couple of patrons.

As soon as Davis Lee and Josie reached the bottom of the stairs, she slipped her hand free of his arm. "You don't have to see me up."

The fact that he again imagined her in that sheer undergarment told him it was probably better if he didn't. "Okay. I'll say good night then."

"Good night." Gripping the banister, she backed onto the first step.

He stood there, startled by the impulse to twine a finger in the silky strand of hair that tickled her neck.

She hesitated then turned and started up the stairs. Davis Lee watched her; he couldn't help himself. Her brownish-red hair was caught up loosely in the back but he pictured it down as it had been all the days she'd lain ill in her bed— a thick, silky curtain across her pillow, falling over her shoulder.

His gaze was drawn to her trim back, the small waist, following the line of her skirt as he imagined the sleek legs beneath. The memory of her body in that see-through thing rode him like a devil.

She had climbed two stairs when he saw her pause, her shoulder resting against the wall.

"Josie?"

"I'm all right," she said faintly.

He reached her in one stride. "You don't look all right."

She lifted her head and gave him a wan smile. "I'm just tired."

"Let me help you up."

"I don't need your help," she said evenly. "I can do it."

"Okay." He stayed where he was in case her legs gave out, which they looked inclined to do. Stubborn female.

She trudged up three more steps and halted again.

"Josie?"

"I'm fine."

He didn't say anything, just waited.

After a bit, she took another step, bracing her hand against the wall. There were at least six or eight more stairs to go.

Dadburned woman. Davis Lee moved up behind her and swept her up into his arms. Stunned at the jolt her sweet body gave his, he said gruffly, "If you wanted me to take you upstairs, all you had to do was ask."

"Oh, put me down!" She pushed weakly at his chest, a blush spreading from her neck to the roots of her hair. "What if someone sees?"

He started up the stairs. "At the rate you were going, it would've taken you an hour to get to your room."

"Hardly." She wedged an arm between them, holding herself stiffly away from him.

He looked down at her, able to see a hint of the valley between her breasts. "You obviously overtaxed yourself tonight."

"My legs are tired, not broken." She struggled feebly to get down. "I'm sure I can walk."

"You can walk tomorrow. Be still. I'm just helping you get to your room."

"You've already done enough." She squirmed. "You'll drop me."

"Nah, you're just a little bit."

"I'm sure I can manage from here."

Her voice was strained and he wondered if he affected her the way she did him. He stepped onto the second floor's landing and turned. Wishing she would look at him, he chuckled. "This is getting to be a habit. The last time we came up these stairs together, I was carrying you."

"I wasn't even conscious," she muttered, not giving him so much as a peek.

The circling shadows were broken by the gentle flow of light from the kerosene lamp on the table in the center of the hall.

They reached her door. "I hope you have your key."

"Yes." She reached between them, searching for the side pocket in her skirt. "You can put me down now."

He found he didn't particularly want to. He liked the way she fit all warm and soft against him. Down at this end of the hall, the lamplight was just a fringe around the cozy darkness in front of her door.

She glanced up. "Davis Lee?"

"Hmm?" His gaze met hers.

"Put me down."

"I'm working my way up to it."

"Now," she demanded.

"Okay." But he didn't. He liked watching the storm gather on her face, getting her all riled up.

She huffed out an exasperated breath. "And Catherine said you were sweet."

"You don't agree?"

She eyed him shrewdly. "If I say Catherine's right, will you put me down?"

He grinned, lowering her carefully to her feet.

She retrieved the key from the pocket of her skirt then slid the metal into the lock.

Light glided over the sweet line of her neck, played deep in her chestnut hair. He knew he was courting trouble, but he braced one arm above her and dipped his head, breathing in the fresh scent of her thick tresses.

"What are you doing?" She spun around, wobbling into the now-open door.

Knocked off balance, she fell. Davis Lee grabbed for her, hooking an arm around her waist and hauling her into him.

Gripping a handful of his shirt, she looked up at him a little dazed. "Oh. That was close."

Very. He felt her all the way down his body—his thigh between hers, her warm breath tickling his throat. Desire raged through him. Trying to ease the tension he felt coiling inside both of them, he drawled, "You throwing yourself at me, Josie?"

Her spine went rigid beneath his hand until she saw he was teasing. "Oh, yes, Sheriff. I just couldn't wait to get you alone up here so I could have my wicked way with you."

The sudden quiver in her voice drew him up tighter than new rope. He wanted to kiss her. The way her eyes went soft and deep told him she wanted him to. Standing so close to her, feeling the line of her thighs beneath the layers of her dress and petticoat, he knew he couldn't think straight. The reminder that she was hiding something was barely enough to force him to remove his hands and step back, but he did it.

Before he could say anything, she slipped inside her room. "Good night, Sheriff."

"Good night—"

The door snapped shut.

Davis Lee stood there for the longest time. Finally he became aware of people's voices downstairs, the chill that had crept into this corner, the shift of shadows on the wall.

He had hoped to learn something new about her at Cora's, but he hadn't. And when he'd carried her upstairs, he'd clean forgotten about getting anything out of her. Her not giving up any information about herself burned him, but it also intrigued the heck out of him.

He should've been thinking of another way to get at her secret, but was he? No. He was thinking he should've kissed her. Hell and damn and back again.

The only thing he'd learned tonight was he wanted her like hellfire. And she wanted him. That could only be more trouble than an acre of snakes.

He wasn't going to put his hands on her again. He couldn't. Davis Lee hadn't thought clearly in the four days since he'd carried her to her room. He hadn't been thinking too clearly that night, either.

The important thing was he hadn't given in and kissed her. And just to be sure he wouldn't be tempted again, he stayed away from her. Of course it helped that she stayed away from him, too. If he was irritated, it was only because he had failed to learn anything new about her. Not because her avoidance pricked his vanity.

He knew she was lying about something and he despised liars. But evidently not enough to keep from nearly kissing them, he thought darkly. When he was with Josie, he just needed to remember that the last time he'd given in to this kind of insistent wanting for a woman, his heart had been trampled and other people had literally paid the price.

He had finally received a reply to the wire he'd sent the other night before going to Cora's for dinner. The telegraph operator had responded, telling him that Galveston's lines had only now returned to working order. He would pass along Davis Lee's message to the sheriff when he returned from searching for a boy who'd gone missing right after the hurricane.

In the few days since he'd seen Josie, he'd handled his usual duties, which included everything from taking care of his prisoner to separating Luther and Odell, two over-sixty citizens who drunkenly challenged each other to a duel at least once a week. And he stayed clear of Josie Webster.

He hadn't seen her in town or spoken to her since that night. But he did spot her looking out her hotel window. At the jail. Every day. And every day, several times a day, he purposely walked out onto the steps of his office and looked right at her. He made sure she knew he was watching her.

He wondered if she wanted to forget the shooting lessons but he wasn't inclined to ask. He didn't think she even had the guts to see him face-to-face. Of course, he was one to talk.

He'd gotten nowhere with her, not by asking, not by listening, not by seeing her in more comfortable surroundings. It tested his patience sorely. He *would* find out why the devil she was so interested in Ian McDougal.

That afternoon, Davis Lee walked out of the jail with Dr. Butler, who had come to check Ian's tuberculosis. The outlaw had first asked for Catherine, who had nursed him some months back at the coercion of his brothers. His now-dead brothers. Catherine didn't want to get anywhere near the outlaw. Which was good, because if she did, Davis Lee knew he'd have to answer to Jericho.

From Josie's perfect perch, she could see everyone who went in and out of the jail. No doubt, seeing Butler would rouse her curiosity. Visitors to the jail were infrequent.

Grinning to himself, Davis Lee glanced up at her window. Yep, there she was in plain sight, her chestnut hair threaded with sunlight.

McDougal had been coughing a lot lately, set off by the wind and dirt, the doc said. Dr. Butler had given Ian a small amount of laudanum to soothe his chest, painful from so much coughing. Butler left a small bottle of the medicine with Davis Lee, who had put it in the bottom drawer of his desk and locked it. As the other man said goodbye and headed in the direction of the telegraph office, Davis Lee looked again at Josie's window.

And blinked. Where the devil was she? He waited a few minutes. When she didn't reappear or come out of the hotel, he decided she must have finally tired of staring out the window. Or perhaps she'd gotten hungry and gone to find something to eat.

He turned to go in, giving one last look in that direction in time to see her step off the hotel's landing and start toward the jail. He had no doubt she was looking for Dr. Butler.

Grinning, Davis Lee leaned against the wall of his office, propped one booted foot behind him and got comfortable with his whittling knife. Just what was his little spy going to do?

Chapter Seven

Stepping off the hotel's landing, Josie immediately realized that Davis Lee hadn't gone back inside his office. He leaned against the wall beside the front door of the jailhouse, watching her. Steadily, insolently. Just as he had for the past four days. A knife blade flashed silver in the midday light. He was whittling.

She tore her gaze from him, searching for the tall, brown-haired man with the black bag she'd seen from her window. He came out of the post office a few yards in front of her and she gathered up her skirts. As she hurried toward him, she fought the impulse to go back to the hotel, duck away from Davis Lee's piercing gaze. If she wanted to have a conversation with the man she hoped was Dr. Butler from Fort Greer, she would.

Trying to ignore the lanky sheriff who watched her with a concentration that made her skin tingle, she caught up to the bag-carrying stranger and asked tentatively, "Doctor?"

"Yes?" He turned, the beginnings of a smile on his lips.

"Dr. Butler?"

He nodded.

She tried to pretend Davis Lee wasn't staring as if he were trying to figure out how to whittle *her.* "I wanted a chance to say thank you. I'm Josie Webster. Last week, I was—''

"You're the snakebite. I mean—'' He gave her a sheepish grin, stepping into the street to make way for passersby on the planked walkway. "Yes, I remember. I'm sorry I said that about the snakebite.''

"It's all right. My father was a doctor. He sometimes referred to patients by their ailments.''

"It's a habit I need to curb.'' He had kind brown eyes and silver threaded sparsely through his walnut-dark hair. "I'm glad to see you're up and about. How are you feeling?''

"Much better. I'm so grateful you had the herbs Catherine needed to make my poultice.''

"And the bite, the swelling?''

"I have a scar, but my leg is back to normal size.''

"Good, good.'' He nodded vigorously, his intelligent gaze attentive. "Catherine said you were versed in the treatment.''

"A little. My father taught me how to treat a snakebite. I wish I hadn't needed to know,'' she said dryly.

"It's lucky you have Davis Lee's protection. He's a good man.''

"Yes.'' First Cora, now the doctor. Josie hoped he wasn't going to extol the sheriff's virtues to her.

"If you ever need work, I could use you at the fort. Catherine is there three days a week.''

"I'm a better seamstress than a nurse, but that's very kind.''

Davis Lee's intense regard shrank the distance between them until it felt as if he stood just inches from her. She shifted, trying to position herself in front of Dr. Butler so that his shoulders blocked the sheriff's view. Hoping to get the information she wanted, she gently prodded, "I saw you coming out of the jail. I hope nothing's wrong with the sheriff.''

"No, he's fine. I was taking a look at—"

"Hey, Doc." A gravelly masculine voice boomed behind her.

"Doc." Another deep male voice.

Drat. Josie turned, her eyes widening at the sight of two huge, dark-haired men. She'd seen them before, talking to Davis Lee in the street several days ago.

"Ma'am." They spoke at the same time, sweeping off their well-worn cowboy hats. Their blue eyes sparkled at her.

"Miss Webster," the doctor said. "May I introduce Russ and Matt Baldwin?"

"Hello." She had to tilt her head back in order to meet their gazes.

The men were two to three inches taller than Davis Lee, one taller than the other by an inch. He had a mustache.

The clean-shaven one grinned broadly and jerked a thumb toward his brother, his eyes sparkling at her. "That's Russ. He's too old for you."

His words startled a laugh out of her. "I guess that means you're Matt."

"Yes, ma'am." He settled his hat back on his dark, wavy hair, his gaze warm as it traveled over her plaid daydress. "And I must say it is a pure pleasure to see you again."

Again? Josie frowned. "I don't think we've—"

"Simmer down, Matt," Russ muttered. "You'll spook her. He apologizes, Miz Webster."

"It's all right." Swallowed up by their size and exuberance, she felt a bit overwhelmed. Goodness, but it would probably take nearly a quarter bolt of fabric to make a shirt to fit their brawny chests and arms.

Though both had rugged, bronzed features, Russ's were slightly more refined—a sharper angle to his cheekbones and jaw, the straight line of his nose. Matt's features were more blunt, but just as handsome.

He flashed a pair of deep dimples. "We haven't formally met until now. You were unconscious."

She lifted an eyebrow.

"Stop teasing her, Matt." Russ took a step closer. "He helped the sheriff get you into the hotel after the snakebite."

"Oh, I see."

"And *I* went for Catherine," he added.

"Thank you," she said warmly. "I'm lucky you were around. How nice to meet you both."

"The pleasure's all ours, ma'am," Russ said with quiet charm.

Josie felt Davis Lee's scrutiny sharpen. Why didn't he just go inside the jail and leave her alone? And as nice as these men seemed, she wished the Baldwins would give her one more minute alone with Dr. Butler so she could try and find out why he'd been in the sheriff's office.

Russ turned to Butler. "What are you doing in town today, Doc?"

She tried to hide her surprise that he had asked the question she had planned to ask.

"Davis Lee wanted me to check the prisoner." His gaze shifted to Josie. "He has tuberculosis."

"He could die from that," Matt said in a hard voice. "Wish he'd get on with it. Beg pardon, ma'am."

"That's all right," she murmured. Davis Lee was right in that the people of Whirlwind didn't seem inclined to let McDougal escape justice this time.

Dr. Butler nodded. "Consumption can be a slow death."

"Too good for him, if you ask me," Russ muttered.

Josie silently agreed. "Is his condition getting worse?"

"Not more severe, just a flare-up."

"I see." She didn't want Ian McDougal dying of that disease. She wanted his death to have a face. Hers.

The doctor shifted his bag to the other hand. "Please excuse me, Miss Webster. I must leave, but I'm happy you introduced yourself. It's a joy to see that you're recovering so well."

"Thank you."

As he walked toward the jail and his buggy, Matt and Russ moved in front of her, forming a welcome obstacle to Davis Lee's unwavering regard.

Matt grinned. "You do look a sight healthier than the last time I saw you."

"I hope that snake didn't scare you into wanting to leave Whirlwind," Russ said.

"Not at all." She wasn't going anywhere until she'd done what she came to do.

Matt's blue gaze easily met hers. "Where you from?"

"Galveston." Despite the solid wall of man in front of her, she felt the sheriff's attention.

"We've never been down to the coast. Are you planning to make Whirlwind your home now?"

"I'm thinking about it."

"We'd be pleased to have you here," Russ said. "Whirlwind isn't as big as Galveston, but it's a nice town. Our Founder's Day dance and horse race are the best in three counties."

"And don't forget the harvest dance," Matt put in. "It's a real shindig."

"It's coming up in about a week." Russ edged closer. "Would you allow me to take you?"

"Thank you, but I'm already going with someone."

He looked genuinely disappointed. "I'll just have to be quicker next time."

"You still staying at the hotel?" Matt's gaze skated over her with obvious interest, but her nerves didn't flutter like they did when Davis Lee simply looked at her.

"Yes."

"Getting settled in all right?" Russ asked.

"Just fine." She would really enjoy talking to them if it weren't for the sheriff's unflinching regard.

"If you decide you need a permanent place, we can help you find something," Russ offered.

"Thank you. I'm still not sure what I'll do about that."

In the small space between the brothers she saw movement, a flash of a blue shirt. Davis Lee was coming toward them. Why? she thought irritably.

He sauntered up with an easy grace that had Josie setting her teeth. As if he had a right to be there, he moved to the left of Matt so that he stood at Josie's shoulder. His shirtsleeve brushed her arm and she edged away. The warmth of his body and the clean outdoor scent of him reminded her of the other night in front of her room.

"Good afternoon, Davis Lee," Russ said while Matt lifted a hand in greeting.

"Boys." The sheriff's gaze, sharp and piercing, moved to Josie as he said with a trace of amusement, "Miz Webster."

"Sheriff," she murmured, fingering her white standing collar.

Matt slid a speculative look at Davis Lee then at Josie, plainly curious. "You like horse races, Miz Webster?"

"Yes."

"There are some good ones in Abilene this time of year. Maybe we can—"

"I saw your pa down at Ef's smithy," Davis Lee broke in. "He looked perturbed. Were y'all supposed to meet him there?"

Josie slid him a narrow-eyed look. How did he know where the Baldwins' father was? Davis Lee hadn't moved from his spot in front of the jail the whole time she'd been talking to the brothers.

"Don't recall that, but I guess we'd better go." Russ's

gaze flicked to Davis Lee. "Sure was nice to meet you, Miz Webster."

"Josie, please. I enjoyed meeting the both of you," she said warmly. "Thank you again for your help after my snakebite."

She noted the sudden tightening of Davis Lee's jaw. And the nearly imperceptible warning look he flashed at the brothers. Then she understood. They thought Davis Lee had some kind of claim on her and he was letting them think that. Encouraging it, even!

Thinking back to the doctor's words about her having Davis Lee's protection, she realized he'd thought the same.

Her blood started a slow simmer and she gave Matt her sweetest smile. "Since I was conscious for this meeting, next time I'll remember you."

He chuckled. "I hope so. I'll make sure next time comes real soon."

She laughed and both men smiled, their avid interest making her face heat.

Davis Lee folded his arms across his big chest and cleared his throat, which seemed to prod the brothers into moving.

Matt tipped his hat to her. "If you need anything at all—"

"Please call on us," Russ finished.

"Thank you, I will."

"And save me at least one dance at Eishen's," Russ said.

"Me, too," Matt put in.

She laughed. "All right."

They started toward the other end of town, going only a short distance before they both looked back. She wiggled her fingers in a wave. "They're very friendly."

"To every woman they meet," the sheriff drawled.

She slanted a look at him, then shifted her attention, staring blankly at a woman and small girl going into Haskell's. She was still weak from the fever. That's why she kept wondering what Davis Lee's kiss would've been like, why she spared it a thought at all. "I think you made that up about their pa, just so they'd leave."

"I didn't *say* he was lookin' for 'em." His gaze sharpened on her face. "What did you want with Doc Butler? Checking to see why he was in my jail?"

"Am I supposed to report my activities to you, Sheriff?" she snapped, annoyed at how vividly she recalled the hard warmth of his chest cradling her. "I must've forgotten."

"Want me to think you're spyin' on me, Josie?" His low tone raised the hairs on her neck.

"I wanted to thank the doctor for the herbs Catherine used to make my poultice," she said defiantly, arching an eyebrow. "All right?"

His prolonged silence unnerved her and she tamped down the urge to squirm, feeling compelled to add, "He said he was glad to see me up and about."

Davis Lee's blue gaze did a slow slide over her, flicking her nerve endings sharply. "How *are* you feeling?"

"I'm fine." She couldn't meet his gaze. Even knowing that the desire to feel his mouth on hers was an effect of her weakened state, she was skittish. "In fact, I feel well enough to resume my shooting lessons, if you would be so kind."

A subtle tension lashed his body. "You sure?"

"Yes." The way he affected her had her reconsidering the lessons altogether. But thinking about her parents and William told her that not learning to shoot was just as risky as being in close proximity to Davis Lee.

His gaze searched her face. "Did you want to start tonight?"

Tonight! She might rather take her chances with the sheriff, but she needed a little time to prepare herself. "Uh, no. How about Saturday? Or Monday?"

"Tomorrow's better than Monday. Same time as last?"

"Between six-thirty and seven would be fine." She glanced around, catching sight of Charlie Haskell standing in the doorway of his store watching her with Davis Lee. The older man gave her a big smile and nodded approvingly.

Something he and his nephew had said yesterday when they paid her a visit made sense now. She lowered her voice. "Are you trying to make people think there's something going on between us?"

He grinned and pushed his hat back, making her stomach do a slow drop to her feet. "Are people starting to think that?"

He looked far too pleased with himself and she narrowed her eyes. "Charlie and Mitchell both told me that you've been asking after me, quite a lot. Just now, the Baldwins seemed to think something along the same lines and so did Dr. Butler. You did nothing to correct that impression."

She crossed her arms and lowered her voice. "And I'm sure Charlie at least has noticed all the attention you've been paying to my hotel window since you've taken no pains to be discreet."

Davis Lee laughed. "The way you have?"

She flushed. Though she had kept her distance since Tuesday night, she refused to abandon her spot at the window.

"Seems to me, people would also notice all the attention you've been paying to my jail."

His husky voice had her toes curling inside her button-up boots. One time when she'd seen him watching her from the street below, she'd waved just to taunt him. Perhaps that had been ill-advised.

She sniffed. "I can hardly help the direction my window faces."

"And maybe I just enjoy looking at a pretty woman, like all the other men in this town."

That irritated her no end and she ignored the pleasure that streaked through her when he said she was pretty. "We both know you're not lookin' because you're sweet on me."

"Are you sure?" His gaze dropped to her lips just as it had the other night.

She didn't like the sudden skip of her heartbeat or the slow heat that rolled through her body. It was caused by the snakebite, she told herself. Not those hot blue eyes. This was simply proof that nothing about her body was back to proper working order. "Yes, I'm sure you're not sweet on me."

She picked up her skirts and turned to go. "You should stop being so obvious. People will talk."

"Honey, that doesn't bother me as much as it seems to bother you."

"Fine. Watch all you want." She lifted her chin and started back to the hotel.

She'd taken only two steps when he asked, "Just exactly what *are* you always watchin' from up there, Josie?"

The low rasp of his voice had her faltering. She knew he was goading her and she wanted to push back. Prodded by some wicked demon, she threw him a look over her shoulder and said sweetly, "Why, Sheriff, I'm watchin' *you*."

That drew him up and heat flared in his eyes.

A shiver chased down her spine and Josie hurried off, biting back a laugh. She hoped she had knocked him off balance the way he frequently did her. It would serve him right for encouraging the impression they were involved. Of course, continuing her shooting lessons with him would only further the impression. The thought of seeing him every day was enough to send anticipation curling slyly through her.

Nonsense. All she needed—*wanted*—from Davis Lee Holt was to learn how to handle a gun. Not how to handle *him*.

* * *

Her voice slid over him like smoky velvet. He wanted to get his hands, his mouth on her. *All over her.* Wanted to thumb open every damn button down the front of her dress.

Davis Lee started after her, moving on impulse and not one whit of common sense. He was steps away from the hotel when he realized what he was doing and jerked to a stop.

Stalking back to the jail, he muttered curses the whole way, ignoring the curious looks from Pearl Anderson and Tony Santos who had both stepped out of their businesses.

Josie Webster was causing all kinds of havoc with his mind—his *body*—and it made him mad as a hornet. That sultry look in her eyes made him want to say to hell with his misgivings about her and get her naked. Which would be the stupidest, most dangerous thing he could do.

It had been plain to him that the Baldwin brothers had imagined her without her blue, yellow and white plaid dress, too. They'd eyed her like she was one of those half-dressed dance hall girls they'd seen in Dallas last year and still talked about. And Josie had clearly enjoyed the attention. Thinking about her being with one or the other of the brothers made Davis Lee's teeth clench.

He shook his head. He only cared about Josie's company because he wanted to know what she had up her sleeve. Maybe she really had simply been thanking Dr. Butler, but Davis Lee didn't think so. He'd bet his last dollar that she had been trying to find out if the doctor had seen Ian McDougal.

She was lying and Davis Lee had better not forget it again. Which would be darn hard after the interest he'd seen in her hot green eyes.

He considered using that advantage, playing on the pull between them to see if he could gain her trust and get the truth out of her. But in the next breath he dismissed the thought. He knew what it was like to be conned, to be *used*.

He couldn't bring himself to do the same to her even if she did drive him to distraction.

There was something about her...some lost look buried deep in her eyes. It made his insides twist up when he looked at her. He told himself he had a soft spot for her only because he'd seen her on the brink of death, but the tangle of emotion he felt when he saw her seemed more than that. He figured that would disappear as soon as he found out what she had planned. And he *would* find out. Even if he had to stick to her like a cockleburr, he would stop whatever she had planned.

The same heat that had moved through his chest the other night returned and he wrestled it down. Thanks to Betsy, his eyes were wide-open. If he let down his guard because of a pair of gorgeous green eyes, he would have only himself to blame.

He had no intention of making that mistake again, not with Josie Webster, not with anyone.

Hours later, when midnight hovered and the town had settled, Davis Lee finally stepped inside the jail and closed the door. He'd kept a close eye on the hotel all night. Josie hadn't stepped foot outside since he'd seen her this afternoon; her room had gone dark an hour ago.

He checked to make sure McDougal was asleep and that the cell was secure. Then Davis Lee pulled the iron bed with its thin mattress from the second cell, through the connecting door and into his office. He settled the bed in the space between the window and his desk. He didn't expect trouble, but he always liked to be near the door in case it came. A quiet, uneventful night would be nice. Right now, Josie Webster was about all the trouble he cared to handle.

After removing his gun belt, he eased down on the edge of the bed and toed off his boots. Thoughts of her had been buzzing around his head ever since this afternoon.

"Why, Sheriff, I'm watchin' you."

As hard as he tried, he couldn't keep the grin off his face. Or the blood from surging to his groin. She was a cool one, keeping her composure even when he knew she was rattled. Sure made him want to see if he could crack that calm veneer.

Grunting, he flopped back on the mattress and closed his eyes, telling himself to stop thinking about her.

Sometime later, he came awake with a start. His feet hit the floor as he registered the clanging of a bell. The fire bell. The town council had placed one cow bell in the livery, another inside the church at the other end of town.

He tugged on his boots, grabbed his gun belt and jammed the keys to the cell doors into his trouser pocket as he ran outside. Flames flared in the pastureland behind Pete Carter's saloon. Davis Lee rushed across the street and into the alley between the saloon and the livery stable. People streamed out of the line of houses situated behind the jail, some from the businesses where they also lived.

"What's happening?" someone yelled.

"Not sure yet!"

The fire burned about fifty yards from Pete's saloon. He and Ef Gerard were already beating at the flames with wet blankets. Murmurs and cries of surprise sounded behind Davis Lee as more people learned of the fire.

He slowed, coming to a stop at Ef's shoulder. The flames were nearly out, dying in a circle of burned earth.

"Did you see what happened?" he asked, his chest heaving as he buckled on his gun belt and reached down to tie the leather thong around his thigh.

"No." The big blacksmith turned, his dark arms bulging with muscle as he brought the blanket down with the force of his hammer. "No damage done, though. 'Cept to the grass. Pete smelled smoke and yelled for me. I guess we got here in time."

Davis Lee's lungs pumped hard as he tried to catch his breath. The fire wasn't close to the livery or the saloon but in a few minutes more it would've been.

Pete beat at some remaining embers. "Probably some kid trying a smoke. It don't look like they meant to hurt nothin'."

The fire was nearly extinguished as people made their way to the site.

Davis Lee shook his head. "Who would—"

The sharp crack of a gunshot behind him cut off his words. He spun. The sound had come from town and not too far away. Something in his gut told him to move and he bolted. As he reached Whirlwind's main street, his gaze passed over the people in pairs or small groups. No one appeared to be hurt, but they were curious about the gunshot. Who had fired that shot and why?

He slowed as he crossed the street to the jail. People had come out of their homes in town as had those whose quarters were above their businesses like Charlie Haskell and the Doyle brothers.

"Davis Lee! What's happened?" The question came from Cal Doyle, whose law office sat next to Haskell's General Store. "I heard a shot!"

"I'm looking into it now. There was a fire behind Carter's saloon, but it's under control."

Pearl Anderson and her youngest daughter stood with Charlie and his nephew, Mitchell Orr, on the porch of Pearl's restaurant.

"Everything's all right, folks," Davis Lee said from the bottom step of the jail. "Ef and Pete have the fire nearly out."

Josie suddenly joined Pearl and the others. He couldn't tell which direction she'd come from and he hoped it wasn't from his jail.

Now that he was close enough, he could hear McDougal

carrying on inside like a stuck hog. Davis Lee mounted the steps to the jail, watching as Josie walked with the small group of people back toward the hotel.

"Somebody just tried to kill me!" Ian yelled as soon as Davis Lee got through the door. "Sheriff!"

"I hear you." He grabbed a lantern and lit it then went to Ian's cell. Someone had tried to *kill* the outlaw? Was the attempt related to the fire? The blaze would have served well as a distraction to get Davis Lee away from here.

"Look at this!" The youngest and only remaining McDougal stood square in the center of his cell pointing at the pine planked floor. "They took a shot at me!"

"Did you see who it was?" Davis Lee searched the shadows around the outlaw's body.

"No, it was too dark for one thing. And they barely peeked through that window."

Davis Lee could see the glint of dull metal now. The lead had plowed into the wood floor.

"It pinged off the bars," McDougal said, his eyes wild. "Then went into the floor."

"You didn't hear or see anything else?"

"No, just that commotion before you ran out. Somebody screamed there was a fire."

"Yeah."

"I was looking out the window and trying to get someone's attention to tell me what was going on when I saw something out of the corner of my eye. Someone stuck a gun in my face and I barely had time to duck before the gun went off."

"They were that close and they missed?"

"You don't have to sound so disappointed." Ian gripped the bars, glancing again at the window. "Whoever it was is a lousy shot."

"I guess they'd have to be. Did you see their face? Anything?"

"Just the gun and the hand holding it."

"Man's hand?"

"I'm not sure. It happened too quick." He coughed, pressing his face to the bars. "Maybe they won't miss next time. I think you should move me to the other cell."

"Later." A lousy shot? Davis Lee didn't like the thought that grabbed hold of him. He turned down the lantern and hung it just on the other side of the door as he walked out.

"Where're you going?" the outlaw demanded. "You can't leave me here."

"Push your bed against the far bars and don't get in front of the window. I'll be back."

"Do you think you know who did this?"

Davis Lee didn't answer. He hoped he didn't know, but he couldn't rid himself of the suspicion chewing at him. He'd seen Josie too close to the jail for him to let it pass without some answers.

With people stopping him along the way to ask questions, it took him a bit longer than usual to get from the jail to the Whirlwind Hotel. Was the fire out for certain? Did he know what had happened? When would he know?

"Simmer down, folks. No one was hurt. No one was even near the flames." None of them seemed near as bothered by that gunshot as he was.

The hotel blazed with lamps and candlelight. Davis Lee stalked inside and headed for the stairs, glancing at a group of people gathered in the dining room.

Catching sight of a silky fall of chestnut hair and a familiar dress, he changed direction and went past the stairs instead. Josie stood with Penn and Esther Wavers, Charlie and his nephew. They were all chattering about the fire.

"Did anyone else hear a gunshot?" Mitchell asked.

"I did." Josie drew a light, soft yellow shawl closer around her shoulders, wearing the same blue, yellow and white plaid dress she'd had on earlier. "Who would be shooting and why?"

Just what Davis Lee intended to find out. He stopped behind her, wondering how she could smell like honey-suckle even so late at night. He gripped her elbow, ready when she started violently at his touch.

"Evenin', folks." He tried to unclench his teeth and sound calm. "Looks like everything is settled now. I need to talk to Miz Webster for a minute."

"I don't—" She broke off when he squeezed her arm in warning.

He turned, feeling her balk. Ignoring the startled looks on the others' faces, he tugged hard. She took a little hop-step and hurried to catch up.

"He's checking on her," Esther said. "How sweet."

Mitchell muttered something Davis Lee didn't catch.

Josie tried to wrestle her arm out of his hold. "I don't know what you think you're doing."

He didn't ease up, just dragged her back into the lobby. He wanted to talk to her in private, but where? Not outside. Too many interruptions. Her room? That wouldn't do for her reputation.

Seeing the door behind the registration desk that led to Penn's small office, Davis Lee snatched up a lit candle from the corner of the wooden counter and hauled Josie behind it.

"What is going on?" She pushed at his hand with her free one, trying to pry his fingers loose.

"Get in there." He released her to open the door.

She lunged away in an attempt to run, but he easily grabbed her around the waist and picked her up.

She gasped, shoving at his arm. "Put me down this instant!"

He elbowed his way inside the dark, windowless room then kicked the door shut and set her on her feet. The candle provided only enough light to see her face. Immediately he was hit with the softness of her scent, the isolation of their location. "I want to talk to you."

"Not in here." She reached for the doorknob. "We're alone."

He slammed a palm against the door and said through gritted teeth, "You don't want me asking these questions in front of an audience."

"What questions?"

He nudged his body between her and the only way out, forcing her back one step then another. The candle's flame flickered with his movement. Even in the poor light, her eyes were luminous, her skin polished like pearl.

Irritated at himself for even noticing, Davis Lee cornered her the way he would a stray cow, crowding her without touch to move to the place he wanted her. He backed her the few feet across the room and set the candle down on Penn's small rolltop desk. The tiny flame threw a small oval of light against the wall.

"I don't like you dragging me off like that." Josie rubbed at her arm, glaring at him. "People will talk. You heard Esther—"

"Where were you a while ago?"

She closed both hands over the edges of her shawl. "You saw me. In the dining room, remember?"

"No, when you were walking back to the hotel. Where were you coming from?"

"Here."

He folded his arms and gave her a flat stare.

Wariness slid into her eyes. "I was," she said evenly. "I walked out of the hotel and started toward the fire but came upon Charlie and Mitchell. They told me it was out so I turned around and went back to the hotel with them to tell Esther and Penn that everything was all right."

She looked concerned. "Everything is all right, isn't it?"

"Not if you were at the jail just now."

She blinked. "I told you—"

"Yeah, I heard you."

"What's this about?" She edged down the wall and he copied her movement, keeping himself between her and the door.

She could easily have slipped out of the hotel, started the fire, waited for his attention to be diverted then made her way back to the jail. But she could just as easily have been returning to the hotel, as she'd said.

His eyes had adjusted to the dimness of the room so he could see her features, but he wanted to see her eyes. He angled his body so that she scooted back toward the desk. The air was thick and Davis Lee felt hot all over, which he figured was on account of being riled up. Not because he was close enough to count the freckles on her nose or see the rapid tap of her pulse in the hollow of her throat.

She watched him with wide eyes. "People saw us come in here, *alone.*"

"If you'd keep your voice down, no one would know where we are. Can you account for your time tonight?"

"Why?" The puzzlement in her eyes looked genuine. "You're making me nervous."

The hand holding the edges of her shawl curled beneath the top of the light wool. Between her breasts.

"Uh-uh." He covered her hand with his, squashing the flare of heat that moved up his arm when his knuckles brushed the soft swell of her breasts. "You keep away from that scalpel."

Her eyes flashed, her hand tightening under his. He could feel the skitter of her pulse beneath his touch. If she thought she could get to that weapon, he knew she'd take the chance.

With one swift motion, he plucked the shawl from her.

She grabbed for it. "Give that back!"

"I'll just hang on to this so I can be sure you're not gonna try gettin' at that blade."

Glaring at him, she wrapped her arms around her waist. The movement pushed her breasts up and against the plaid fabric of her bodice. Her chest rose and fell rapidly, her hair sliding over her shoulder. His gaze unwillingly tracked down her body and back up, stopping at her breasts. Her nipples were hard; he could barely make them out in the pale light but there was no mistaking it.

She was enough to make his mouth go dry. Didn't she have on any undergarments under there? It registered now how soft and unrestrained she'd felt when he picked her up a minute ago. Hell.

She glanced down and drew in a breath. Even in the dim light, he could see her flush. Folding her arms so that her breasts were hidden, she pressed back into the wall. That grating note of cool slipped into her voice. "Just what is it you think I've done, Sheriff?"

"Tell me how you spent your time tonight."

Her chin lifted stubbornly and for a long moment he thought she wouldn't answer. That went all over him. "If you'd rather take this to the jail—"

"I had dinner in the hotel dining room, then I went to my room and cut out the bodice for Catherine's wedding gown and then I went to bed."

"What time?"

"I don't know." At his arched eyebrow, she said, "An hour or two ago."

"Your lamp went out only an hour ago." The scent of her drifted into his lungs and his fingers curled tighter into her wrap.

She exhaled loudly and spoke with exaggerated patience. "If you know that, why are you asking me?"

"To see if you're telling the truth."

She stilled. Just as she had during Cora's questions the

other night. Just as she had when Davis Lee had asked her about what she'd said during her fever.

"What do you think I've done?"

"I think you just came from my jail."

"I didn't!" She held his gaze steadily, but he caught a flash of fear in her face.

"Someone took a shot at Ian McDougal tonight."

Her eyes rounded. "Is he—?"

"No," Davis Lee bit out. "He isn't dead."

"I heard a gunshot," she said slowly. "So did Esther and Charlie and Mitchell. None of us knew what it meant."

"Don't you?"

"I said I didn't." Hurt darkened her eyes.

He didn't want to notice that or feel regret over causing it. "McDougal wasn't even hit."

She threw her hands in the air. "Then what's all this about?"

"Whoever set that fire did it to get me away from the jail so they could go after my prisoner."

"And you obviously think it was me."

He leveled his gaze into hers. "I'm wonderin' why you didn't want to resume your shooting lessons tonight."

"Maybe I had something else to do."

"Like try to kill my prisoner?"

For one instant, raw pain filled her eyes. Her mouth tightened.

He stared flatly at her. "Josie?" he snapped.

Anger vibrated in every line of her slender body. Despite the way she narrowed her eyes, Davis Lee wasn't prepared when she said, "Okay, I did it."

"What?" He stiffened.

"I tied my sheets together and climbed out of my hotel window. Right in plain view of everyone. Then I ran to the other end of town and started a fire. Then I dashed over to the jail to shoot McDougal and managed to get back to my room and come downstairs with Penn and Esther.'' Her voice, trembling with anger and hurt, sliced at him. ''And I was so sure you wouldn't catch me. Aren't I silly?''

His blood boiled. He leaned toward her, perversely glad when she pressed harder into the wall. ''Why don't you tell me what I want to know?''

She angled her chin at him but he swore he saw fear in her face again. Her gaze flickered to the door. For the first time he wondered if she were afraid of *him*, rather than what he might find out.

''It sounds like you want me to say I tried to shoot your prisoner.''

''Did you?''

''You really think *I* shot at him?'' She looked incredulous.

''Do you have a gun on you?''

She spread her arms wide, looking down at herself. ''Do you see one anywhere?''

She clamped her lips tight as if she hadn't meant to say that.

''There's not one hidden in the pocket of your skirt?''

''No,'' she said shortly, crossing her arms again. ''And don't even think you're going to feel my…touch my…do what you did before.''

If his whole body hadn't been hard before, it was now.

''You, of all people, know I'm a terrible shot. You said so. I've only had one lesson. How could I hit anything?''

''Whoever shot at McDougal missed him.''

''Oh.'' For a long moment, she was silent. ''Well, it wasn't me.''

The way the light slid down her throat, played at the edges of her standing white collar had Davis Lee's fingers itching to touch her. He'd better get out of here before he did something stupid.

"If I find out it was you, I'll stick your pretty little hide in jail." He turned, stepping toward the door.

He heard her rush at him and spun, expecting to see the glint of her blade. Grabbing her around the waist, he yanked her tight against him, restraining her. "When are you going to learn your lesson, Josie? I've taken that blade from you before. I can—"

"Give me my shawl," she said thickly, her hands flattened against his chest. Pushing at him.

Her hands were empty. There was no sign of the scalpel. She strained away from him, but her hip bumped his groin. The sudden smoky explosion of lust in his belly had him thrusting the shawl at her, releasing her so quickly she stumbled back as she clutched at the fabric.

"Remember what I said," he growled, reaching around her to pick up the candle before opening the door of Penn's office. After a quick look at the lobby, he said, "No one's out here so you can go on back to your room knowing your reputation is safe."

"I'm not going anywhere until you leave." Her voice cracked, but she kept her eyes narrowed on him.

He could've sworn he saw tears. Why? Because she *had* taken a shot at the outlaw and Davis Lee had found her out? Or because he'd hurt her?

He didn't like the way his conscience pinged at him, didn't like that he wanted to apologize for dragging her in here, for accusing her of lying and attempting to kill his prisoner.

Apologize? For trying to find out what she was up to? No way in hell.

Chapter Eight

Infuriating, insufferable bully! That's what she thought of Davis Lee Holt. Approaching her in a group of people then hauling her behind closed doors! Josie was still fuming about it the next day as she settled into her place at the window of her hotel room.

The morning saw fat gray clouds scudding in from the west, but by midafternoon the sun was out, drenching the earth with soft warmth. Catherine's wedding was to be held in mid-October, less than a month from now. Josie made good progress on stitching together the wedding gown's back bodice. She worked the pale blue silk easily, which enabled her to pay ample attention to the jail.

She was not going for her shooting lesson tonight. Davis Lee Holt could wait until Judgment Day for all she cared.

As the day passed, Josie saw McDougal twice, both times when Davis Lee took the prisoner behind the jail to the outhouse. The sheriff's gaze rose straight to her on leaving *and* returning to the jail but she refused to look at him except when his back was turned.

The man made a rattlesnake look cuddly and more than once during the day Josie found herself wanting to scream in frustration. How dare he accuse her of shooting at

McDougal! She didn't like Davis Lee's attitude, his high-handedness, his certainty that she'd been involved.

His distrust of her stung deep. She didn't like him thinking that she had made an attempt on Ian McDougal's life, which was complete and utter nonsense because she'd come here to do that very thing.

Since *she* hadn't tried to kill the outlaw—yet—who had? Ian and his brothers had murdered several people throughout the state, and threatened even more. With the deaths of his three brothers a few months ago, Ian was left to accept the punishment for what they'd all done and Josie probably wasn't the only one who wanted to see him pay for the crimes. In Whirlwind alone, she could count three people who had good reason for vengeance.

Catherine Donnelly's fiancé, Jericho Blue, had more against the outlaws than their coercing and blackmailing her into doctoring Ian's tuberculosis. The McDougals had killed his partner, also a Ranger and injured Jericho severely.

Susannah Holt had escaped death only by luck when the gang and their horses rushed her wagon, causing it to crash. If her husband, Riley, went after Ian, Josie didn't think it would be under cover of darkness. Not if Riley was anything like his brother, the sheriff.

If Cora Wilkes, whose husband, Ollie, had been murdered by the outlaws, had been the one to shoot at McDougal, she probably wouldn't have missed. The woman seemed competent in every area. Besides, Josie couldn't see the woman taking the law into her own hands.

Since Josie planned to do exactly that, she needed to find someone else to teach her to shoot. There had to be someone who was willing, someone *polite* who didn't make her want to scream. Aggravated, she huffed out a breath. She needed someone with frequent access to the outlaw so she could continue to check up on him. That person was Davis Lee.

And if she didn't appear this evening for her lesson, he

would view that as an admission of guilt. It didn't matter that she'd told him she hadn't shot at McDougal. Davis Lee would think he'd been right about her. Which had her clenching her teeth.

The hurt she felt had nothing to do with the *sheriff's* opinion of her and everything to do with what Davis Lee, *the man,* thought of her. That realization didn't sit well. At all. She was forced to admit for the first time in two years that she wasn't sure she could carry out her plan.

Oh, but she *had* to. She might be the only justice her parents and William ever saw. Calling their faces to mind, replaying the horror of finding them dead in the house, had her spine stiffening and her heart clenching. The only man she'd come to Whirlwind for was Ian McDougal and she wasn't leaving until she got him. Davis Lee Holt was going to help her do that.

She would go for her shooting lesson if for no other reason than to prove he was wrong about her.

After dressing in her dark blue split skirt and a plain white bodice, she braided her hair. She left her hotel room just before six o'clock and paid a visit to Jed Doyle, the town gunsmith. By the time she knocked on Davis Lee's office door at five minutes before seven, she had corralled her emotions. Mostly. Seeing the fleeting astonishment in his blue eyes when he opened the door to find her went a long way toward soothing her wounded pride.

He really hadn't expected her to show up. Well, she had, and now he would have to deal with her.

He was without his hat, his walnut-dark hair furrowed as though he'd run his hands through it repeatedly. One thick lock fell over his forehead, making her want to smooth it back into place. He studied her for a moment, some undefinable emotion in his eyes.

Wishing her pulse would stop jumping around at the sight

of him, she cocked her head and asked in her sweetest voice, "You didn't forget about my lesson, did you, Sheriff?"

He leaned one shoulder against the doorjamb, his gaze speculative as if he didn't quite know what to do with her. "I didn't forget."

"You look surprised to see me."

"I wasn't sure you'd come."

Knowing she'd been right didn't dim the hurt she still felt over the fact that he believed her guilty of last night's shooting. "I knew if I didn't, you'd think I was off shooting someone again."

Was that regret that flashed across his face? Unlikely. And why did she care anyway? "I'm ready if you are."

Stepping back, he opened the door wide and jerked a thumb toward a brawny, black-haired man who sat on the far corner of Davis Lee's desk polishing a rifle. "This is Jake Ross, one of my deputies. Jake, this is Josie Webster."

She leaned into the room and smiled at the man who appeared to be about Davis Lee's age. "Hello."

"Ma'am," the man said gruffly, his dark gaze barely meeting hers before skipping away shyly.

Davis Lee motioned her inside. "Come in while I get your gun."

She wasn't moving any closer to him than she had to. "If you're getting the .45 for me, there's no need."

Reaching his desk, he glanced at her over his shoulder. "Why not?"

She patted the pocket hidden in the front of her skirt. "I took your advice and bought one of those pocket revolvers."

He turned, looking confounded for the second time since she'd arrived. "Did Jed help you?"

"Yes."

One of Davis Lee's big, sun-weathered hands slid down the inside of his thigh to check the leather thong of his gun belt. At the sight of his hand there, she got a funny ache in her throat. She jerked her gaze back to his face.

"Did you get bullets?"

"Even though I'm new at this, I'm pretty sure you need them for target practice," she said coolly.

His mouth tightened a fraction and Josie heard a smothered sound from his deputy.

She lifted a small package wrapped in brown paper. "I have two boxes here."

He nodded. Sweeping up his hat from his chair and settling it on his head, he started toward her. "Jake, I'll probably only be about an hour."

"No hurry," the other man said in a quiet drawl. "Nice to meet you, Miz Webster."

"You, too." She smiled again then moved down the steps as Davis Lee shut the door to the jail and followed her. "Are we going back to the same place outside of town?"

She had worn her split skirt again so that she could ride.

"No. We're going out behind Catherine's."

As they stepped into the street, Josie frowned up at him.

"I've already asked and she said it would be fine. The chances of seeing a snake there are much less."

"Oh. That's good." She didn't know if his thoughtfulness was out of deference to her snakebite or the fact that he didn't want to be too far away from town. Either way, she was glad.

Davis Lee started east in the direction of the hotel. "Catherine and her brother live just up the hill past the church."

Josie fell into step with him, wishing she knew what he was thinking, then in the next breath, glad she didn't. She waited for him to say something about her watching the jail today from her window, but he didn't. Since the hotel was situated at the edge of town, they were out of Whirlwind quickly and passed no one on their way to Catherine's. Davis Lee remained quiet during their walk to the small pale yellow house.

It wasn't anger she felt from him but something she couldn't define. Catherine and her brother weren't home so Davis Lee led Josie around the house, past a root cellar, a small garden and a springhouse. They angled toward a nice-size barn, its double doors pushed wide.

Josie waited outside the barn while he went inside and returned with a hay bale hoisted on each shoulder.

"What are those for?" she asked.

"Thought we'd try something besides cans this time."

"A bigger target?" Her mouth quirked. "Do you have hopes I might be able to hit one of these?"

"Yes." He smiled, causing a tickle in her stomach.

She looked away, making herself recall the way he'd spoken to her last night. He strode behind the barn, walking into the pasture beyond. Late-day sunlight, the color of old gold, shifted across the prairie, running over the tips of endless buffalo grass. The muscles in his arms strained at the sleeves of his blue shirt.

Several yards away from the weathered building, he stopped in a gentle dip of ground and dumped one rectangular bale on top of the other.

He started past her toward the barn again then stopped. "Josie?"

She looked up, her nerves prickling at the intensity in his eyes.

"I'd like to apologize."

She blinked. "W-what?"

He braced his hands on his hips and faced her, his eyes glittering beneath the brim of his hat. "I was too harsh last night; I shouldn't have handled things that way and I'm sorry."

Stunned, she stared at him. "You obviously thought I was guilty."

"I did. I don't now."

"Why not?"

"I just...don't think so."

"So you do believe that last night I was where I said I was?"

"Yes."

Why did he believe her now? She shoved down the pleasure she felt at his apology. "I don't understand."

"If you were guilty, you wouldn't have shown up tonight."

"And if I really had been the one who took a shot at McDougal, I probably would've left town after your accusations."

"I figure that's right."

Though she was glad Davis Lee no longer suspected her, there was something... "I understand," she said softly, stifling a twinge of disappointment.

"Understand what?"

"The reason you believe me isn't because I told you I didn't shoot at him. It's because you watched the hotel all night to see if I would go anywhere. And since I didn't, you've decided maybe I was telling the truth."

He kept his gaze trained on hers and she knew by the implacable look on his face that she was right. Why did that hurt so much?

"Did anyone see me last night who could confirm where I was?" Her voice sounded ragged. "I'm sure you asked around."

He nodded. "I'm apologizing because I was too harsh."

"And arrogant?"

After a slight pause, he acceded with a nod.

"And a bully," she added.

"Going for blood?" He grinned. "And a bully."

His admission had her lips curving, but as glad as she

was to hear his apology, he was much less dangerous when he wasn't being so likable. "Thank you. I accept."

"Good." He smiled into her eyes and her heart skipped a beat.

His fierce questioning of her last night had left her wondering. "If something happened to McDougal while he was here, would you be held accountable?"

"Yes. He's in my jail, after all."

Josie didn't want that. Davis Lee had saved her life and now she could be endangering his job. The last thing she wanted was to hurt him, but McDougal had to pay for murdering her loved ones.

She watched him stride back to the barn, long legs eating up the distance. She wanted him to believe her because he *trusted* her. The admission sent a jolt of panic through her, had her backing up mentally. No, she didn't care if he trusted her or not. The reason she was here with him was twofold: to learn to shoot, and to use him to find out information about the man she intended to kill.

Davis Lee returned with two more bales, stacking them atop the others to make a straw tower. The pressed hay sat considerably closer to her than the cans had at her first target practice.

"Do we need to start at the beginning?" Davis Lee came to stand beside her.

"No," she said shortly. "I remember what you taught me."

She dipped into her pocket and pulled out her new weapon. She popped the chamber and held it up so he could see it was empty. "After I load it, I sight the target—do I just aim for a place on the bale?"

"I'll get something." He walked back to the front of the barn and disappeared around the corner then returned with a burlap bag. Walking the twenty or so feet to the hay bales he stretched the feed sack the length of a bale and tucked it beneath the thin rope that held the hay together. He turned the marked side toward her so that the name of a feed company and some words too small to read were visible.

"Aim for the circle of words."

She nodded, desperate to hit the target today, to finally learn how to do this.

He moved up beside her. "What else do you remember from last time?"

You yanking off my corset. "Don't point the gun unless I'm prepared to use it."

He nodded. "Ready when you are."

"All right." She opened the box Jed Doyle had filled with bullets.

She slid six into the gun's chamber and clicked it into position. She lifted both arms and leveled the gun, sighting down its length to the black words marked on the burlap bag. She pulled the trigger, flinching at the noise.

The bullet went off into the air. She'd forgotten how loud the gunshots were, how hard the weapon kicked, how lousy she'd been the first time. Resolved to hit the target at least once before leaving today, she sighted it again.

"Here." Davis Lee reached toward her, sliding his hand over hers and pushing her grip down. "If more of your palm covers the handle, you'll be steadier."

She squeezed the trigger again, amazed that the weapon's kick did lessen. "Yes, I can tell a difference."

"You didn't close your eyes this time. That's good," he murmured.

His words sounded almost caressing and made her as jittery as a painted lady at a prayer meeting. She didn't know how many lessons she would be able to survive with Davis Lee. How long she'd be able to keep up her guard against him. She emptied the chamber, hitting absolutely nothing.

She stared at the weapon in frustration. As she reloaded,

Davis Lee laid a hand lightly on her shoulder. "Try to relax. Your shoulders are too stiff. That's part of the problem."

"The other part being that a blind man has better aim?"

He grinned. "This isn't something you can learn in a day."

"For some of us, maybe not even a year."

"You'll get it. It just takes practice."

She *would* learn how to do this. Ian McDougal wasn't getting past her again, the way he had that awful night. As she stared at the bale of hay, she wondered if she could really shoot the outlaw given the chance. Could she really kill him the way he'd killed her parents, her fiancé? She shoved the doubts away. She'd come to kill him. She would.

Josie didn't know how long she stood there with Davis Lee, shots cracking through the air as the sun sank lower in the sky behind them. A couple of times he jogged over to the hay bales and told her she'd hit the ground just to the side of them or just in front.

That gave her enough encouragement to load another six bullets. Her forearms ached and she found it more and more difficult to keep her attention solely on the task at hand. Her mind and her attention kept wandering to the big man beside her who encouraged and directed and stood altogether too close.

She wanted to stay mad at him, but the anger slipped away as easily as the time. There were only a dozen or so bullets remaining in the box. She fired three more, lousy good-for-nothing shots and lowered her arm. "Why can't I do this?"

"Squeeze the trigger slowly," he said. "Picture in your mind that you're blowing a hole in that feed sack."

"I have been," she said through gritted teeth.

He smiled, reaching over to nudge her forearm up. His hand circled her wrist, his thumb resting on her pulse. "Don't stop yet."

His palm was hot and callused against her skin. She pictured hitting the target then squeezed the trigger. A hole appeared in the bag at the left edge.

For a second, she stared. She took a couple of steps forward and her mouth dropped open. "I—I hit that! Do you see? I hit it!"

He chuckled. "Yeah, I see."

"I'm going to do it again." She moved back beside him, taking aim.

When she was ready, she fired. Another hole appeared, this one near the bottom center of the bag. *"Ohmystars!"*

In her excitement, Josie spun toward Davis Lee. He was closer than she thought and she bumped him, hard. The gun flew out of her hand. Before she could react, a sharp explosion cracked the air.

She shrieked and launched herself at him, her arms locking around his neck. She pressed against him, tight as a steel spring bustle. "What was that?"

"Your gun." His arms wrapped around her as he looked over her shoulder. "You're lucky it's pointed the other direction. You could've shot off your foot or mine."

She exhaled in relief, sagging against him. "I got so excited that I finally hit something. I'm sorry."

"No harm done. This time." His breath drifted against her cheek.

Josie realized with a start that she was plastered to him. Every inch of her. Against every inch of him. She swallowed hard.

"You gotta be careful." His voice stroked over her, velvety and hypnotizing.

Her gaze met his. There was no mistaking the hunger in his eyes. Hunger that should've had her wrenching herself out of his arms and putting her feet on solid ground. She licked suddenly dry lips. "I will. I promise."

His eyes darkened and her senses narrowed to the man holding her.

The burn of gunpowder, the excitement of hitting her target for the first time, disappeared. Davis Lee's chest was solid muscle against her breasts. The deep male scent of him slid into her lungs, heady and delicious. His body cradled hers all the way down to her button-up boots.

"I'm gonna kiss you, Josie," he said gruffly. "I have to."

Her breath caught. "Are you trying to scare me?"

"If you're scared, you better run. Now."

She didn't want to run. She wanted to feel his mouth on hers.

He dipped his head. "Are you goin' for that blade?"

She shook her head. Waiting, aching for him to kiss her. Her heart pounded painfully in her chest and her arms tightened around him.

He had to taste her. Filled with the scent of her, he curled her tight into him and settled his mouth over hers.

She stilled for a second then parted her lips, letting him in. The soft noise she made kicked off a scalding desire inside him. He had imagined the taste of her, but he'd come nowhere close to the dark sweetness of her mouth.

She touched his tongue with hers. He dragged one hand up her back, cupping her nape so that his thumb rested in the hollow of her throat. He drank her in, his mind blank of all reason as a savage swirl of need pulled him under.

He angled her head, went deeper and slower with his tongue. There was no fight in her. She was all give and soft woman.

He let her slowly drift down his body until her feet touched the ground. She stood on tiptoe, still kissing him, her stomach against his arousal, her breasts flattened against his chest. She smelled delicious, tasted like honey-drenched sin.

One arm slanted down her back, holding her to him. He lifted his other hand, gliding his thumb over her cheekbone, burying his fingers in her hair.

It was like thick, hot silk. He wanted to unbraid it, drown his face in it, feel it on his bare skin, his belly. The whole time they kissed he told himself he was in control. That it was *her* body shaking, not his. That he was only trying to keep her off balance.

She moaned, gripping the front of his shirt. He lifted his head, his breathing rough and loud. Hard with need, he throbbed against her belly and she felt it, her eyes widening slightly.

Her pulse thrummed wildly beneath his touch. She was flushed, her eyes deep and soft with desire as she lifted a shaking hand to his face. "Oh...my," she said hoarsely.

He kissed her again, harder this time, again demanding total surrender.

He got it. She melted into him, her hands curving around his nape then slipping into his hair. She was sweet and hot.

Davis Lee thought his knees might buckle. He dragged his lips from hers and set his teeth on her neck. He nipped and laved his way to her ear, biting gently on her lobe.

She wiggled closer, making a sound somewhere between a whimper and a moan. Aching, he nuzzled her temple, her cheek, savoring the fine texture of her skin, drawing in her light honeysuckle scent. He brushed her lips with his just as he heard a noise behind him.

He lifted his head.

"Noooo," Josie moaned, trying to pull him back down.

"Shhh." He pressed her close, trying to hear over the roar of his blood.

The murmur of a voice, the jangle of harness, the soft blow of a horse. Someone was in the barn. Catherine.

Josie finally heard the sounds, too. She stiffened and wiggled out of his arms. Her face was flushed, her hair loose where he'd thrust his fingers. Her breasts rose and fell rapidly.

Davis Lee balled his hands into fists and forced himself to step away, which was damn hard when he wanted to pull her back against him and finish what he'd started. Dragging in air, he waited for her to slap him or run.

She stared at him, her eyes huge and moss-green in her beautiful face.

The violent hammering of his blood finally quieted enough for his brain to work. She probably expected him to apologize for taking such liberties, but when she spoke, she said, "I think we should go."

She turned away, kneeling to pick up her gun. She carefully checked to make sure the chamber was empty before she stood and slid it into her skirt pocket. As she smoothed her hair into place, her color deepened. Her lips were still wet from his.

The sight of her set off a primal hunger inside him. He wanted to taste her again, take her. She was *his*.

The thought exploded in his mind and suddenly he couldn't breathe. His lungs burned, laboring as if an invisible weight pressed down on him. He had to get away from her.

"I'll come back later and return the hay bales to Catherine's barn," he said. "I should get you back to the hotel before dark."

"Yes. All right."

She didn't look at him as they walked silently back to town, making a path that kept them away from Catherine as well as other people and brought them up behind the hotel.

One look at Josie and it would be clear she'd been thoroughly kissed. By him. What was he going to do? "Josie?"

"Please don't say anything. Please." She knew it would

never happen again. It couldn't. But she didn't want to hear him say he regretted it.

Somehow she'd find a way to put the memory aside so she could continue her lessons with him.

He walked her to the front of the hotel, his handsome face set in unyielding lines. The day had only begun to shift into evening, a soft gray haze blurring the edges of the setting sun. Voices drifted over from the Pearl as people finished their dinner. Lanterns there and in the hotel spread golden light onto the street.

They stopped in front of the hotel's landing. She tried to ease the tension arcing between them by giving a little laugh. "It's a good thing you didn't have to kill any snakes for me today."

He nodded, his eyes dark and serious in a way she'd never seen.

"I hope I'll be able to hit that target again. Do you think it was just an accident that I did?"

"I can't do it, Josie," he said baldly.

"Do what?"

"The, um—" He cleared his throat. "I won't be able to take you out for lessons again."

Shock stiffened her spine. "But I was just getting somewhere."

"I know. I'm sorry."

"Is it because I dropped the gun? I didn't mean to, I swear."

"No, that's not why."

She stared at him for a moment. "It's because of that ki—because of what happened, isn't it?"

"It's not that." But he looked so uncomfortable that she knew it was.

"We can forget about it." She didn't know how she would. She'd never been kissed like that in her life, not even by the man she'd pledged to marry. "I mean, it was just a kiss. Or two. Right?"

His face hardened. "Some things have come up that demand my attention. All my attention."

"I thought you had Jake to help you."

"I do." Davis Lee's gaze flicked away. "He will, but I'll still be too busy to spend the time with you."

"We don't have to meet every night." She didn't understand why she felt so desperate.

"I'm sorry."

"But—"

"I hope you'll understand."

No, she didn't!

He tipped his hat, murmuring, "I'll see you soon."

And with that, he was gone. Josie watched his steady purposeful gait as he moved toward the jail. She wanted to wail, to scream. She needed him—his *help,* she corrected. Only that. Even so, she fought the sinking feeling that she'd lost more than shooting lessons.

Chapter Nine

Knowing he'd been right to tell Josie he couldn't continue the shooting lessons did nothing to ease the need that had throbbed below Davis Lee's gun belt since kissing her.

Need that only sharpened the next day in church, when she slipped into a seat on the back row across the aisle from him. The drift of her soft scent lured his mind back to the way she'd felt against him yesterday. It was difficult to keep his attention on Reverend Scoggins.

After the service ended, she rose, barely sparing him a look as she walked out. By the time Davis Lee answered questions about the fire and gunshot on Friday night and got outside, she was walking down the middle of Main Street, flanked by Cora and Loren.

Her bronze silk gown gloved her high breasts and tapered in at her small waist. Her skirts swayed gently. Her long hair was gathered high on the back of her head to cascade in a dark fall to her shoulders, exposing the sweet line of her neck. She looked like honey and cream, and Davis Lee wanted another taste.

He curled his hands over the brim of the hat he'd taken off for church, unable to stop thinking about the way her eyes had gone all smoky after she'd been kissed. The now-familiar hard knot of need coiled in his gut. He was beginning to wonder if it would ever go away.

He'd just had to get his hands on her—his *mouth*—and now he couldn't stop thinking about her.

Her voice was a murmur on the air and he heard the faint sound of her laughter. His gut pulled tight. As she, Cora and Loren passed the Pearl Restaurant then the jail, Davis Lee figured they must be going to Cora's for Sunday dinner.

He was glad she wouldn't be eating alone. Sunday dinner together was a long-held Holt family tradition. He never missed that meal with Riley, and now Susannah since she'd married his brother.

"If you like her, why don't you bring her to dinner?"

At the sound of Susannah's voice, his head jerked around. His blond sister-in-law stepped up beside him, adjusting a jaunty flat-brimmed hat made of the same dark green as her dress. Her gaze followed his down Main Street.

"Who?" he asked nonchalantly.

"The new dressmaker who's got your eyes poppin' out of your head." Riley walked up holding his seven-month-old daughter. "You haven't taken your eyes off her since church let out."

Before Davis Lee could tell Riley and Susannah that he still thought Josie was up to something, Matt Baldwin's deep voice stopped him.

"You not seeing Miz Josie anymore, Davis Lee?"

"Why do you say that?" he hedged.

The big man pointed in the direction Davis Lee had been staring. "'Cuz she's leaving with Cora and her brother. You're still here."

"I always have dinner with my family on Sunday. You know that. And Cora wanted to invite Josie today."

"Didn't look like you brought her to church." Russ joined them, his eyes gleaming speculatively at Davis Lee.

"I didn't see y'all taking roll at the door."

Both brothers grinned and walked back toward the church steps where J.T., their pa, stood.

Riley handed the baby to his brother and Davis Lee snuggled little Lorelai into the crook of his neck.

Susannah smoothed the baby's blanket over her back. "I didn't know you were seeing her, Davis Lee. She seems very nice."

"I'm not."

"But you just said—"

"Well, uh, the Baldwins said that. Not me." He shifted from one foot to the other.

His brother chuckled, glancing at his wife. "I think there's a story here, darlin'. What's going on, Davis Lee? Why do the Baldwins think you're courting Miz Webster? Are you?"

"Not…exactly. I've been giving her shooting lessons."

"Hmm." Riley considered him for a long moment.

Susannah tilted her head, her blue eyes puzzled. "Then why do people think there's more going on?"

He settled his hat on his head. "I kinda let them."

Riley grinned.

Susannah squeezed Davis Lee's arm. "Then you *do* like her!"

He scowled. "I've been asking a lot of questions about how she spends her time. If people choose to think that means I'm sweet on her, I can't help that."

"If you've been asking about her, doesn't that mean you're interested?"

"He is, darlin', but maybe not completely in the way you're thinkin'." Riley slipped an arm around her waist, looking at Davis Lee. "Did you ever figure out if she's interested in your prisoner?"

"She's interested, but she's not 'fessin' up to it."

Susannah frowned. "Riley told me you suspected her of

having a connection to McDougal, but she's a dressmaker, Davis Lee. What could she have to do with him?''

''I don't know yet, but my gut tells me she does. I still haven't been able to get a direct answer out of her about anything, although I did learn she had a fiancé who passed away about two years ago.''

''Oh, no,'' Susannah murmured sympathetically.

He glanced at his brother and sister-in-law. ''Remember the fire Reverend Scoggins mentioned this morning?''

''He said no one was hurt.'' Susannah snuggled into Riley. ''And there was no damage to any of the buildings in town.''

''That's right, but I'm pretty sure someone set that fire deliberately, as a diversion to get me out of the jail. While I was over behind Pete's making sure the fire was under control, someone took a shot at McDougal.''

''And you're thinkin' Josie Webster did both?'' Riley guessed.

''I did, but I don't now. People saw her and I don't think she had time to pull it off. I didn't find any signs of the shooter outside the jail the other night. Not footprints, not anything. Still there's something about her that doesn't sit right.'' Davis Lee shifted Lorelai to his other arm as the infant grabbed at his ear. ''I've sent a couple of wires to the sheriff in Galveston to see if he knows anything about her but there was a hurricane down there about a week and a half ago. He hasn't gotten back to me yet.''

''What will you do if you learn something bad?'' Susannah asked.

''Depends on what it is, I guess.''

Riley grinned. ''Have you considered maybe she's just turnin' your head? You're probably ripe for some lovin'.''

Davis Lee gave him a quelling look.

Susannah swatted her husband on the arm. ''Riley Holt!''

His brother grinned, hugging his wife close and nuzzling her hair. "He's not denyin' it, darlin'."

Davis Lee snorted, shifting Lorelai once again to his other shoulder, submitting to the clumsy pats of her baby hands on his face. Why couldn't women stay as uncomplicated as they were at his niece's age?

He had put a stop to his little flirtation with Josie just in time.

Where the hell was Jake Ross? The next evening, Davis Lee paced to the window of the jail for the fourth time in as many minutes and looked outside for the rancher who also served as his sometime-deputy. Jake was supposed to relieve Davis Lee so he could go to dinner. The man was never late.

McDougal was hungry and prowling nervously around his cell. Davis Lee would bring the outlaw's meal from the Pearl when he returned. If he ever got to the restaurant.

He stepped outside, his gaze automatically going to Josie's hotel window. She wasn't there. Surprised, he wondered if she had taken a break for supper. Reminding himself he'd come out here to look for Jake, he shifted his gaze to the other end of town, scanning the livery, the new hotel. No sign of him. Or Josie, either.

The shy Ross wasn't near Haskell's store, Cal Doyle's law office or Jed's gunsmith shop. Davis Lee shot a look at the church, the gentle slope behind the white frame building.

He froze. A man and a woman were walking down the hill behind the church and into town. Even from this distance, he couldn't mistake the fall of chestnut hair, the easy grace of her movements. Josie. And Jake. Coming from the direction of Catherine's house.

Davis Lee's eyes narrowed. Why was she with Jake? Had they been at Catherine's? Why? How long had they been together? The questions hit him like bullets and set off a throbbing pain behind his eyes.

He watched as Jake walked Josie to the door of the hotel. Kept watching as they talked. Josie looked to be smiling at Jake. A lot.

Davis Lee folded his arms. What in the Sam Hill was going on? Had she asked Jake to give her shooting lessons? The thought caused his muscles to seize up.

Jake swept off his hat, said something to Josie then opened the hotel door for her. She patted the man's arm then disappeared inside. The deputy stepped into the street, starting toward the jail.

Davis Lee waited. Ross kept a steady pace but didn't hurry, pausing along the way to speak to a few people. Davis Lee tried to squash the impatience that was quickly edging into irritation.

All day he'd fought missing her. He let himself believe it was because they'd spent so much time together when she was ill.

Jake passed the Pearl and finally saw Davis Lee. He smiled and raised a hand in greeting. Davis Lee nodded, not understanding the savage emotion that knotted his gut.

His deputy started up the jailhouse steps. "Hey, Davis Lee. Sorry I'm late. Got tied up."

Yeah, Davis Lee had seen exactly who had tied Jake up. He took a deep breath, making an effort to speak casually. "What were you doing with Josie?"

Before the other man could answer, Davis Lee asked, "Were y'all coming from Catherine's?"

"Yes." Jake reached the landing, looking confused as he met Davis Lee's gaze.

"Why?"

"You know she wants to learn to shoot." The other man eyed him warily. "I told her I'd help her."

Shooting lessons. So she *had* asked Jake for his help. A

red haze clouded Davis Lee's vision. He knew what *he* and Josie had done behind the yellow house. Just the thought of her doing any of that with Jake, getting close enough to do it, had Davis Lee's hands clenching. "Why did she ask for your help?"

His deputy answered slowly, "I didn't figure on this being a problem."

"It's not. Why you?" Why hadn't she asked the Baldwins? Or Mitchell Orr? Not that Davis Lee wanted her spending time with any of those men, but why Jake?

"I don't know why she asked me." The man thumbed his felt hat back, his black eyes measuring. "All I know is she said you'd been helping her but had to beg off. That you were too busy."

Davis Lee grunted. What she did and with whom was none of his business unless it involved his prisoner. He didn't want it to be his business. He had to stay away from her. Too often his thoughts were of her naked, beneath him. Not about what he should be doing to find out more about her and what she might be hiding. The things he wanted to find out had to do with getting his hands on her again. He realized Jake was talking.

"I guess you haven't had a chance to tell me about all the work that's come up. What do you need me to do?"

"I can handle it." Especially since the only thing to handle was trying to forget kissing Josie. Davis Lee couldn't think about her going behind Catherine's with Jake or he would do something stupid, like tell the man to stay away from her.

For a long minute, Jake didn't say anything. Davis Lee had known the man since they'd been in knee britches. He was a mild man for the most part, but his nerve and his will were solid steel. "Is there something going on with you two?"

Davis Lee shook his head.

He wondered what would happen if Josie dropped her gun when she was with Jake and climbed him like a tree the way she'd done Davis Lee. As far as the deputy knew, she was available. "I have some suspicions about her."

The stiff set of Jake's shoulders eased slightly. "You still think she has some connection to McDougal?"

"Yes."

"If you're wantin' to keep an eye on her, why did you beg off her lessons in the first place?"

Davis Lee's teeth clenched so hard he thought his skull would crack open. "I'm going to go eat."

Not ordering Jake to stay away from Josie was one of the hardest things Davis Lee had done since telling the people of Rock River that his woman had stolen their money.

He now knew the burn that had sizzled in his blood since kissing Josie wasn't going to disappear. Still, he wouldn't give in to it. Not when his instincts told him she was hiding something.

She had asked Jake for his help. Jake, who also had access to McDougal.

Davis Lee might want Josie until he ached, but he couldn't trust her. Forgetting that would get him in a heap of trouble. He had to keep both eyes on her. And his hands off.

Four days later, Josie was still thinking about that kiss. Even William had never kissed her like Davis Lee had. As if he'd been waiting years just for her.

Which was a ridiculous notion. If her gun hadn't gone off when she dropped it, she wouldn't have jumped into his arms. And that kiss wouldn't have happened.

Now, as she rode out to the Eishens' place on Friday night with Cora and Loren to attend this annual event that signaled the coming pecan harvest, Josie resolved to stop thinking about Davis Lee. And that kiss. And the fact he'd backed out of giving her shooting lessons.

"I don't imagine you'll see Davis Lee here tonight," Cora commented.

Wishing her friend hadn't mentioned him, Josie groaned under her breath.

"Why not?" Loren asked.

"He never comes to the harvest dance. I'm not really sure why."

Good, Josie thought. That should help keep thoughts of him out of her mind. If Cora didn't talk about him all night.

The Eishens, who lived about two and a half miles from town, had hosted the dance for the past twelve years. Cora pointed down the slope of a hill and Josie followed her gaze, stunned at the thousand acres thick with tall, mature trees. The nut harvest would begin in two or three weeks.

She shifted her gaze to the Eishens' home. It was bigger than Cora's and the white frame home was extravagant. Framed by the lush foliage, it was sprawling with a veranda that went around the whole house. The trees sat some distance from the house. Spaced well apart to allow for their full, spreading branches, they formed a wall of sorts around the sides and back. Nothing obstructed the front view of the house with the wide porch as they rolled up the road, packed hard from years of wagon use.

Behind the main house, Josie saw a springhouse and a garden and a couple of large buildings. She'd heard the Eishens were one of the wealthiest families in Taylor County. Her eyes widened. "How many barns do they have, Cora? I can see two from here."

"Only one is a barn." Her friend pointed to the building closest to the trees. "The place we're going is a cleaning room for the nuts."

"A cleaning room?" Josie had never heard of such a thing.

Loren looked interested, too. "How do you know that, Sister?"

"Sometimes for extra money—" the other woman's voice cracked "—Ollie worked the pecan harvest."

Josie reached up from her place in the back to pat Cora's shoulder. Loren passed his sister a handkerchief.

"I'm all right," the widow said, pointing to the building's doorway, which was wide enough for two wagons abreast. "After the pecans are knocked out of the trees with padded sticks, they're tossed into the wagons. The wagons drive inside the cleaning room and deposit the nuts there throughout each day's harvest. Then the hulls are removed, the nuts are loaded into burlap bags and driven to the train in Abilene where they're transported back East."

"I never knew there was so much involved in getting pecans."

"It's long, tiring work, especially the cleaning. The Eishens hire a lot of people from around here to help."

"How long does the harvest usually last?"

"Oh, usually anywhere from about mid-September until December, depending on the weather. It's starting a couple of weeks late this year because of the rain we got in August."

Josie was amazed at the number of waiting horses, wagons and buggies parked in front of the building where Loren braked their wagon.

After he helped her down, she adjusted the velvet wrap she wore over her evening gown and followed Cora inside, carrying an apricot pie. All the women wore their best finery and even a lot of the men had put on their dressier shirts.

The smooth pine floor was amazingly clean. The only bits of red Texas dirt in the place were being tracked in by the guests. Two rows of solid wood columns that marched from front to back separated the sides from the big center area and formed a long rectangular dance floor. To the left of the columns two trestle tables were shoved end to end, already filling up with pies and cakes. Large pewter bowls at either end held punch. The right side of the room bustled as people arrived and greeted one another.

Josie followed Cora to the far end of the tables and was introduced to their hostess, Lettie Eishen. The large, raw-boned woman took their wraps and gloves, pointing across the room to her husband, Glen, who was built just like her. After a few minutes, Josie and Cora added their pies to those on the long tables. A sudden spate of whispering drew Josie's attention and she glanced up at the women on the other side of the table.

Esther Wavers, Pearl Anderson and a woman Josie didn't know stared at a point over her shoulder. She turned, her stomach fluttering as Davis Lee strode through the door, removing his hat. He walked toward his brother, who must've arrived while she was speaking to their hostess.

Josie tried to squash the pleasure she felt on seeing him, reminded herself of the way he'd backed out of her lessons. The way she'd gone as soft as butter the second he kissed her. As annoyed as that made her, she couldn't take her eyes off him. The square line of his jaw looked freshly shaven. A black shirt and trousers molded the powerful lines of his body. The brilliant blue of his eyes glittered in the burnished copper of his face. Her throat closed up and she turned away, greeting Catherine and Susannah as they walked up to the table together.

"Can you believe it?" a woman said behind her. "I never thought we'd see *him* here."

A quick glance back told Josie that the woman was talking about Davis Lee. From the sound of more hushed voices around her, several people were surprised at his appearance.

Catherine tugged Josie over to join her and Susannah, away from the whispering women.

"Cora said Davis Lee never comes to this dance," Josie

said. "Judging from all the attention he's getting, I guess she was right."

"Yes." Susannah's brow furrowed as she studied her brother-in-law thoughtfully. "He only occasionally goes to the Founder's Day celebration. He must be here for you."

"Me! No." Josie shook her head. "I don't think so."

Her gaze traveled across the room and crashed into his. He nodded. He had so much work to do that he couldn't spare her an hour in the evenings, but he could come to the dance? She fought back a stab of irritation.

The Doyle brothers, Cal with a mouth harp and Jed with a fiddle, started the dance with the quick-paced "Turkey in the Straw." Couples hurried onto the floor to polka.

"Rumor has it the two of you are courting."

Susannah's words had Josie jerking around. "We're not."

"That's what he said, too." The blonde eyed Josie curiously before shifting her gaze to Davis Lee.

Josie squirmed, turning to Catherine and changing the subject. "When is your fiancé due back in town?"

"With any luck, in the next two weeks or so. He's been down in Houston wrapping up some business. When he comes back, he'll have his mother and sisters with him."

"I guess if he's delayed, the wedding can be moved back a day or two."

"Jericho won't be delayed," the dark-haired woman said softly, certainly.

Josie accepted a dance with Mitchell Orr and they moved onto the floor along with several other couples. Davis Lee and Riley stood across the room, their legs spread, their arms folded across their chests, watching. Josie didn't see Jake Ross anywhere, which probably meant the deputy had stayed at the jail with McDougal.

The song ended but before Mitchell returned her to the edge of the crowd, Matt Baldwin claimed her for a polka.

After him, she danced with Russ and later their father, J.T. Through every song, she felt Davis Lee's gaze on her like a touch and she fought to ignore it.

When the Doyle brothers took a break, Josie was ready for one, too. She moved to the side of the room with Loren, her latest partner.

She and Cora fetched a cup of punch then joined Catherine and Susannah down at the opposite end of the table. Across the wide expanse of floor, Davis Lee still stood talking with his brother. She caught the flash of a blade in his hand. He was whittling. This time both he and Riley were looking at her. She turned away just as the Baldwin brothers joined them.

"Josie, your dress is beautiful." Susannah eyed the pale pink silk admiringly. "I guess you made it?"

She nodded. "I saw a pattern in *Godey's Lady's Book* but used it only for the skirt. The bodice draped off the shoulder and I wanted something a little warmer so I put on the high neck and sleeves."

"I love the lace edging your neckline." Catherine pointed to the high collar that opened down the front to the base of Josie's throat. "It's so delicate it looks like it might melt."

"I bet Josie could put some on your wedding gown," Cora said.

"Yes. Would you like that?" she asked Catherine. "I can add it before your last fitting."

"Oh, yes." The bride-to-be looked delighted. "Thank you."

Josie glanced up and this time found Davis Lee's gaze on her as well as that of the Baldwins and Riley. They stared at her as if she were a broken doll they were trying to piece back together.

"When Jericho sees you in that gown, he's liable to promise you the moon," Susannah predicted.

The other women laughed softly. Cora moved off to

speak to May Haskell. As Susannah and Catherine discussed the wedding, Josie sipped at her punch, her skin prickling under the intense regard from across the room.

"He's a good man. It's a shame he hasn't settled down yet."

Josie caught the words uttered in a sympathetic voice and saw that they came from Pearl Anderson. She was with the same unfamiliar woman Josie had seen before.

The other woman, small with dark eyes, *tsked.* "I think he was more hurt by that Rock River incident than any of us knew."

What incident? Josie wondered. Who were they talking about?

"Did anyone ever find out exactly what happened?" Pearl asked.

"No. Only that there was a woman involved and Davis Lee was run out of town."

Josie choked on her punch. Davis Lee Holt? Run out of town? She couldn't fathom it. She looked up and saw that Catherine had heard, too.

Susannah frowned and walked off, motioning for Josie and Catherine to join her behind one of the support columns. The music started again, this time with a banjo playing "Buffalo Gals."

Susannah's lips tightened in disapproval as she bent her head close to Josie and Catherine. "Don't listen to them. Millie Jacobson is the worst gossip in town."

"Is any of it true?" Josie didn't see how it could be.

Catherine leaned in. "I know Davis Lee was the sheriff in another town before Whirlwind. Was he really run out of there?"

"Over a woman?" Josie couldn't imagine Davis Lee losing his head over anyone enough to jeopardize his job as a lawman. Despite their short acquaintance, she knew that about him.

Susannah flicked a look over Josie's shoulder, her blue eyes softening. "I can't talk about it. Riley swore me to secrecy."

"Susannah, you *have* to tell us what happened," Catherine breathed. "We won't repeat it to anyone, will we, Josie?"

"Of course not." Even with her back turned, Josie could feel the men looking at her again. "*Please* tell us."

"I can't."

"Not even a smidgen?" Catherine looked hopeful.

"No. I will say that I think Davis Lee's paid enough for that mistake. Just because he followed his heart doesn't mean he was at fault for what happened."

"Well, if they're saying he did something bad, I won't believe it." The dark-haired woman glanced fondly in his direction. "He's one of the best men I've ever known."

"Me, too," Susannah said quietly.

Josie's mind raced with questions. What had happened in Davis Lee's past that Susannah couldn't discuss? Was that why almost every person at the dance had done a double take upon seeing him arrive? Had the woman involved been his intended? His wife? The possibility jolted her. She didn't know if he'd ever been married or engaged. Until now she hadn't thought about it.

Catherine glanced at her. "Why do Davis Lee and the Baldwins keep staring at you, Josie?"

"I don't know." She wished they would stop.

"Here comes Davis Lee," Susannah said. "We can ask him."

"No!" Josie's spine went rigid. Before she could take a step away, she felt him behind her. His nearness caused her nerves to twitch.

"Evenin', ladies."

"Davis Lee." Catherine and Susannah smiled easily at him.

Josie didn't even want to look at him, but she turned anyway. As handsome as he'd looked across the room, he was even more so up close. He was without his badge. Dressed all in black, he was tall and whipcord lean. He smelled like male and the outdoors and soap, but it was the deep blue intensity of his eyes that had Josie's belly quivering. She hadn't been this close to him since they'd kissed.

The soft poignant strains of "Silver Threads Among the Gold" surrounded them. There was a hot, proprietary look in his eyes as his gaze slid down her dress to her black kid boots. "This is my dance, isn't it, Josie?"

She stiffened. "I don't recall you asking."

He grinned. "May I have this dance?"

She didn't want to dance with him. She'd had enough trouble sorting out her thoughts the last time he'd held her. "I'm a little tired. I think I'll sit this one out."

The smile he gave her was charming enough to melt her stockings off. "This is my favorite song."

Of course it would be a waltz. Her heart started hammering hard. "I don't really ca—"

"I knew you wouldn't want me to miss it." He tugged her onto the floor as if she hadn't spoken a word.

"I said no," she muttered under her breath as he drew her into his arms. "Are you just dancing with me so the Baldwins can't? I saw y'all talking over there."

He didn't answer and she looked up, surprised to find him studying her, his eyes warm.

As he whirled her around the floor, she caught glimpses of people who were either slack-jawed with amazement or openly curious. As if Davis Lee's showing up here were the equivalent of hell freezing over.

He held her lightly, their bodies a respectable distance apart, but she felt every inch of him as they moved—shifting, brushing, touching. Hard to soft, curve to muscle. His hand was hot and big on hers, causing sensation to slick through her.

All she could think about was the way he'd kissed her, how she wanted him to do it again. She didn't look at him, afraid he would see it in her face, but she was helpless to stop her body from straining toward his. Friction traveled between them every time her skirts teased his legs.

His overwhelming maleness frayed her nerves. She felt scrutiny from every corner of the room. "Your coming to the dance has put all the women in a tizzy."

"Including you?" His voice so close to her ear sent a delicious shiver down her spine.

Her gaze shot to his. "Of course not."

The satisfied smile on his face told her he'd said it only to get her to look at him. Well, now she had and her chest grew tight. She had missed him. The admission had her squeezing her eyes shut briefly. She wanted to press her lips to his throat, his jaw, his mouth. The urge was strong, strong enough that her hand tightened on his shoulder as she forced herself to remember why she'd come to Whirlwind. Reminded herself that Davis Lee didn't trust her.

Some part of her mind registered the start of a new song. "With the way all the women were carrying on about you being here, I was beginning to think you didn't know how to dance."

"I know how," he growled.

"You're very good."

"I've had lots of practice."

"In Rock River?"

He faltered, his foot coming down hard on hers.

She jerked in reflex. "Oomph!"

"Sorry." The hand at her waist steadied her as his gaze narrowed. A muscle ticced in his jaw. After a long moment, he asked, "How are your shooting lessons with Jake going?"

"Fine." Her question about Rock River had caught him by surprise. Josie wondered if he ever talked about it.

"Why Jake?"

She frowned up at him.

"What made you ask him in particular?"

You're leaving me high and dry. "Since he's a deputy, I figure he must be good with a gun."

"Is that the only reason?"

She tilted her head, wondering if he guessed at her other motive. "What other reason could there be?"

"Answer my question."

"He's a good shot. Well, I think he is anyway. And he's a good teacher. He's very...patient."

Davis Lee's hand tightened on hers. The look in his eyes seared straight to her soul. "Josie?"

"Hmm?"

"About that kiss."

She inhaled sharply, her gaze darting around even though the music was loud enough to keep anyone from hearing him. "I can't believe you're bringing that up."

"I reckon we should clear the air."

"You're not going to apologize, are you?"

"Do you want me to?"

No. She wanted him to kiss her again. Now. "We shouldn't do it again."

"I know."

Disappointment slashed through her, but she knew she couldn't get further involved with him. She realized suddenly that he had partnered her through four dances. She tried to disentangle her hand from his. "We've danced together too long."

"Too long for who?"

Want slid slyly through her, tugged hard. "People will certainly think we're a couple now."

He stopped in the middle of the floor. "All right."

As he walked her back to Catherine and Susannah, Josie tried to determine what he was thinking. She couldn't read anything on his rugged face. He bowed politely over her hand and thanked her then walked away.

"Four dances?" Susannah had a mischievous gleam in her eye.

Catherine grinned. "There's no denying he's interested now, Josie."

"I guess not." But she knew his interest was more about suspicion than romance. And heaven help her, she wanted it to be the other way around.

Chapter Ten

For the next two hours, Josie watched him surreptitiously. Her invitations declined considerably after their dance and she knew it was because people believed the same thing about her—*them*—that Susannah and Catherine did. Why didn't he just leave her alone?

While he danced with Susannah and Catherine, Cora and Pearl and nearly every other woman in the place, Josie answered inquiries about her seamstress services. As people began to leave, she walked down the table searching for her pie tin. She found it, glad to see only crumbs remained. Cora had disappeared after her dance with Davis Lee so Josie turned to look for her friend.

"I told Cora and Loren I'd see you home."

She whirled at the sound of Davis Lee's voice. How had he snuck up on her like that? A quick scan of the building showed no sign of Cora or Loren. In fact, there were only a few people left and they were gathering up wraps and dishes to leave. "I can ride back with Catherine."

"She's gone, too."

Josie's nerves fluttered as she searched the remaining faces and saw he was right.

"If you're worried you might have to ride, I brought a buggy."

"It's not that." Why had he agreed to take her home? He'd made it clear the other night that he preferred not to spend time with her. She licked her lips. "I can't go back with you alone. People will talk, Davis Lee."

"They already are."

"That doesn't mean we have to add fuel to the fire."

"I'm taking you," he said firmly.

What choice did she have? Her friends were gone and she didn't fancy walking back. Still it irked her that she was at his mercy. "If I say yes, can I ask you a question?"

He gave her an impatient look. "Why is everything a negotiation with you?"

"Can I?"

His gaze turned sharp. "All right, but not until we're in the buggy."

She nodded and went to retrieve her coat and gloves from Lettie Eishen. "Thank you for a lovely time," she told her hostess as she took the items.

The woman's smile softened her square face. "I've been admiring your coat. Did you make it?"

"Yes."

"Are you looking for work?"

"Yes, ma'am." She had finished the tablecloths for the hotel and soon Catherine's dress would be finished. After that she had only one current order, nightshirts for Lemuel Tucker back home.

As Josie slid her arms into the coat, Lettie touched the dark gray velvet, its edging of white fur. "I like how it's longer in the back than in the front and is fitted to the body."

"It makes a nice look over a dress, with or without full skirts."

"Could you make me one in dark green velvet?"

"Yes. Would you like white fur trim?"

The woman thought for a minute. "Is there another color you'd recommend?"

"Gray or black would be nice. The green will be striking though, no matter what."

Lettie thought for a moment. "I believe the gray. That would be different, plus it wouldn't show wear as quickly as the white."

"All right." Josie pulled on her gloves. "I can start as soon as I get your measurements."

"I'll come to town tomorrow."

After they agreed on a price, and a time to meet the next day, Mrs. Eishen called her husband over and had him give Josie half the cost of the garment so that she could buy the fabric.

Josie said goodbye and turned toward the door. Davis Lee waited for her there and when she reached him, he lightly cupped her elbow and led her to his rig.

"Getting acquainted with Lettie?" He bundled her into the buggy and walked around to climb in beside her. Pulled by a single horse, it was built for two people. The leather seat was soft and more comfortable than she'd expected. The hood shielded them from the cool air and occasional gust of wind.

Josie huddled into her wrap. Davis Lee reached beneath the seat and pulled out a lap robe, spreading it over her legs.

"Thank you," she murmured.

He snapped the reins against the horse's rump. The buggy lurched into motion but quickly settled into a smooth ride. Davis Lee leaned forward, elbows resting on his knees, big hands controlling the reins easily.

Sitting so close to him made her body tingle. His heat wrapped around her in the confined space and every breath brought the scent of him into her lungs. With shaking hands she tucked the lap robe under her legs. The big man beside her, the clip-clop of the horse, the sound of her own breathing—all played against Josie's nerves. "Can I ask my question now?"

"Go ahead," he said gruffly.

"Have you ever been married?"

He sat up, looking at her sharply. "No."

"Close?"

"No." His gaze narrowed. "That's two questions."

"Then what happened in Rock River?"

His eyes glittered like steel in the mix of moonlight and shadow.

Well aware of the way Davis Lee's body had gone rigid, Josie proceeded tentatively. "I heard some women talking. They said something happened there, that there was a woman involved and you were run out of town."

His face went carefully blank and Josie felt an inexplicable tug of regret at asking him. Whatever the secret, he had been hurt by it. Suddenly she didn't want to know, didn't want him to recall painful memories.

"I'm sorry, Davis Lee," she said quietly. "It's none of my business. I shouldn't have asked."

He looked back to the road. Silver light drifted across the hard angles of his face, and for an instant he looked so remote, so alone that Josie ached for him.

"I was in love once," he finally said. "Her name was Betsy Mays. That's what she told me, anyway. I met her when she came to Rock River pretending to be on the run from an abusive father."

He faced her; his gaze changed from raw to calculating, gauging her reaction to his words. "By the time I figured out she had lied, she'd conned half the town out of their money by saying she planned to use it to help abused women like her to start a new life."

"And they ran you out of town because of her?" Josie asked incredulously.

"I vouched for her. People didn't take kindly to their sheriff having such lousy judgment. Who could blame them? I'm a lawman. I should've at least *suspected* something about her wasn't right."

No wonder he was so diligent about watching the stage, checking in with every new arrival. The cold gleam in his eye had Josie swallowing hard.

"As you can probably guess, I have a special aversion to liars." His voice was soft, ragged with an edge Josie had never heard from anyone. "And I'm real careful about who comes into my town. I'll never let something like that happen again."

"It wasn't your fault."

"I trusted her when I shouldn't have. Other people suffered for it."

Josie fought the apprehension spreading through her. He had good reason to be suspicious of everyone, of *her*. She was lying to him, just as that other woman had. If he ever found out, ever looked at *her* with that same unforgiving bleakness in his eyes, she wouldn't be able to bear it.

She should've changed the subject, done something to keep from giving in to the urge to soothe him, but all she cared about was the pain beneath his words, the blow his pride had suffered. All she wanted right now was to erase the self-loathing on his face.

Without thinking, she lifted a hand and cupped his cheek.

Looking startled, he reined the buggy to a stop, his eyes dark and hot on hers.

"Davis Lee, I haven't known you all that long, but I know you're an honest man, a good man. You care deeply about this town and everyone in it. I'm sure it was the same in Rock River."

"That doesn't excuse—"

She placed her fingers against his lips, shivering at the feel of his hot breath through her gloves. "We can't help who we fall in love with. You weren't at fault for the things that woman did. She's the only one responsible.''

Riley had told him the same thing, but somehow, coming from Josie, the words took on a new significance. They were at the edge of town; the sounds of raucous laughter and voices drifted from the saloon. Friday and Saturday nights always saw the cowboys from neighboring ranches coming into Whirlwind to blow off some steam and spend their pay. Only occasionally did they cause any trouble.

Right now his mind was on the trouble sitting next to him. He reached up and gently removed Josie's hand, folding hers into his much-bigger one. ''Josie—''

''Do you know what I see when I look at you?'' she asked softly. ''A man who would nurse a near-stranger back to health. A man who has the compassion to bring a puppy to a widow to help ease her pain.''

A man who wants to drag this woman into his lap and kiss her senseless, he added silently. The dark thrum in his blood urged him to do it; so did the soft look in her green eyes. Somehow he resisted, managed to put the buggy in motion and start through town while still holding her hand.

She stunned him. Amazed him. He had thought to tell her about Betsy only to see how she would react, see if guilt would cross her face when he talked about the lying woman from his past. But somewhere in the telling, he found himself confiding in her because he wanted to.

His hand squeezed hers. ''I've never told anyone except Riley.''

Emotion flared in her eyes. ''You can trust me not to say a word to anyone.''

Trust her? Instinct told him he shouldn't trust her at all, yet he'd done just that. They reached the hotel and he released her hand, but instead of stepping out of the buggy to help her down, he turned to her. ''Since I've been honest with you, Josie, why don't you be honest, too? Why did you really come to Whirlwind?''

He saw her pulse jerk in her neck. "I told you why."

Maybe she'd told him part of the truth, but his gut knew she hadn't told him all of it. "I considered that maybe you came here because the memories in Galveston were too painful."

Her whole body locked up.

"Was it too hard to stay there because you're still in love with William?"

"No." Tears welled in her eyes, but she blinked them away.

"Does your coming here have something to do with the time I found you in my jail?"

She looked down, her voice trembling. "Is that why you're interested in me? Because you think I'm hiding something and you want to know what?"

"No," he said quietly. His only interest in her *should* be to discover her secrets, but it wasn't. "I'm just curious as to why you would leave your family and move so far away? What's here for you?"

"There's nothing *there* for me." She fisted her hands in her lap. "My parents are dead."

His heart clenched. "I'm sorry."

She fiddled with her gloves, the edges of her coat.

"You have no other family?"

She shook her head.

"Why Whirlwind?"

"Why not?"

He waited, sensing a struggle within her. She gave a hoarse laugh. "I got on the stage, and when it stopped here, I thought this was a nice town. I wanted to stay."

"So you just ended up here?" he asked skeptically.

Her gaze leveled into his. "Haven't you ever ended up somewhere you hadn't planned to?"

Yes. Back here, by way of Rock River. "I guess so."

He knew she was holding back, but he also felt that she was starting to trust him. He wanted that as much as he wanted answers.

She looked so pretty in her ice-pink gown with the moonlight touching her face, skimming the hair she'd gathered back loosely. He wanted to kiss her again, wanted to do more than that.

The Baldwin brothers' blunt questions from earlier tonight replayed in Davis Lee's mind. They didn't think he was involved with Josie the way he'd led them to believe. They had made their intentions toward her very clear, especially Matt. And something inside Davis Lee had snapped. He'd claimed her for a dance, knowing that if he didn't, every man there would know inside of five minutes that she was available. And she wasn't.

He might not trust her, but he wanted her. Until he figured out what to do about it, the only man she spent time with would be him.

He stepped out of the buggy and went around to help her out. At the hotel's front door, he opened it, holding her arm for a moment longer than necessary. He managed to keep from wrapping a tendril of her hair around his finger.

She looked up at him, thoughtful and unguarded. "Thank you for telling me."

He nodded. As certain as he was that she was up to something regarding McDougal, he was just as certain that she would keep his confidence. "Good night."

"Good night." She started inside.

"I'll pick you up tomorrow evening at six-thirty."

"What?" She pivoted. "Why?"

The look on her face—part eagerness, part apprehension—had him grinning. "For your lesson."

She stared hard at him. "I thought you were too busy."

He stepped down onto the street and shrugged. "I've worked things out."

"I've already made other arrangements."

"Change them."

Her chin came up. "But I'm doing fine with Jake."

She wasn't going to be doing fine or anything else with Jake from now on. "I'll feel better knowing exactly what instruction you're getting."

"Why have you changed your mind?" Her eyes narrowed.

He climbed into the buggy. "I thought you wanted *me* to teach you."

"I do. I did." She shook her head as if trying to clear it. "Why?"

"Don't worry about telling Jake. I'll see he finds out."

She crossed her arms, looking at him expectantly. He just grinned. When she realized he wasn't going to bend, she said grudgingly, "All right."

He waited until she was inside the hotel before he turned the buggy around and headed for the livery. The low din of noise and off-key piano music from the saloon rumbled around him. Two cowboys staggered across the street up ahead and Davis Lee kept an eye on them until they slumped down in front of Ef's blacksmithy and nodded off.

Slowly he was gaining Josie's trust. She had told him her parents had died, as had her fiancé. Had those deaths somehow compelled her to come here, to Whirlwind? One way or another he would figure out why she had come.

Chapter Eleven

Davis Lee had lain awake a long time last night, thinking about Josie's hand on his face, her fingers on his lips, the fiercely earnest look in her green eyes. He sure did like her even though he knew she wasn't shooting straight with him.

That fact should've blistered him up more than it did. He should be thinking about how to get her secrets out of her, not how to get her out of her clothes, which was where his mind had stayed since he'd kissed her. He'd gotten about as far with her as he had with finding out who'd taken a shot at his prisoner.

But on this Saturday morning, he couldn't work on either one. Luther and Odell demanded his full attention. About an hour before lunch, Davis Lee stood in Pete Carter's saloon, eyeing the two over-sixty gentlemen whose antics had brought him here at least once a week every week for the past two years.

Luther Grimes and Odell Pickett were mostly harmless until they got too much liquor in them. Then some old feud—to this day no one in town knew about what—caught up to them and they threatened to duel.

Late-morning sunshine bounced through one of Pete's large windows, shooting sharp points of light from the glass scattered across the scratched wooden floor. Besides Pete and his boy, Creed, Davis Lee, Luther and Odell were the only ones in the saloon. It being the weekend, those two weren't the lone drunks in town, but they were the only ones causing problems at the moment. The cowboys who'd come to town last night to spend their pay on whiskey were now sleeping it off either upstairs or outside.

The culprits leaned back against the bar and Davis Lee eyed both of them, knowing the counter at their backs was the only thing keeping them propped up.

"So, now y'all have gone and busted Pete's mirror."

"It weren't not me," Luther slurred.

"It was'n, too," Odell yelled.

Davis Lee pinched the bridge of his nose. "I've had more than one complaint about y'all today."

Odell Pickett was slight with a knobby frame and neatly trimmed hair. He set great store by his thinning, gray-streaked hair and had Tony Santos trim it every week. Usually right before he and Luther got busy in Pete's saloon.

Luther Grimes was no taller than Odell, both hitting Davis Lee right about the chin, but he was built like a bull, and nearly as strong as one. The man didn't have an ounce of fat on him, just thick hard muscle and an even worse aim than Josie. Davis Lee smiled at that.

So far he had been saved from carting one or both of them to the undertaker in Abilene because they could barely hit a target when they were sober much less drunk. And half the time their guns weren't even loaded.

After the second time he'd been called to the saloon because the old men were shooting up the place, he had made some rules. If they wanted to drink, they had to turn their bullets over to Pete and they couldn't get the ammunition back until they were sober. Over the past two years, a bullet or two had been overlooked, which was why Pete's floor, ceiling and walls had gouge marks from where stray lead had dug into them.

Until today that had been the only damage. One of the old coots had shot the mirror behind the bar, which had Pete sending Creed for Davis Lee.

"Y'all are gonna have to pay for the mirror."

"I'm not payin' 'cuz I didn' hit it." Odell glared at him.

"Well, *I'm* not payin' for it, either." Luther poked Odell in the shoulder.

The other man rounded with a raised fist, lost his balance and grabbed the edge of the bar.

"You're both paying."

They mumbled incoherently.

Davis Lee braced his hands on his hips. "This has been going on for two years and I want it stopped."

"You gonna make us, Sheriff?" Odell blustered. The old guy swaggered toward Davis Lee then wilted to the floor.

Davis Lee shook his head, glancing at Pete, who looked as if he couldn't decide whether to laugh or spit nails. Luther pushed away from the bar and lurched toward Odell, waving his gun around like a dadgum flag.

Davis Lee stepped over the man on the floor and plucked the weapon out of Luther's hand. "I'm gonna count to three then y'all better scoot."

Luther wobbled over to a table, sank down into a nearby chair and flopped over to rest his head on his folded arms. "I'll just sleep it off in here."

Davis Lee looked at Pete who nodded. "Sure, as long as he sleeps."

"You heard him, Luther."

The old man wheezed out a breath in answer. Davis Lee turned and held out a hand to help Odell to his feet. "Let's go."

"I'm gonna stay here, too."

"No. Getting y'all separated is the whole idea of me coming down here."

"Well, that ain't your call, Sheriff."

Davis Lee pushed back his hat and said drolly, "Seeing as how I'm sober and standing, *and* have bullets in my gun, I'd say it is. Get up."

"Ain't gonna."

"All right then." Davis Lee wasn't angry but he was fed up. He stepped over Odell, grabbed the back of his shirt just below the neck and started dragging him toward the swinging doors.

Odell put up a fuss, yelling and hollering like his head was being pulled off. He started kicking his feet.

Davis Lee held on tight, pushed his way outside and hauled the man to his feet. As the old cuss teetered and wobbled, Davis Lee was aware that a couple of people stood behind him under the saloon's awning. He took a hold of Odell's arm and half pulled, half pushed him into the street and straight for the horse trough that sat between here and the livery.

Odell held up a hand to block the bright sun and stumbled. The old man squinted against the light. "Where are we goin'?"

"To sober you up."

"Noooooo!" He squealed like a schoolgirl who'd had her pigtails yanked. "Sheriff, don't be dunkin' me in that horse trough again. I don't like it!"

"You should've heeded my last warning."

"There's horse spit and all kinds of things in there."

"I told you to quit your warring with Luther, but you didn't. And then you resisted authority in the saloon." Davis Lee added that last for good measure, hoping it would shock some soberness into Odell's liquor-soaked brain.

The old man planted his feet, trying to dig in his heels with his slight weight. He twisted and strained back toward the saloon. Since he didn't weigh more than a drowned rat, Davis Lee easily reeled him around and pushed him face down into the trough. Water splashed all over Davis Lee's black wool trousers and the tops of his boots.

Odell came up sputtering and coughing. Davis Lee forced the old man's head back under the water for a second. After another dunk, he surfaced, shaking his head hard and spraying Davis Lee's pants and shirt. "All right, Sheriff." He panted the words. "I give."

Davis Lee helped him up and nudged him toward the livery. "Go home. Don't come back over here today. Next time I break up one of these fights, I'm takin' both you and Luther to jail."

"All right." The man staggered off, his shirt and dark trousers sticking to his spindly frame. He was so skinny his shadow had holes in it.

Davis Lee looked down at his shirtsleeves, wet past his wrists. The thighs and knees of his trousers were damp. He shook his head in disgust, rolling back his sleeves as he turned around. He caught sight of Josie standing under the awning, one gloved hand wrapped around a support post, her green eyes dancing.

"Hey," he said in surprise. Beneath a brown velvet bowler hat, her hair was swept up into some kind of twist that bared her nape and her dainty ears. "Not thinking about going in there to drink, are you?"

"Lands, no." She glanced in Odell's direction. "I certainly don't want you dunking *me* in the horse trough."

His gaze slid over the dark-honey-colored bodice that gloved her breasts and waist. The brown velvet buttons down the front matched the same color in the brown, cream and black striped skirt. "I wouldn't mess up that pretty dress."

She smoothed her skirts and gave him a little smile that darkened her eyes.

A little smile that had him thinking about what else she might do with that mouth. "I thought I wouldn't see you until tonight."

"So we're still having a lesson?"

"I'm planning on it."

"Good."

She looked so pleased that Davis Lee figured he better gather up what common sense he still had and use it. "So, if you're not here to drink, why are you here?"

"I'm looking at the stagecoach schedule."

"Why? Are you leaving town?"

"Yes." She turned away from him to study the paper stuck to the other side of the post. "It's for my business."

She was leaving? Davis Lee's stomach dropped to his knees. He had been kidding. He hadn't considered for a moment that she might leave. Forcing the words past his suddenly dry throat, he said, "I guess you'd get more customers in a bigger town."

She glanced over with a smile. "I'm only leaving for a day. I need to go to Abilene for some fabric."

Only a day. His chest felt strangely light. "The stage ran there yesterday. It won't go again until Wednesday."

"That's four days," she groaned.

"You in a hurry?" He grinned as he edged closer, admiring the smoothness of her peach-tinted skin. She smelled fresh and sweet, especially after Odell.

"I need some lace for Catherine's wedding gown. It has to be sewn on before I can finish her dress. She's expecting it next weekend, and if I have to wait until Wednesday to go to Abilene, the dress won't be ready. Once I finish that, I can start on Mrs. Eishen's order."

"Lettie's been to see you?"

"Yes. We talked last night about me making her a new coat and she came this morning so I could take her measurements." Josie tapped her foot then turned to him with a hopeful look on her face. "Exactly where is Abilene?"

"Due east."

She frowned, her gaze moving from the church at the far end of town then back past the saloon where they stood. A sheepish smile crept across her face. "Which direction is that?"

He grinned and pointed over her shoulder. "That way. We're on the west end of town now."

She thought for a minute. "Can you recommend someone I could hire to take me there? I don't fancy going alone."

"You shouldn't." The smartest thing he could do would be to give her the names of a couple of men he trusted, but evidently he was fresh out of smart because he said, "I'll take you."

Her eyes widened. "Oh, no. I couldn't ask you to do that."

"You didn't." Where had that come from? He hadn't thought about offering, hadn't even thought about *thinking* about it.

"Surely I'll be able to manage Abilene if I can just get there. I'd hate for you to wait on me while I shop."

"I have some business with the marshal over there." Which could be taken care of by wire, but it wouldn't hurt Davis Lee to talk to John J. Clinton in person. "Besides, Abilene can be rowdy, even during the week. On the weekends, it's more rough than it is here."

"Yes, I heard a lot of laughing and singing and hollering last night."

"You'll hear it tonight, too. Saturday nights seem to be a favorite for causing trouble."

"Was that gentleman—" she pointed to the horse trough "—one you consider rowdy?"

"No." Davis Lee pushed his hat back. "Odell's obstinate and mostly harmless. But some of the cowpokes who pass through here and Abilene are downright mean and looking for trouble."

"Oh." She stared thoughtfully at the stage schedule. "Can you have someone else watch the jail, your prisoner?"

"If Jake can't guard McDougal that day, I can ask Cody Tillman, one of Riley's ranch hands."

He leaned a shoulder against the post, unable to keep his gaze from sliding over her. "Is there some reason you don't want me to take you?"

"No, of course not." Her gaze flicked to his lips. "No."

He wanted to kiss her. Something fierce. But he wouldn't. "Is Monday soon enough for you?"

She fiddled with the glove on her left hand. "Are you sure about this?"

"Is that a yes?"

"Oh. Yes." A flicker of uncertainty passed through her eyes. "Thank you, Davis Lee. I really appreciate it. What time should I be ready?"

"Well, if we leave before eight, we can get there in plenty of time for the noon meal. We can eat before or after you shop."

"That sounds perfect."

"How much are you plannin' on buyin'? Do I need to drive something bigger than the buggy?"

She thought for a minute. "Could you get a wagon?"

His eyes widened. "Are you kiddin'?"

"Yes." She laughed, the sound wrapping around him like warm velvet.

"You better watch out or we'll take my horse," he said gruffly, biting back a smile. "I'll make you ride behind me and all you'll have room for is what will fit in my saddle-bags."

She grinned. "I'll try to behave."

Suited him fine if she didn't. "We're all set, then."

"I'll see you tonight?" she asked as he backed toward the saloon doors.

His gaze slid down her body again. She looked like a caramel-candy confection and he wanted to lick her all over. "You gonna wear that for your lesson?"

"No." She rolled her eyes as if that were the most ridiculous thing she'd ever heard.

He couldn't seem to wipe the stupid grin off his face. "See you at six-thirty sharp."

She nodded and turned in a swirl of skirts. He watched her as she walked past the office of the *Prairie Caller* newspaper then disappeared inside Haskell's General Store. He wondered at the kink in his gut when he'd thought she was leaving town. Maybe she *should* leave. That would at least put his mind at ease about her having a connection to McDougal. But Davis Lee didn't want her to leave.

Offering to take her to Abilene wasn't what he should've done. He had gone with his instincts and offered because he wanted to. He didn't even try to tell himself it was for any other reason.

Chapter Twelve

Josie needed to go to Abilene. Why shouldn't she go with Davis Lee? Riding over there with him didn't mean anything. She refused to dwell on the fact that ever since he'd shared the Rock River incident with her she'd been hard-pressed to remember she was supposed to keep a distance from him.

Her heart had ached at the self-reproach she'd seen on his face. His sharing with her an occurrence that she knew had hurt him deeply touched something inside her, a place that hadn't been reached by any man except William.

Monday morning dawned bright and breezy, the air cool with the advance of fall. She pulled her hair back into a low chignon and since she decided to wear her hooded wool cape, she didn't add a hat. The wrap covered her cinnamon traveling dress and provided some protection from the wind and the dust as did the collapsible hood of the buggy when raised.

When Davis Lee walked into the hotel lobby to fetch her, her nerve endings sizzled. He brought in the chill with him, a sweeping gust of wind that he cut off when he pulled the door shut. His cheeks were reddened, his blue eyes glowing in his bronzed face. The supple deerhide coat he wore made his shoulders look even broader. His light blue shirt tucked neatly into the waist of dark gray trousers that emphasized the powerful lean muscles in his long legs. The pants hem brushed the tops of his polished black boots.

The slow smile he gave her sent a tingle to her toes and made her as aware of him as if she were wrapped in his arms. Her own mouth curved. He wore his hat down low, thumbing it back as his gaze traveled from the top of her head to the tips of her black boots peeking out from under her skirts.

He helped her into the buggy then reached across her for the lap robe and arranged it over her legs. Going around to the other side, he climbed in beside her and snapped the reins against the horse's rump. Leaning forward with his elbows resting on his knees, Davis Lee kept the mare at a brisk pace.

Josie's gaze was caught by his strong, bronzed nape, the glimpse of dark brown hair peeking out from beneath his hat.

He asked what all she needed to buy in Abilene and acted interested when she told him. His questions turned to her sewing. How had she learned? Did she use patterns? His ma hadn't. But he was most taken with hearing about Galveston and what it had been like to grow up on an island just off the Gulf of Mexico.

Davis Lee's knowledge of the island city was minimal. He recalled his folks talking about the frequent threats of yellow fever and how nearly three-fourths of the population suffered one of its worst onslaughts in 1867. And he remembered hearing about hurricanes. Even so, he still wanted to visit there someday and see the gulf.

They were in the wagon at least three hours, but it felt like minutes to Josie. Before she knew it, they were there. They entered Abilene on First Street, which separated the north part of town from the south. The tracks for the Texas and Pacific Railway ran straight through the middle of the street, all the way through town. Davis Lee told her the growing community already claimed a post office, a newspaper, several churches and a public school. Not to mention numerous saloons.

When lots were auctioned by the railroad back in '81, the town had sprung up, mostly in tents. But as fast as lumber could be transported in, more permanent structures were built. Some were constructed of pine, like the huge Texas Crown Hotel and Fulwiler's Livery Stable, and some of stone, such as the depot and Taylor County Bank.

Buffalo Gap, fourteen miles south, was the county seat but with the railroad passing through Abilene and the growth that had resulted, an election was scheduled for next month to vote on moving the seat here. Davis Lee stayed on the north side of the tracks. They passed Hickory Street and Josie could see the train depot up ahead.

He maneuvered the buggy around a group of people gathered in front of a half-finished building listening to a man proclaim the benefits of *Corey's Stomach Bitters,* a concoction guaranteed to settle the stomach better than *Hostetter's Celebrated Stomach Bitters.* Hostetter's could be bought in almost any general store, but Josie had never heard of Corey's.

Davis Lee reined the buggy up at the corner of First and Cedar, in front of a two-story frame building identified as the jail by black lettering on its windows.

People teemed in the streets; some crowded around the train depot while others congregated in the road.

Davis Lee leaned toward her. "Believe it or not, it's even more noisy than this on the weekends."

"Because of those cowboys you told me about?"

"Yeah." He set the brake. "Do you mind if we stop here first? My business with the marshal won't take long and he can tell me the best place for you to buy what you need."

"All right." Josie counted two grocery stores, a saddle shop, a jeweler, a watchmaker and an ice house farther up the road. Merchants on the north and south sides of First had opened their doors and a steady stream of people went in and out. She edged closer to Davis Lee. "Is it always this crowded?"

"It has been nearly every time I've come over. Seems like people are always moving in or moving on."

He stepped out of the buggy, his gaze sweeping the throngs of people on the street. Three rough-looking men leaned against the wall of a frame building across the street, making general nuisances of themselves whenever a woman walked past. Davis Lee came around to her side. "I'd feel better if you went inside with me."

"I think I would, too."

He helped her down, seeming not to realize that he kept his hand at the small of her back until they stepped inside the jail.

She waited in a chair next to the marshal's desk as the man with an Irish accent and Davis Lee stepped through a back doorway where she saw a staircase leading to the cells on the second floor.

The office was bigger than Davis Lee's, but not fancy. A dark heavy desk commanded the center of the room. One chair sat behind it and two plain wooden chairs in front. Two gun racks mounted end to end on the opposite wall each held six rifles.

Josie had just removed her gloves when Davis Lee returned, saying he was finished. It had been so quick, she wondered if he had really needed to make the trip over.

He held the door open for her. "He gave me the names of a couple of places where you can find what you need."

"Thank you." His consideration had been evident all day, from making sure she was warm enough for the trip to finding out about the stores. He made it all too easy for her to want more from him.

Back in the buggy, they continued up First Street. He pointed to a large, imposing hotel at the corner of Cypress called the Texas Crown. "Riley and Susannah were married there."

He had her laughing with a story about Cora disguising herself as a man and winning every horse race here and in Whirlwind last spring. The older woman had needed extra money because a banker here had suddenly and unfairly raised her mortgage payments.

Davis Lee and Josie passed the train depot then Pine Street. Raucous piano music underlaid by loud voices caught Josie's attention. She glanced back, noting several tents and a couple of flimsy frame buildings lining the street.

"Saloons," Davis Lee said. "Marshal Clinton said there are quite a few on Pine and Chestnut Streets."

Halfway up the block, he reined to a stop in front of a large store bearing the name Trent's Dry Goods.

An advertisement affixed to the glass panel in one of the front double doors drew her attention. *Imported Dress Goods From New Orleans.*

She turned to him in surprise. "How do they get here? Does the owner go to New Orleans?"

"Probably goes to Fort Worth or has the goods sent from there. That place has turned into a considerable supply source."

Trent's Dry Goods store was easily twice the size of Haskell's. Through the large windows Josie's gaze swept tables of fabric, sewing notions, baskets and shelves of merchandise containing everything from stockings to sachet. "I'll probably be in here a little while. What time do you want to meet?"

"I'll go in with you."

Her gaze swerved to his. "Are you sure? I tend to forget the time when I look at fabric."

"I'll help you carry stuff. Besides, I don't fancy leaving you here by yourself any more than I did at the jail. Especially with those saloons only half a block away."

Josie couldn't say she minded him staying, either. "All right."

They stepped inside, teased by the subtle scent of apples and vanilla and leather goods. A long, glass-front counter sat directly in front of her. A dozen jars filled with different candy marched in a precise line across the top of the counter. Below and behind the glass were snuff boxes, plugs of tobacco and watches. To her right, Josie saw fancy soap, work boots and ready-made shirts, but her attention quickly moved to the left side of the store.

It was filled with table after table of fabric. The Wool Table, the one closest to her, held a copy of *Godey's Lady's Book* and *Peterson's Magazine,* from which ladies could order clothing patterns of the latest styles as well as some ready-made garments.

Davis Lee held the door open for an elderly woman who was leaving.

"Aren't you a dear?" She patted him on the arm then gave Josie a smile. "My husband will never come in here with me."

"Oh, but he's not my—"

"Have a good day, ma'am." Davis Lee spoke before Josie could correct the woman.

A stately, middle-aged brunette sailed out from behind the counter and introduced herself as Mrs. Trent. Josie explained what she needed and that she'd like to look around.

The woman gestured toward the stock of fabric. "Each table is marked with a price, but if you have any questions, all you have to do is holler."

"Thank you." Josie took off her gloves and slid them

into the pocket of her skirt's right side seam. She passed the Wool Table, the Gingham Table, the Silk Table and stopped at the Velveteen and Velvet Table. Davis Lee stayed behind her.

She soon found two shades of dark green that she liked and pulled out the bolts to lay them side by side.

Davis Lee leaned over, his breath tickling her ear. "These prices are pretty steep."

"That's why Mrs. Eishen went ahead and paid me for half the job."

He moved to the other end of the table and fingered a length of deep burgundy. "What about looking down here? The cost is more reasonable."

Josie glanced at him. "Those are velveteens. Unless the material comes from France or Italy, the colors are prone to fade. The velvet's color is more steadfast and Mrs. Eishen did say she wanted velvet."

He grinned. "I don't know why you won't take my suggestion. Since I know so much about sewing and all."

She laughed.

After a few minutes, she made her choice and measured out the necessary yardage, using the scissors tied with a string to the table for customers who chose to cut their own material. She folded the fabric lengthwise and draped it over her arm, but Davis Lee took it from her.

"Here, I'm good for something. I'll carry and your hands will be free."

"I didn't intend to work you in here."

"I don't mind. Gives me something to do." This way he could watch her. Which he'd probably done too much already. But he liked seeing the tiny frown form between her brows when she compared fabrics and colors. Liked the way she tapped her index finger against her lips as she considered the choices.

"All right." She relinquished the fabric to him and he

folded it in half, making a bulky mound that he carried in both arms.

She walked to the next aisle, stopping at the Trim Table to look over fur and braid and feathers. Here she cut a length of dark gray fur, giving Davis Lee an impish smile when she tossed the long rope of trim onto the velvet he held.

The tail of the fur fell over his arm and she caught it before it touched the floor. Rather than returning it to the top of the velvet, she threw it playfully over his shoulder.

"Hey," he growled. "I didn't say I would wear any of this stuff."

"But you look so pretty." She laughed and tugged the trim away from him, arranging it on top of the velvet as she'd originally intended.

Her eyes sparkled and Davis Lee was surprised to find himself enjoying the shop full of fabric and fripperies.

At another table, she chose a solid black lining for the coat, then he followed her to a table frothing with lace. Wide, thin, stiff, soft. The stuff was organized on spools in every imaginable pattern and colors from white and black to pastels and something he finally decided was green.

She searched for a while, finally finding a delicate-looking lace about a half-inch wide and holding it up. "This is for Catherine's dress."

He shifted the bundle in his arms, managing to rescue the fur before it slithered off. "It looks like the lace on that pink dress you wore to the dance."

"It is." Her eyes warmed.

She looked surprised that he'd recognized the trim. *He* was certainly surprised. He'd never noticed much about women's clothes except how to get them off.

She added the delicate lace to her growing pile and he followed her down a long aisle to the back wall. At the White Table, she quickly found what she sought. She pulled a bolt of fabric from the bottom of a stack and rolled out about a yard, passing it over her hand.

It was sheer white, and Davis Lee could see every line in her palm, the blue tracing of veins when she turned her hand over. "You can see right through that."

She glanced up. "Yes?"

"What do you do with it? Put it over something else?"

"You can. I'm buying it to make something for Catherine."

"Like what?"

She started to answer, then must've thought better of it. "Never you mind."

Her prim tone had realization zipping through him. It was for one of those combination chemise-drawers things like she wore. Davis Lee would bet his hat on it. "Did Catherine order that?"

"No. I want to give her something special, a little extra for nursing me after the snakebite."

"Hey, I was there, too. What about me?" He'd gotten plenty of reward just seeing her in the see-through undergarment the first time, but he wouldn't mind seeing her again.

"Want me to make you a shirt out of this?" Her eyes danced mischievously.

He grinned and leaned toward her to whisper, "That's for underwear, isn't it?"

She blushed. "Davis Lee!"

He straightened, unable to keep his gaze from sliding to her breasts. The image of her naked body teased by that sheer piece of nothing would stay with him until his last day on earth. His mouth dried up. "Jericho will think he's died and gone to heaven," he murmured.

She turned away as if she hadn't heard him, but he knew by the flush on her neck that she had. He chuckled, following her to a section full of ribbon.

She chose a thin white satin as well as ten different shades of pink, green and blue. Sunshine filtered through the window behind them, and Davis Lee thought how beautiful her hair was in the golden light. He wanted to pull out her hairpins and release the silky curtain, bury his hands in its thickness. A ribbon the same moss-green as her eyes caught his attention. Her hair would be pretty caught back with that ribbon, but so far she hadn't bought anything for herself.

Josie added her selection to the stack of goods he held, noticing as she did so that his attention was riveted on her hair. "Davis Lee?"

"Mmm?" His gaze moved to hers.

She smiled, wondering at his thoughts. Turning, she walked up the aisle toward the door and the sewing notions she'd spied upon entering. She chose thread and fastenings for Mrs. Eishen's coat, and pearl buttons for Catherine's combination.

Davis Lee lagged behind and she couldn't imagine what he was doing back there, but by the time she put her goods on the counter, he appeared behind her with the rest of her purchases. She carefully counted out her money. As Mrs. Trent packaged everything in brown paper, Josie noticed the fancy wrapped soap in a bushel basket off to the side.

Before she could talk herself out of it, she stepped over and picked up a cake perfumed with the scent of honeysuckle. When she returned to the counter with the box, Davis Lee was leaning against it and the storekeeper was giving him a sly smile.

Josie looked at him, not caring for the stab of jealousy she felt at the other woman's attention. He just smiled, thanked Mrs. Trent and carried Josie's packages out to the buggy. After paying for her soap, she followed him, pulling on her gloves.

He adjusted then readjusted the biggest parcel under the middle of the seat. The other packages were under her side.

He glanced over his shoulder. "Maybe I should've brought a wagon, after all."

The way his gaze warmly held hers had her forgetting all about how the other woman had smiled at him. He helped her into the buggy, his big hand hot enough to send heat through her gloves.

After he climbed in, he drove farther up First Street and turned left on Walnut. "How about some lunch?"

"That sounds good. I'm hungry."

He passed empty lots and several doctors' and lawyers' offices. Turning left onto Second Street, he pointed ahead to the Taylor County Bank, an imposing two-story stone building. "I bet we find some places to eat around there."

Josie nodded, noting fewer people in this area of town and liking the quieter atmosphere. "Thank you for bringing me today. I'm glad I didn't come by myself."

"You're welcome."

"I appreciated your help at Trent's, too. You can carry so much more than I can that I'm wondering if I should take you any time I need to buy things."

"So you decided I wasn't in the way, after all?"

She looked over, saw the teasing light in his blue eyes. "Well, I didn't say *that*," she murmured.

"Sass." His gaze drifted over her face.

He stared so long she squirmed. "Davis Lee." She looked away, noticed the buggy wheel was about to scrape against the curb in front of the bank. "Davis Lee!"

He jerked his gaze back to the road and righted the buggy, grinning.

Josie's entire body thrummed with awareness. He continued down Second and reined up in front of a small restaurant with a hand-lettered sign. He set the brake, glancing at her hair as a thoughtful look settled on his face.

Self-conscious now, she lifted a hand to her chignon.

"What is it? Has one of my pins fallen out? Is my hair loose?"

"No." The deep gruffness of his voice sent a wave of sensation through her. He reached in his coat pocket. "I was going to give this to you later, but I can't wait."

She frowned, her eyes widening when he brought out a length of green ribbon. "Davis Lee?"

"I thought it would look pretty in your hair."

Her mouth dropped open. She stared at the satin then at him. "You bought me something?"

"If you don't like it—"

"Of course I like it." Tears stung her eyes. "How could I not?"

"It's the color. You don't like the color."

"I love it."

"Then why are you about to cry?"

She answered without considering her words. "Because you are the dearest man and I…I can't believe you bought me something."

"If I'd known it would make you cry, I wouldn't have done it." He pressed it into her hand.

She inched forward, reaching back to wrap the ribbon around her chignon and secure it with a hairpin.

He laughed. "Josie, you don't have to wear it now. It doesn't match your dress."

"I want to wear it." She patted her hair and angled her head so he could see. "How does it look? Do I need to retie it?"

"No." His fingers brushed the ribbon and she straightened in her seat.

"Thank you."

"You're welcome." His hand stayed in her hair, the pad of his calloused thumb stroking just behind her ear.

She could barely keep from arching into his touch. His

eyes darkened. He slid his palm under her hair, cupped her nape and drew her toward him.

She never even considered pulling away. Anticipation pooled in a delicious heat low in her belly.

His lips touched hers and she sighed. She yanked off her right glove and curved her hand around his neck, felt his warm skin, the pulse throbbing against her palm.

He held her there with the barest touch. This kiss was nothing like the other one, but it was every bit as wonderful. His mouth moved over hers, tender and soft, dizzyingly sweet. She melted into him. He didn't press for more, didn't take the kiss further, just drew on her gently until she couldn't tell his breath from hers.

When he lifted his head, it took a second for her to open her eyes. She saw tenderness and desire in his face. Her heart hammered against her chest. "Should we…have done that?"

"Probably not."

She wasn't sorry, though it unleashed a flood of emotion inside her.

"Guess we'd better go in," he said.

She blinked. "A-all right."

Her legs were still wobbly when they walked into the newly built restaurant, and she gratefully sank down into the chair at their table.

As they waited for their meal, Josie could hardly keep her eyes off him. She wanted to know more about him, more than the fact that he was sin-temptingly handsome and could kiss the starch right out of her.

"Is Riley your only sibling?"

"Yeah. I'm older by three years. Do you have any brothers or sisters?"

"No. I had two younger brothers, but they both died soon after birth."

"That's too bad." His attention fixed on her as if everything she said was important. "So, you really are all alone?"

She nodded. "What about your parents?"

"They're gone, too. Pa died about two years ago. Our ma passed on a year before that. Dr. Butler said her heart just gave out."

"So it's just you and Riley."

"And now Susannah and Lorelai. Our ma was named Lorelai. Susannah chose that name for the baby because Riley helped deliver her. Have I ever told you about that?"

"No."

He told her how Susannah's brother, one of Riley's best friends, had sent her here under the impression that Riley wanted to marry her. Riley hadn't known a thing about the arrangement.

"But she and Riley ended up together anyway?"

Davis Lee grinned. "Yeah, no thanks to my hardheaded brother."

"From what I've seen, that trait runs in your family."

The crooked grin he gave her sent her pulse skittering. He hadn't worn his badge today. His light blue shirt turned his eyes an even more intense shade of the same color. The bottom three buttons on his placket were fastened, but not the top one. The hollow of his throat was visible, and Josie's gaze returned there several times before she realized why.

He ducked his head to peer at her. "Why are you studyin' me so hard?"

She looked at him. "Your button. I— Who sewed that on for you?"

"I did," he said rather proudly. Seeing the grimace on her face, he frowned. "Why?"

The button was hardly visible beneath a mound of thread that could've been used to sew on a dozen buttons. She bit the inside of her cheek. "How much thread did you use?"

"Enough to make it stay on."

She hesitated over the next question. "Did you do it in the dark?"

He laughed, his eyes crinkling at the corners. "Just say what's on your mind."

"I need to fix that." She glanced around, keeping her voice low but unable to stop the urgency. "You've *got* to let me fix it."

"I think it'll hold."

"I'm sure it will hold until the Judgment. It's not that. It's—"

"You think I look unpresentable?"

"Not you." She didn't want to hurt his feelings. "First impressions are important," she hedged. "You are a lawman, after all."

"Okay. When it falls off, I promise to let you reattach it."

"Oh, no, you can't wait until then. I need to fix it right now."

One dark eyebrow arched.

"You know what I mean. When we return to Whirlwind, I want you to bring me the shirt. Along with any of your other clothes that need to be mended."

"Aw, now, Josie, I don't want—"

"*I* want to. Please. I want to do something to repay you for bringing me today."

"I was happy to do it."

"And for taking such good care of me when I was ill."

He considered her for a minute then shrugged. "All right."

Their food came and they ate in companionable silence. When a young woman picked up their empty plates, Josie declined dessert, but Davis Lee ordered a piece of apricot pie for himself and coffee for both of them.

When the dessert came, he offered her some.

"Maybe a bite." Her silverware had been taken away so

Davis Lee held out a portion on his fork. She took it, enjoying the burst of fruit on her tongue, the sweet pastry crust.

She sipped at her coffee, her stomach doing an odd flip when his mouth closed over the fork exactly where hers had been.

''It's good,'' she said.

''Not as good as yours.'' His big hand dwarfed the delicate china coffee cup.

She sat up straighter. ''You tried my pie?''

''Yeah, the other night at the dance. More than one piece, too.''

That pleased her far more than it should have. *It's just pie, you ninny.*

He contemplated her over the rim of his coffee cup. ''Would you tell me how you met William?''

She thought back to the night when her fiancé had first knocked on their door. ''He was a doctor. Late one night, he came to see my father about a patient because he was unsure of his diagnosis.''

''And it was love at first sight?''

''He says it was for him. I certainly liked him right off.''

''When were you supposed to be married?''

''In August, about three months after we met. He wanted to get his family to Texas for the wedding. They were in Ohio.''

''But then he—''

''Yes.'' She cut him off. She didn't want to talk about William's death or her parents' deaths, either.

Davis Lee didn't say anything for a long moment, just looked out the window at the people passing by. ''Do you still love him?''

With her index finger, she traced a circle on the white tablecloth. ''I guess a part of me will always love him, but not in the here and now. Do you know what I mean?''

"You're ready to move on?"

She nodded, trying not to allow the thought that she might like to do that with him.

"Got anybody special in Galveston?"

She looked up, her gaze locking on his. "No, not in Galveston."

"Me, either."

She couldn't resist. "You don't have anyone special in Galveston?"

He grinned, his eyes burning into hers until she glanced down, pleating and unpleating a piece of her skirt.

Davis Lee wiped his mouth with the cloth napkin and leaned back in his chair. "You said your pa taught you and your ma to defend yourselves using that scalpel."

She nodded.

"What made him do that?"

She wasn't sure she wanted to tell him everything about herself, but he'd answered her earlier questions without hesitation. "An old beau of my mother's tried to force himself on her one night when my father was out."

"Your parents were already married?"

"Yes. The man who attacked her was someone my mother had asked not to call on her again after she met my father. He could never accept it."

"Never?"

Josie shook her head. "He still lives in Galveston. He never married, and he never forgave my mother for choosing another man over him."

"Did he cause more trouble after that?"

"Only once," she said quietly. She didn't want to think about Judge Shelton Horn and how he'd refused to hold Ian McDougal for trial or even one hour in jail, all because of a bitterness that had festered for more than twenty years. She didn't want to remember the reason she'd come to

Whirlwind. The reason she shouldn't be spending time with Davis Lee.

His hand touched hers. "Hey, I didn't mean to bring up bad memories."

"It's all right." She worked up a smile.

"You sure?"

"Yes."

He gave her hand a quick squeeze. "I guess we should be getting on back to Whirlwind. Don't want to be travelin' much after dark."

She stood, reaching for her cape but Davis Lee was there first. His big hands settled the wrap carefully over her shoulders then lingered.

"Thank you."

His hold tightened fractionally then he stepped away. After plucking up his hat from the back of a chair behind his own, he shrugged into his coat.

He left money for their meal and they walked out, his hand light on her elbow. In the buggy, she arranged the lap robe over her skirts while he climbed in and took up the reins, urging the horse into motion.

As they drove out of town, Josie commented that there seemed to be even more activity now than there had been when they'd arrived. Davis Lee told her the place would be wild come dark and he didn't want to be anywhere around when that happened.

"I'm off duty today," he said with a grin that curled her toes.

His words reminded her that she could no longer pretend that they were simply two people enjoying the day.

They rode for a while in silence, straight into the sun. He pulled his hat lower to shield his eyes from the glare.

After a bit, he slanted a look at her. "If you want, you can rest. I won't mind."

"Maybe I will." Sleeping might get her thoughts off the

gnawing truth she was trying to escape. And closing her eyes would keep her from gazing at the big man beside her, which she couldn't seem to stop doing.

She settled back into the corner and pulled the hood of her cape over her head. The edge of her garment kept the worst of the sun out of her eyes.

Sleep didn't come, but she didn't talk, either. When they were more than halfway to Whirlwind and the sun had started to sink below the horizon, the wind picked up. A cold gust blew across the buggy floor and up Josie's skirts. She unfolded the lap robe and spread half of it across Davis Lee's legs.

"Thanks."

"You're welcome." She leaned back in the seat, her thoughts churning. She'd come to Whirlwind for one reason, and until they'd left Abilene a while ago, she hadn't given Ian McDougal or what he'd done a single thought.

Even before Davis Lee's kiss had driven every thought out of her head, all her attention had been centered on the handsome man who'd brought her.

She was reluctant to reach Whirlwind. For a brief time today, she'd been just a woman enjoying herself with a man. A man, she forced herself to recall, who could come between her and the vow she'd made to her family, to William.

Davis Lee turned his head, stared at her for a long minute. "You're awfully quiet."

She couldn't meet his gaze. "Just thinking about the work ahead of me."

"Was today too much for you? It didn't occur to me that you might not have your strength back yet."

"I'm a little tired, but I'm fine." Why did he have to be so considerate? Make her think he really cared?

That sweet kiss earlier told Josie that he *did* care about her. And she cared about him, too. Enough not to want to hurt him. Enough not to want to lose whatever this connection was between them.

But if she went through with her plan, he wouldn't be able to stand the sight of her. She had intended to kill Ian and leave, but now she didn't want to go. She wanted to stay with Davis Lee. Because right or wrong, she could no longer deny that what she felt for him was something more than desire.

Chapter Thirteen

For the first time, Josie considered foregoing her plan to kill Ian McDougal. The emotions sweeping through her surprised her. And frustrated her. In the two years since the deaths of her loved ones, she had never questioned her plan for the McDougals. Never doubted her intentions for Ian, the sole survivor of the outlaw gang. Now, after less than two months in Whirlwind, she wasn't sure if she could kill the man who had cold-bloodedly murdered her family and her fiancé.

She had no doubt she could pull the trigger. Her uncertainty stemmed from imagining the way Davis Lee Holt would look at her afterward. She'd known the man less than two months. How could she feel more for him than she did about getting justice for her family?

What kind of person was she that a kiss—okay, more than one—could make her forget justice for the people she loved? That she could put aside the vows she made to them for the chance to explore her feelings for Davis Lee? But if she stayed on her course, the tall, lanky sheriff would look at her with only contempt. He would certainly never kiss her again.

She hated having this secret—any secret—between them.

She'd already gotten too close to him so she couldn't undo that. The only thing she *could* do was keep as much distance between them as possible.

Except for the hour each evening spent on her shooting lessons, she stayed away from him whenever possible. Giving up her lessons wasn't an option. Her skill was improving, but the circuit judge could be here in as little as two weeks and Josie was not ready if the outcome of the trial didn't go as it should. Cora invited her to dinner with Davis Lee again, but Josie begged off. Being guarded with Davis Lee now was difficult. She liked him too much. She *wanted* him. His tender kiss in Abilene had turned her inside out. She couldn't stop thinking about it, wanting more.

So for the next several days, when she and Davis Lee spent time together behind Catherine's house, Josie clamped down hard on her emotions. She couldn't be cold to him and didn't want to be, but her heart broke a little more each time they were together. And every evening, she grew more torn about her plans for McDougal.

It didn't help when she received a letter from William's sister in that week's mail. Josie had written to Rosemary and told her she was leaving Galveston for Whirlwind. She and the other woman had stayed in touch after William's death, but Rosemary had never sent such awful news. Still unable to cope with William's death, his mother had tried to kill herself. As a result, she was under constant sedation.

The news weighed on Josie, made her feel an even greater burden to make sure Ian McDougal paid for William's murder as well as that of her parents. That responsibility, combined with the uncertainty Josie already felt regarding her plans for McDougal, and her developing feelings for Davis Lee had her ready to scream. She could get no peace.

On Saturday night after her shooting lesson, Davis Lee saw her back to the hotel then went to relieve Jake for dinner. Josie spent the rest of her evening putting the final touches on Catherine's wedding gown. The task took three times longer than it should have because she kept looking out the window. For him.

She cut out the back and sleeves for Mrs. Eishen's coat, her thoughts seething. When she was with him, nothing else seemed to matter. And when they were apart, she was painfully aware of what *should* matter. Doubt churned inside her. The walls of her room seemed to close in. She couldn't separate one thought from another. The turmoil in her mind sent her downstairs and outside for some air.

It was well past ten o'clock. The full moon glowed angel-white in an inky sky and spread light over the town that had mostly closed down. The saloon at the other end of town was well lit and loud with piano music and voices. A lantern glowed inside the livery stable next door.

At first, she simply stood outside on the hotel's landing and breathed in the chill air, wrapping her shawl tightly around her. But she couldn't escape the guilt and disloyalty she felt to her family for wavering in her intent to kill McDougal. Couldn't dodge the fact that the reason was her feelings for Davis Lee. She wished she could simply turn off the thoughts.

She stepped off the hotel's landing and began walking toward the other end of town. As happened frequently on the weekend, plenty of visitors had come into Whirlwind, but so far she'd heard none of the ruckus that had been so prevalent last weekend. Silvery moonlight shone through the darkened window of the telegraph office. The Pearl Restaurant was also closed for the evening. A lamp shone inside the jail and as Josie passed, she saw Jake move in front of the window.

She wondered if Davis Lee had already started his nightly ritual of walking the town. He'd told her that every night he checked to make sure the merchants' doors were locked, that there were no mischief-making kids or secret trysts in the livery's loft.

The memory of his face when he told her about the woman he loved and how she had lied to him kept circling through her mind. Josie wouldn't be able to bear Davis Lee looking at her with the cold implacable mask she'd seen the night he told her about the con woman in Rock River.

Her head ached. Frustration burned inside her, making her feel helpless and disloyal to her family, to William. And deceitful to Davis Lee.

Noise finally penetrated her turbulent thoughts and she found herself in front of Pete Carter's saloon. Piano notes clanged above the sound of raucous laughter. The smell of liquor was strong enough to be noticed over that of the horses in the nearby livery stable. The place was crowded, the air laced with the odor of unwashed bodies. Lamps burned bright on the other side of the swinging doors.

She hadn't realized she had gone so far from the hotel. The loud off-key singing of several men carried to her, the words to their lewd song unfamiliar. Though she wasn't frightened, she angled back to the opposite side of the street.

A noise sounded behind her and she turned her head, placing the sound in the alley between the saloon and the livery. It came again. A moan? "Is someone there? Do you need help?"

"Yes." The voice was male, slurred with either pain or drink.

Josie twisted around as a young man stumbled into the light. Under six feet tall and spare with ragged blond hair, he didn't look as old as she was. Pale eyes glittered in the half-light. "Can you help me?"

She turned toward him, but stayed where she was. His white shirt and dark pants were grimy. He smelled like cattle. "Are you hurt?"

"Yeah. Why don't you kiss it and make it better?"

Disgusted, she spun to leave. He moved quick, hard fingers biting into her right arm.

"Let go!" She jerked at his hold but he was stronger than he looked. His gaunt features were mean.

He dragged her toward him and Josie fought to pull away.

"You're not as friendly as the other girls here."

"Let me go right now!"

His grip like a trap, he dragged her into the alley.

"Stop it!" she yelled, shoving at him, her shawl falling to the ground.

He clamped his other hand on her left arm. "I just want to show you a good time. You'll like it if you give me a chance."

His breath was rotten with alcohol. She reached for her scalpel. He saw her movement and reached, too, grabbing her breast and squeezing.

Fury and fear exploded inside her. She whipped out her blade and slashed at his windpipe. He jerked his head away at the last instant. Blood welled from a cut on the underside of his jaw.

Even as she went for him again, he roared in outrage and backhanded her. She reeled, crashing against the saloon wall, her weapon flying out of her hand. She lunged and tried to run.

He grabbed at her skirts, snapped her back, ripping seams. Screaming, she struggled against his hold, hoping someone in the saloon would hear her. *Please hear me.*

He seized her hair and yanked, wrenching her around to face him. She cried out, pushing at him. He slammed his fist into her jaw, sending her to her knees, her mind dazed.

Her cheek burned, her jaw throbbed. She scrambled away, but he caught her legs. His hands hard and clammy through her stockings, he twisted painfully until he flipped her onto her back.

His hand clamped over her mouth, muffling her scream.

She writhed and kicked. The sharp heel of her boot stabbed into his thigh. She bit his hand. The resulting blow from his fist left her limp and dazed, staring up at the night sky.

He climbed on top of her, his hand once again crushing her mouth. He smelled dirty and sick and she tried to buck him off. He ripped at the collar of her green-sprigged calico, dislodging buttons and tearing the bodice over her left breast. Sharp pain stung her chest.

The feel of his hot breath against her skin sent her into a frenzy. She clawed at his face, trying to reach his eyes.

He threw one leg over hers and curled it tight around her ankles, imprisoning her while he rucked up her skirts. She boxed his ears. Bellowing, he recoiled slightly. When his hold slackened, Josie strained to escape, to free her legs.

Suddenly his weight was off her. She scrabbled across the dirt, trying to get to her feet and run. A tall, broad-shouldered man slammed her attacker against the wall of the saloon. In a patch of moonlight she saw Davis Lee's face—hard as rock, his eyes cold enough, sharp enough, to kill in one vicious slice.

Josie sagged back against the wall. Her heart pounded painfully in her chest as her stunned mind tried to understand what she saw. Davis Lee's fist smashed into the other man's face again and again. Blood spurted from his nose; his head snapped back after each punch.

She huddled against the wall, her entire body quaking. Her jaw hurt, her cheek stung. Cold bored deep into her bones. Davis Lee shoved her attacker to the ground then knelt and did something she couldn't see. Ragged sobs broke from her.

Davis Lee rushed to her, going to his knees and cupping her shoulders. "Josie, are you all right? Talk to me."

She was crying so hard she couldn't see him. His arms went around her and she collapsed against his solid chest. He was big and warm and safe. Reassured by the clean, male scent of him, she finally understood that he was asking her a question.

"Honey, are you all right?"

"I—I think so," she sobbed. She told herself to stop crying, to let go of him or at least loosen her hold, but she couldn't. "Get me away from here, please."

Her voice was thick and foreign. Davis Lee held her tight, rocking her, murmuring soft words until her sobs abated.

He eased her back. "Look at me, honey. Let me see your face."

She did, her limbs trembling and useless. His hands moved over her face carefully, skimming her aching cheekbone. He barely touched her jaw and she winced.

He cursed, his eyes turning savage, but there was only tenderness in his touch when he helped her stand. Soon, he would ask why she was out here. She couldn't tell him that it was because thoughts of him, of *them* were driving her crazy.

He found her shawl, draped it around her shoulders, going stock-still when he got a look at her. "Your dress is ripped." Fury vibrated the air between them. "Honey, did he—"

"No. You got here before he could."

Davis Lee cupped her uninjured cheek, searched her eyes. "You can tell me if he did."

"I would."

He pulled her gently to him. "I'll take you to Catherine."

"No!" Panic and embarrassment flooded her.

"Cora then."

"Only you. No one else." She hugged him so hard she felt a button on his shirt dig into her cheek.

"Catherine should look at you," he said cajolingly.

"I don't want her to know. I don't want anyone to know."

"It wasn't your fault, Josie."

"Please." She buried her face in his chest. "Please?"

"All right. It's all right." His big hands stroked her back. "Let me take you to your room, then I'll—"

"Someone will see me. I don't want anyone to see me like this."

"How about my house? Will you go there?"

"Yes." He bent to scoop her up and she said in a shaky voice, "I can walk."

"I'll feel better if I carry you." Putting one arm beneath her legs, he lifted her easily. "I need to get you home. Then I can deal with this worthless piece of humanity."

Fighting the picture of her on the ground with her skirts pushed up and that bastard on top of her, Davis Lee carried her down the alley. Behind the saloon, the newspaper office and finally Haskell's.

She laid her head on his shoulder, her breath shuddering out. Rage twisted a vicious knot in his gut. What if he hadn't heard her scream? What if he hadn't gotten there in time to stop the guy from violating her?

"D-did you kill him?" He could hear her teeth chattering.

"Not yet." His jaw clenched. He thought he still might.

Josie huddled into him, her entire body shaking. They reached his small house, lit only by the moon since he hadn't been home yet tonight. He cleared the one step of his front porch and shouldered open the door, closing it with his foot once they were inside.

Aside from a few pine shavings courtesy of the whittling he'd done every night since taking her to Abilene, the house was clean. Built five years ago by the townspeople for Whirlwind's sheriff, the place was more modern than what Davis Lee was used to. Now he was even more glad for the indoor pump and the bathing room at the back of the house.

This large room served as the center of the house. Through the shadows he could see the cupboard and sink on the wall straight ahead, the stove to his left, making the kitchen almost a separate room.

The fireplace along the left wall kept Davis Lee's bedroom on the other side toasty during the winter. A second bedroom led off the right side of this room. Mixed with the lingering scent of wood smoke was a hint of shaving soap and kerosene. The air was cool.

With his foot, Davis Lee hooked a dining chair by its leg and dragged it over to the stove, setting Josie down carefully. But when he tried to step away, she clung to him.

"I'm lighting the lamp," he said soothingly. "Then I'm going to start a fire and get you a blanket."

Her eyes were huge with terror. "I don't want you to leave."

The alarm in her voice had him stroking her hair. "You'll be able to see me the whole time."

Finally she released him. He quickly lit the lamp on the dining table, then moved around her and past the stove to shove kindling into the fireplace. After starting a fire, he went through the door that led into his bedroom and returned with a quilt his ma had made.

He wrapped Josie up and crouched before her. "I've got to go back and take that guy to jail. Will you be okay for a few minutes?"

"I don't want you to go."

"I know, honey." Leaving her alone for even a minute went against every protective instinct inside him. "But if you want what happened to be kept secret, I have to be the one to move the bastard or tell Jake to do it."

"All right," she whispered, her face ashen, tears streaking her cheeks.

He squeezed her shoulders. "Let me get Charlie or his wife—"

"No, just you."

"I don't like you being here alone."

"I'll be okay. Just hurry."

He wasn't worried about her attacker going anywhere because he'd used the man's own rope belt to hog-tie him, but Davis Lee didn't want the sonovabitch drawing any attention, either. He took an extra pistol from the mantel and laid it in her lap. "You use this if you need to."

She nodded but didn't touch the gun. He smoothed a hand over her dark hair, half of it loosened from her chignon. "Bar the door behind me. I'll be right back."

He waited until he heard her slide the long piece of wood into place then he raced to the alley and made sure his prisoner hadn't moved. He hadn't, so Davis Lee checked his breathing and made sure he was still alive. He was, which was slightly disappointing.

It was a wonder Davis Lee had heard Josie scream with all the racket coming from the saloon, especially since he'd been checking Jed Doyle's gunsmith shop several doors away.

Concerned at being away from her a minute more than necessary, Davis Lee ran to the jail and told Jake to go fetch the guy in the alley then lock him up. Whatever questions the deputy wanted to ask would just have to wait. Davis Lee was back at his house in less than five minutes.

When Josie heard his voice, she opened the door so fast he figured she must've been standing there the whole time. She was huddled into the blanket, and when she saw him, sharp relief broke across her face.

"Is he in jail?"

"On his way." He barred the door behind him and shrugged out of his coat.

She closed the distance between them and laid her head on his chest. His throat tightened.

Reaching behind him, he hung his coat on the peg next to the door. "Let's go over here."

He picked her up and walked to the chair she'd used

before. Sinking down into it, he closed his eyes and inhaled her light scent, let it soak into him. She trembled in his arms and Davis Lee remained silent until the jagged edge of his fear subsided. "I found your scalpel. It's in my coat pocket."

"I cut him."

"I know, honey." He stroked her hair out of her face, careful to keep his touch easy. "That was good."

Her lashes lay in dark velvet crescents on her cheeks; she was pale as milk. Her shawl was draped over the back of another chair and he caught sight of something green and white on the floor behind the table. Her dress.

Her gaze followed his. "I had to get it off."

"Are you—do you—" *Damn.* "Do you need some clothes? You can wear one of my shirts."

"That's okay. I didn't…take off anything else."

"You're not cold?"

"No."

He tucked the quilt tighter around her, refusing to let his mind picture what she looked like beneath the covering. Her small black boots peeked out and he caught a flash of a white stocking.

"Thank you for not telling anyone."

"You're welcome." He pressed her head to his shoulder. "Tomorrow, Jake will take the guy to Abilene. I don't want that sonova—him anywhere near you."

She nodded, exhaling a ragged breath.

"Feeling a little more steady now?"

"Yes."

"I'll get some water and a cloth."

"No," she said quickly. "Not yet."

"All right." He slid out her hairpins and placed them on the table. Running his fingers through her hair, he got out what dirt and tangles he could. "What happened, Josie?"

"I went for a walk," she said quietly. "Until I reached

the saloon, I didn't realize how far I'd gone. When I started back to the hotel, I heard a noise behind me. Like someone was in pain.''

"And you tried to help?"

"Yes."

Davis Lee had seen it before—a man pretending to be sick or injured to trick a woman into getting close to him, then hurting her. "That's when he attacked you?"

"Yes."

"I'm glad you had your scalpel."

"Me, too."

He gathered her hair in his hand and smoothed the silky length to the middle of her back. "Why were you walking so late?"

"I...couldn't sleep."

"Something was troubling you?"

She nodded against his shoulder.

"Wanna tell me?" If he hadn't been holding her, he wouldn't have known that her body tightened almost imperceptibly. Why wouldn't she want him to know what bothered her? Surely she hadn't been meeting someone. Or trying to sneak into the jail again.

"Don't you know by now that you can trust me?" he asked softly.

"It isn't that," she whispered, so low he had to strain to catch the words. "I just...went for a walk."

His gut told him she had started to say something else, but he let it go for now. Finally the thunder of his heartbeat slowed. She breathed easier, too. "Let me get that water now. You'll feel better once we get some of the dirt off of you."

"Okay." She stood stiffly beside the chair as he got a basin from the shelf over his sink then pumped the bowl full of water. He added a warmed brick piece from the fireplace. After dropping a cloth into the basin, he set it on the table then turned to the small cupboard behind and took out a bottle of Old Farm whiskey and a glass.

Filling it with a moderate amount of liquor, he stepped over to her and pressed it into her hand. "Drink this. It'll help steady you."

She sipped slowly, grimacing distastefully at the first swallow.

He laid his palm between her shoulder blades and rubbed her back until she finished the drink. Pulling the rocking chair over from the corner, he settled it in front of his seat and motioned for her to sit.

He did the same, picking up the basin of water. "I'll hold the washbowl for you."

She finally relaxed her stranglehold on the blanket and it gaped slightly at her neck. Reaching toward him, she took the cloth and squeezed out the excess water. Her hands were visibly shaking and she clasped them tightly together, her gaze fixed on them as if she could order them to stop trembling.

After a long minute, when she still hadn't moved, Davis Lee set the basin on the cold stove and lifted her onto his lap, fitting her against his left shoulder so he could use his right hand. He gently pried the cloth from her.

"I feel silly," she said, looking down.

"There's nothing silly about letting me help you. Especially tonight."

She nodded, her eyes locking on his.

"I'll try not to hurt you." He dabbed at her cheek, already slightly discolored, then ran the cloth lightly over the delicate lines of her face, careful of the bruise on her jaw.

"I'm so glad you found me," she said close to his ear.

As he moved the rag down her neck, the blanket parted enough to reveal one lace-edged strap of her undergarment. He nudged the blanket aside just enough to reach below her collarbone, and froze.

A vicious scratch angled from just beneath the hollow in her throat to the swell of her left breast.

He went rigid with the effort to hold back the brutal, black tide sweeping through him. "Why didn't you tell me you were hurt here?"

She glanced down. "I didn't know."

"Are there any other marks on you?"

"I don't think so."

A long minute passed before he had himself under control. He carefully cleaned the flat plane of her chest, unable to keep his jaw from tightening as he neared the bloody mark on her tender flesh.

The thought that she'd been hurt was bad enough, but that she could've been hurt even worse rocked him. Hating that he hadn't been there to prevent the attack, feeling he should give her *something,* he bent his head and put his mouth gently on the scrape.

She made a little sound of surprise. Her warm breath fluttered against the back of his neck. "I don't know what I would've done if he—"

"Shhh." He looked up, his mouth barely an inch from hers. "You're all right."

Tears filled her eyes, spilled down her cheeks.

"Oh, honey, don't cry. I've got you now."

"I—I know," she sobbed, covering her eyes. "I can't help it."

The shudder that went through her body kindled every protective instinct he'd ever had, made him want to promise her that nothing like this would ever happen again. But he couldn't promise something like that. All he could do was be here for her now.

He took her hand from her eyes. Unable to help himself, he kissed the tears from one cheek, then the other, registering the slight taste of salt. He thumbed away more tears.

The absolute trust on her face released something inside him. "Seeing you in that alley scared the hell out of me."

Her eyes, deep green and wet, met his. He still held the damp cloth to her chest, and beneath his hand he could feel her pulse pounding wildly, could feel the slope where her breast began to curve.

She leaned into him and touched her lips to his; some barrier inside him crumbled. Hungrily, tenderly, he fed on her mouth, reining back the reckless impulses shooting through him. At first their lips were barely open, her breath mingling with his. She looped one arm around his neck and made an urgent sound in the back of her throat.

Mindful of her bruised jaw, as carefully as if she were spun glass, he moved his hand to cup the back of her head and angled her to him for a better fit. Her mouth parted, inviting him in. He went, the slow mating of their tongues helping to reassure him that she was all right.

She shrugged her shoulder free of the blanket and brought her other arm around his neck. Short nails grazed his nape as her fingers delved into his hair. His arm wrapped around her small waist, his reach far enough that his fingers brushed the underside of her breast. She turned fully into his chest.

She was warm and soft, the flavor of woman and aged whiskey. Compelled to taste the rest of her, Davis Lee's lips moved to her neck, up to the tender patch behind her ear, down to the sensitive curve where her shoulder began.

She kissed his nape, her small hands tugging his shirt from his trousers and sliding the fabric up so she could splay her hands flat against his bare back.

The powder-soft texture of her skin, her faint honeysuckle scent swirled around him, making his arousal rock hard.

Her breasts burned into him. He shifted her so he could reach all of her. His lips glided down her elegant neck. Her head went back, baring her throat to him, dissolving every last ounce of his common sense. He laved the dip in the center of her collarbone, touched his tongue to the tiny mole there, then once more opened his mouth over her torn flesh. He pressed his lips to the swell of her breast, repeating the butterfly kiss on the other.

He couldn't stop kissing her there. She made a little sound in the back of her throat, his name spilling brokenly from her lips. "Please, Davis Lee."

Compelled by the rush in his blood and feelings he could no longer escape, he opened the first three buttons at the top of her one-piece undergarment. He slipped his hand inside to the smooth warm flesh beneath, curving his fingers around her small, plump breast.

He felt her pulse hitch when he brushed his thumb across her nipple. It budded in response as she brought his mouth back to hers. She kissed him long and deep with an edge of wildness. Emotion rushed through him. He wanted to devour her, shelter her, claim her. He opened another button then another, pushing aside the thin fabric and dragging his lips from hers so he could look at her.

Her nipples were rosy and tight, touched with gold firelight. The sight of his rough-skinned hand on her pale, perfect flesh had his chest tightening. Transfixed, he brushed his thumb along the curve of her breast.

"You're the most beautiful thing I've ever seen," he said just before his mouth closed over her.

Her hand slid up the bare flesh of his back and she held him to her, her entire body quivering. The ragged moan spilling from her throat went straight to his heart then lower.

He arched her slightly over his arm so he could taste more of her. His big palm splayed on her stomach, the tip of his little finger touching the seam at the apex of her thighs.

His tongue curled around her. She held him close, her breathy cry driving a spike of pure burning need through him.

He moved his mouth to the sensitive skin of her throat,

scraped her gently with his teeth, then covered her lips with his. The kiss was hot and deep, desperately intense. She turned full into him so that her breasts flattened against his chest, trapping his hand between them. One slender arm went around his neck; the other was moving under his shirt, stroking his waist, his back. Every inch of her torso touched his.

His hand slipped down over the soft give of her stomach, the finespun lawn of her undergarment to the heat between her legs. She lifted into his touch.

He unerringly found the opening in her drawers and eased two fingers inside, stroking the heated satin of her inner thigh.

"Please, Davis Lee." Her hips rose as her arms tightened around him. "Love me."

He brought his hand up to touch her face, drinking in the sight of her. Her face was flushed, her eyes a dreamy green. The top of her undergarment was spread wide, revealing her breasts pushed high against his chest, moist and glistening from his mouth. Blood pounded in his ears, his groin.

She pressed kisses to his palm, raised up to do the same to the corner of his mouth, his jaw, his ear. "Davis Lee, take me to bed."

Even in his right mind, he couldn't have resisted her. He buried his face in her neck, the thick cloud of her hair, filling himself up with her scent, her warmth, her softness.

"Make me forget," she whispered brokenly. "Make me forget."

The words reached through the haze of desire, cleared enough of his mind to know something was wrong. He realized then how far they'd gone, what she was doing. What *he* was doing.

Several seconds passed as he dragged in a steadying breath and tried to restrain the ruthless need swirling inside him. He withdrew his hand, settled it at her waist. "Josie."

"Mmm?" She was kissing the side of his neck, the hot tickle of her breath in his ear straining the edges of a control he'd barely regained.

He was breathing hard, shaking, and realized she was, too. "Look at me."

Finally she did, her lashes half-raised, desire smoldering in her eyes. Her dark hair was tousled, her lips wet and red from his.

The sight, the feel of her naked flesh threatened to pull him under. "We can't do this, honey," he said hoarsely.

"What?" Her eyes reflected the struggle to comprehend, and he saw the moment when she finally understood. She sat up. "Davis Lee—"

"Listen." He cupped her face in both his hands, grazing his thumbs lightly along her cheekbones. "I want to love you, Josie, but when we come together, I want it to be something good. A memory that isn't tainted by what happened earlier."

"But I need you."

The ache in her voice tore at him. He pressed a soft kiss to her lips. "Not like this. I don't want us to be together as a result of your being upset. Our loving should be only between the two of us, without the bad memory of another man and what he did to you."

She trembled. "But you can make those horrid things he did go away."

"Is that all you want between us? A way to forget?"

"No," she said on a ragged breath.

"I'm not turning *you* away, honey." His hands delved into the hair on either side of her head. "Tonight just isn't the right time."

In the play of firelight, he could see color flush her cheeks. Her gaze skittered away and she shifted, looking ill at ease. "I'm…sorry. I wasn't trying to tease."

"I know that."

"I thought you wanted me the way I wanted you."

"I did. I *do*. Till I can't see straight, but I don't want to take you this way." He gently nudged her chin up with his knuckle. "Tell me you understand what I'm saying, honey. Why I'm saying it."

She shuddered, her gaze going to his lips then back to his eyes. "You're right. I know you are."

Relief sliced sharply through him.

"Do you want me to go?" Her hand fisted nervously in the fabric of his shirt.

Slightly taken aback, he asked, "Do you want to?"

"No. I don't want to be alone tonight."

"All right then." He hugged her close, trying not to think about how easy it would be to blank his mind and peel off her clothes. How damn sweet it would be to slide into her body. But he didn't want their first time together to be shadowed by what had happened tonight.

He tugged the blanket over her and grinned. "All my good intentions won't be worth a damn if I don't cover you up."

"And you'll really stay with me?"

"Yes."

"All night?"

"Whatever you want."

A sweet, sad smile curved her lips. "Like this?"

He looked into her eyes, knew that holding her after his body was already primed would be agony, but he couldn't deny her. "Yes, if you want. Except…"

"What?" She looked stricken.

He rubbed her back. "Won't you let me put you to bed?"

She paused for a heartbeat then a tiny spark lit her eyes. "That's what I've been trying to get you to do."

With those words, a tightly wound tension inside him released. She was going to be all right. "I'll sit with you. I won't go anywhere."

"Can't you lie beside me? Just hold me?"

Could he? All he had to do was think about what she'd been through tonight. She didn't need sex. She did need *him*. "Yeah, I can do that."

"Thank you." She kissed his cheek then nestled her head in the crook of his neck.

He stood and carried her into his bedroom, his knees weak as realization flooded him. Secrets or not, smart or not, he was falling for this woman. Hard.

Emotions he couldn't begin to sort out tangled inside him. He'd told himself not to let things go further between them until he knew more about her, but it was too late. And he wasn't sure he gave a damn.

Chapter Fourteen

"**I**'m all right." The next morning Josie watched Davis Lee prowl around her hotel room for the second time in five minutes. "Now that you've checked everything, I don't mind being alone."

"You know you don't have to." He turned, wearing the same somber, determined look he'd worn all morning. "I can stay until church lets out, then I can get Catherine or Cora or anyone you want."

His blue eyes were dark with concern. She wanted badly to reassure him, but so far she hadn't been able to. She walked over and laid the bundle of his clothes she'd brought on the low dresser that held a washbasin. "I'm bruised, but I'm not afraid."

"Are you sure?" He braced his hands on his hips, his gaze sweeping the small space again. "I don't mind staying outside in the hall for a bit."

"I appreciate it, Davis Lee, but you've already done so much."

His jaw tightened at that and Josie wondered why. He'd been tense ever since she'd woken this morning in his arms. Part of it was concern for her, she knew. But there was something about his manner that she couldn't decipher.

"I'm fine. Honest. You locked up that man and he can't hurt me again."

A shadow passed across his face as he studied her. Earlier this morning, he had told her that if they waited until church started, nearly everyone would attend and he could get her back to the hotel without anyone seeing her or knowing she'd spent the night at his house. And he had. "Thank you for sneaking me back over here. If anybody asks why we missed church, I'll say I had to tend to some business."

He nodded. "I'll say I didn't feel like going, which I didn't."

She wished he would hold her again, but in the daylight, here in her room, she felt too forward to ask. And something about the leashed restraint in his rangy body held her back.

He had loaned her a needle and thread and she'd tacked down the rip on the front of her dress so the bodice once more covered her underclothing. A couple of whip stitches reattached her skirt to its top.

He had shaken out her shawl as best he could, but it needed a good washing. He'd done everything for her, including hold her all night long against the safe wall of his chest. At first she'd been too wound up to close her eyes. Her breasts, her whole body still tingled from his touch, his kisses.

But she had soon gone to sleep. Waking up this morning with him, both of them fully clothed and in their stocking feet, felt more right than anything in her life ever had.

His gaze turned hard as he looked at her cheek. "How's your face?"

"It's still sore." She smiled. He'd asked her four times since breakfast. "How does it look?"

"Like it hurts." He took a step toward her then stopped, folding his arms across his chest. "And your jaw?"

"It's not uncomfortable enough to keep me from eating." She grinned, not caring that the movement made her bruised face sting. "I must've eaten at least three of your biscuits besides the eggs and coffee you made."

He smiled, but it didn't quite reach his eyes. His stance was guarded and his eyes narrowed as he took in her damaged dress. "Are you going to repair that dress and keep it?"

"I haven't decided for sure. I know it's frivolous to get rid of it, but I don't think I can stand to wear it ever again."

"You shouldn't." Somehow his jaw became even harder.

Not knowing what else to do, she closed the distance between them and put a hand on his arm. "I'm okay."

His face gentled and she saw a combination of protectiveness and searing need in his eyes. Her stomach gave a funny flip, the same way it had last night when his hands moved over her body. The hot look in his eyes told her he remembered everything that had gone on between them at his house. And the ache in her body reminded her of what hadn't.

She regretted that they hadn't made love, but Davis Lee had been right to pull back. Adrenaline and fear had addled her brain; her body had taken over. He'd saved her from more than rape. He had most likely saved her life and he had certainly safeguarded her reputation by getting her back here without anyone seeing her leave his house.

"Thank you for breakfast." She wanted to lose herself in his blue eyes. Go away with him somewhere and forget everything except the two of them. "And for letting me use your tooth powder. *And* for taking such good care of me last night."

"I'm sorry I didn't get there sooner, Josie—"

"No." She put her fingers against his warm lips. "Don't you dare. You got there in plenty of time and I'm thankful."

A dark dangerous light came into his eyes. For an instant, he looked like he wanted to sweep her into his arms. Josie wished he would. Instead, he said gruffly, "I'm glad you're all right."

"Me, too." She wanted to kiss him, but she settled for squeezing his taut forearm.

Their relationship had changed. She knew he felt it, too.

"I'm just a holler away if you need me."

She nodded.

"For anything."

"Okay."

"All you have to do is come to the window."

"I know." What was going on in his head?

"Keep your door locked. It would probably be a good idea if you jammed a chair under the knob, too." His eyes were intense, his shoulders stiff.

"I'll be careful, Davis Lee. I won't be careless, like I was last night."

His gaze, sharp and urgent, swerved to hers. "That was *not* your fault, Josie. Not at all."

She nodded, wanting to feel as sure as he sounded. "Please don't worry about me. I'll stay busy today with your mending. I doubt I'll go out at all."

She pointed to the stack of his clothes. "It won't take me long to fix the buttons on those two shirts so I can probably get them back to you this afternoon. Mending the trousers and darning your socks will take a little longer."

"I'll come get the shirts."

"It's no trouble for me to bring them."

"I'll feel better if I come. Send word when you're ready."

"I certainly won't complain about seeing you." She smiled, trying to figure out what was bothering him. He wasn't being overprotective exactly, just cautious. "Davis Lee," she said gently, "I know you need to get to the jail. It's okay to go."

The disquiet she caught in his eyes caused a tug of sadness inside her. She didn't know what was going on, but she didn't like it. Even more confused than before, Josie gave in to the urge that compelled her to reach for his hand.

At her touch, he stilled. She could feel the strength, the power in his whipcord-lean body. "Please don't worry about me. I'm all right."

He stared down at her, his features grim, his eyes softening. He didn't try to move away, didn't act as if he minded her touch. He didn't act as if he felt…anything, but she knew he did. His manner was restrained, almost reluctant. As if he blamed her for what had happened in the alley or later at his house. But she was certain he didn't blame her. He wouldn't.

She squeezed his big hand with both of hers. "Because of you, I'm just fine. Now get out of here before you make me cry. I did enough of that last night to fill up two water buckets."

At the mention of last night, his shoulders went as stiff as cordwood. "All right, but I'll check in on you later."

"I'd like that."

He gently disentangled his hand from hers and walked out. She didn't hear him move away from the door until she turned the key in the lock. She crossed to the window. After a minute, she saw him step into the street. He turned and looked up at her, his face so fiercely resolute that her heart thudded hard.

She gave him a little wave. Just the thought of leaving town, leaving *him,* ripped at her. She couldn't do it. She wanted a chance with Davis Lee. All she had to do—without killing the outlaw herself—was figure out a way to see that McDougal got the justice he deserved.

Throughout the day, she tried to keep her mind off the attack and stay focused on Davis Lee or her work. Fixing the buttons on his shirts helped; she removed them all and neatly sewed them back on whether they needed it or not.

The well-worn fabric held his dark, woodsy scent and inhaling it helped settle her nerves as did glancing out the window every few minutes. He checked on her twice, but he didn't stay more than a minute each time.

Just before she turned down her lamp to go to bed, she went to the window. Hazy moonlight spilled onto Main Street and Josie saw Davis Lee standing outside the jail. Lamplight from inside his office outlined his broad shoulders, touched his hat and black shirt with amber. His gaze was trained on her window.

She touched the glass to show him she saw him, knowing he was there to put her mind at ease. The thought had her going all soft and shivery inside before she sighed and went to bed.

When she woke the next morning, her first thought was of him. As much as she enjoyed being with him, as safe and right as it felt, she couldn't forget about Ian McDougal. Every time Josie felt the growing urge to turn her back on the plans she'd made for the outlaw, Rosemary's letter and the awful news about William's mother popped into her mind. Josie wanted to forget, leave the past where it belonged and move on. With Davis Lee.

Though still conflicted about her plan for McDougal, she was certain of her emotions regarding the sheriff. Her feelings for him were not going away, even if she left Whirlwind. Maybe not ever. Losing a chance with him would be something she would grieve over the rest of her days.

Since the day they'd spent in Abilene, her resistance to him had been steadily eroding. After Saturday night, she didn't have one defense left against him. Her mind had been filled with nothing except him. No McDougal, no William, no murders. She was tired of focusing on vengeance, tired of trying to balance her feelings for Davis Lee with what she felt for her family.

She had to do something. The attempt last week on

McDougal's life made clear that someone else wanted the outlaw dead. If she could figure out who that person was, maybe she could let *them* do the deed.

There was a good chance Cora would know about everything the outlaws had done and the people they had hurt, but Josie didn't have the heart to broach the painful subject so close to the anniversary of Ollie Wilkes's death.

She could ask around town, but she didn't want to be that blatant. The last thing she needed was for someone to tell Davis Lee she'd been asking about all the crimes committed by the McDougal gang. How could she find out such a thing?

It hit her then that accounts of the outlaws' vicious misdeeds, at least in this part of the state, had probably been documented in Whirlwind's newspaper. The *Prairie Caller* sat in a small brick building between Pete Carter's saloon— a place Josie would do her utmost to avoid—and Haskell's General Store.

She didn't know if she would uncover any information or what she would do with it if she did, but she had to try. Learning something would help her figure out a way to fulfill her vow to her parents, to William and his family without destroying Davis Lee's feelings for her.

He never should've touched her. Even on Monday evening as Davis Lee and Josie stood behind Catherine's house, he couldn't stop thinking it. Images of that bastard on top of her kept stabbing through his mind. What that thug had done to her, what he could've done, twisted viciously at Davis Lee's insides. She'd been hurt, nearly violated and how had he responded? He'd put his hands on her, his mouth.

She had wanted to be close to him, to feel safe and he'd nearly peeled her clothes off. He would've taken her then if her soft plea to make her forget hadn't reminded him of exactly what had happened.

They'd both been rattled; that was to be expected. But his common sense had unraveled faster than a frayed rope. The urge to have her had consumed him. How could she feel safe with him now?

When he and Josie had first arrived at Catherine's small yellow house outside of town, she and Andrew had come out to say hello, but now he and Josie were alone. Though a couple of times he caught her watching him with a perplexed look on her face, she seemed comfortable with him. Which reinforced his decision to keep his hands off her.

Neither of them said much as she practiced shooting. Because the days were growing shorter, Davis Lee had called for her an hour earlier than the usual time. The sun was setting in a blaze of reds and oranges, the falling temperature putting a snap of color into Josie's cheeks. The scent of wood smoke skimmed the air, floating from Catherine's house as well as from town. Before that bastard had attacked her on Saturday night, Josie had hit four out of six targets consistently. She did the same tonight.

"You did real well," he said when she decided to stop for the evening.

She beamed. "I have a good teacher."

He hadn't kissed her since Saturday night at his house and he wouldn't, but he sure wanted to.

"Can you believe we're already into October?" She rubbed her arms, though she'd told him she was warm enough in her long, dark green wool bodice and skirt. "Pretty soon, it will be too cold to continue my lessons. And too dark."

He murmured in agreement, but his attention wasn't on the weather or her lessons. There was still enough light that he could see the bruise on Josie's cheek and the edge of her jaw. His fists clenched every time he looked at her. Whirlwind was his town and he was supposed to protect its people, especially women. Especially her. And he'd failed.

He cleared his throat. "Josie, I haven't been able to get that polecat to the jail in Abilene yet."

She looked a little surprised, but not bothered. "All right."

"One of Jake's ranch hands rode in yesterday with the news that there had been an accident at his ranch. He's been out there ever since Sunday morning so he wasn't able to take the prisoner to Abilene."

She studied him thoughtfully. "Thanks for telling me."

"Cody Tillman, one of Riley's ranch hands, is relieving me for meals and your shooting lesson, but since I have no other help right now, I can't make the trip, either."

She looked as if she didn't understand how this affected her. "Cody's at the jail now, watching over that snake who tried to hurt you. I don't want you to worry that he can escape."

She said slowly, "I'm not worried."

He had to admit she didn't appear concerned, but his mind still wasn't settled about the issue. "Come hell or high water, tomorrow I'm getting that lowlifer out of Whirlwind and away from you."

"Davis Lee, I know you will. I know you'd never let him hurt me again."

"You can bet on it." But what about himself? Did Josie know she could trust him not to peel her naked the first chance he got, though that was exactly what he felt like doing?

The cream-and-honey taste of her, the feel of her magnolia-smooth skin against his tongue and his hands, had only whetted his hunger for her.

Since he'd held her half-naked in his lap, the thick, dark throb of desire in his veins had become relentless. The woman turned him inside out, but he wanted more than her body. He wanted her to confide in him. He refused to be caught unaware again, the way he had been with Betsy. He would do everything in his power to make sure he found out what he needed to know about Josie. Before it was too late to protect his heart.

So yesterday he had wired his cousin, Jericho Blue, who was in Houston. Catherine had gotten word from the Ranger a couple of days ago saying he thought his business there would be concluded this week.

Being as Davis Lee still hadn't heard from the sheriff in Galveston, he asked if Jericho could spare the time to ride to Galveston and ask around about Josie. He knew it would be a day's ride to the port and out to the island. It would probably take at least a day for Jericho to locate the sheriff or someone who might have pertinent information.

His cousin's reply had been quick. He would do what he could, though it would be at least three days before he got back to Davis Lee. In the meantime, Davis Lee hoped Josie would tell him on her own why she had come to Whirlwind.

He walked to the targets; she had graduated from hay bales to tin cans. While he picked them up and put them into a burlap bag, Josie emptied her gun and cleaned it. He moved back to her, cans clanking against his leg. "Ready?"

"Not yet."

"Something wrong?"

"I'm not sure." She smiled, wondering how to broach the issue of his manner. While not distant, he was nonetheless different with her. She wanted to know why. "Thank you for the length of calico you sent this morning."

"You're welcome."

"You didn't have to do that."

"I wanted to. Your dress was ruined the other night. Now you can make a new one whenever you have time." He paused. "If you'd rather have a different color or something, Charlie said you could swap it out."

"I love the small black vines and the red, green and blue flowers, but you needn't feel—"

"It shouldn't have happened."

His taut words fostered suspicion. Surely he didn't feel responsible for her attack or anything related to it? He'd been quiet all evening. And just as he had yesterday in her hotel room, he'd been careful not to touch her, not to crowd her, not to get within a foot of her. So excruciatingly careful that she wanted to scream.

"I appreciate your thoughtfulness, Davis Lee, but you have to stop buying me things."

"Why?"

"It might be viewed as improper."

"Rumor has it we're already involved."

"I guess so."

His gaze searched her face. Was that uncertainty in her eyes caused by him or something else? "Are you okay about keeping the cloth?"

She nodded, looking solemn and intent. As if she had something important to say.

"You're still planning to stay in Whirlwind, aren't you?"

"I...haven't decided yet."

He didn't like that her hesitation caused a snag in his gut. "I hope you won't let what happened the other night make you leave."

She shook her head. "I think I'm safer here than anywhere else."

He arched a brow. "You do? Why's that?"

"Well, I know the sheriff." She lowered her voice conspiratorially. "He's pretty quick on his feet and he's got a knack for taking care of people."

The flirty, sweet smile she gave him hitched up his pulse, made him want to pull her to him. Instead he turned to leave, expecting her to follow.

"Davis Lee?"

He glanced over his shoulder, stopped when he saw she hadn't moved.

"I know something's wrong. Is it me? Is it that you can't look at me now, after what that man did?"

"No!" He dropped the bag with a clang of metal and reached her in two strides. "Why would you think such a thing?"

"You've been acting uneasy around me."

"It certainly isn't because of anything you did, Josie." He hated that he had put pain in her green eyes.

"So, if it's nothing I did..." She wrapped her arms around herself. "You're being so careful not to touch me."

"Honey, I damn near took you—" He broke off, gritting his teeth against the urge to haul her to him and kiss her until their legs gave out. "You can trust me."

"I do." She took one step, bringing her body within an inch of his. Her honeysuckle scent drifted around him, teasing and tempting. "Right now, you're about the only man I do trust. I think you're feeling guilty about what happened between us the other night. You don't need to."

"I should've had more control." He clenched his fists so he wouldn't reach for her. "You never have to worry about me doing anything you don't want."

"I know that," she said quietly.

She sounded completely sure of herself, of him. And he couldn't mistake the trust shining in her eyes. "Good."

He exhaled a sigh of relief, which jammed right back in his throat when she said, "Are you saying that I don't need to worry about you touching me again?"

"*Do* you worry about it?" He stilled at her choice of words. Hell. "Because if you do—"

"No, I don't! And I don't want you to, either. I'm more worried that you'll *never* touch me again."

"Josie." He briefly closed his eyes against the painful confusion on her face. "You went through hell the other night and I put my hands on you. All over you. That was not what you needed.''

"It was, Davis Lee.'' She flattened a palm on his chest. "I *needed* you to touch me that night. I wanted you to. I still do.''

"You had a real jolt, hon. I want you to know you're safe with me.''

"I *do* know it.'' Her eyes were earnest, pleading with him to believe.

"Yeah?''

She nodded.

Relieved, his gaze caught on a wisp of her hair blowing gently against her neck, right below the tender patch of skin behind her ear.

"So it's okay that *I'm* touching *you?*''

He glanced down, saw her hand still on his chest. "Yes.''

Her tongue slicked across her lower lip. "Then maybe you could touch me, too? Just put your hands on my waist, like we're dancing?''

"Okay.'' He settled his hands there, her body heat warming his palms, her small waist taut beneath his touch.

She laid her free arm along his forearm, stroking his bicep. "You can tell I'm not in the least afraid, can't you?''

"Yeah.''

"Do I look like I'm ready to skedaddle?''

He chuckled, his arms sliding around her waist and pulling her close. "All right, I understand.''

Her green eyes sparkled as she smiled up at him. "I'm not made of glass, you know.''

He hoped that was an invitation because he took it that way. He bent his head and she met him, her arms going around his neck as his lips touched hers.

His chest felt strange, warm and light at the same time. She smelled luscious, felt so damn good against him. The same ruthless, reckless lust that had hooked into him the other night grabbed hold and he lifted his head, cautioning himself to go easy. "Better now?"

"I'd say we're finally seein' eye to eye," she said on a dreamy sigh.

The heat inside him spiked. He wanted to kiss her again, do more than that, but he wouldn't. Trying to hold on to his one remaining thread of common sense, he eased back enough to see her face, but kept his arms around her. "Since I told you what's on my mind, why don't you tell me what's on yours?"

Her spine went rigid. He saw panic in her eyes the split second before she shuttered them against him. "What do you mean?"

"Honey, we both know something's going on."

"It's…just the attack."

He lifted her chin. "Josie, it's been between us since the day I confronted you in the alley."

She closed her eyes and when she opened them, they were dark and stormy. The turmoil on her face looked as if it were causing her physical pain. "I just can't talk about it yet. Give me a little time?"

"How much time?" Irritated, he dropped his arms and stepped back. "I want to know why you really came to Whirlwind."

She swallowed hard. "Davis Lee—"

"Why's it such a big secret?"

"Who said it was?"

He gave her a pointed look, nettled by her sidestepping. "If it isn't, then why don't you tell me? Don't you care that it makes me wonder if you're involved in something bad?"

"I can't help what you think."

"You can, but you won't. I'm going to find out what's going on and it would be better if you were the one to tell me."

"Or what?" Apprehension sprang up inside her and her voice rose. "You'll throw me in jail?"

"Do you think I won't?" His voice was low and dangerous.

Her stomach churning violently, she gave a disbelieving laugh. "You have no cause."

"General provocation."

He shot out the term so fast, she wondered if there were such a thing. "You can't arrest someone for that." In response to his stoic look, she said tentatively, "Can you?"

"Tell me what I want to know." He took a step toward her, a fierce light in his eyes. "Tell me my trust in you isn't misplaced."

She turned away from the accusation in his blue eyes. She had come to Whirlwind with a straightforward plan and now it was a maze of secrets and emotions she'd never expected.

Davis Lee moved up behind her, closing in tight the way he had the night in Penn's office. His voice was rough, edged with anger and disappointment. "I've been patient, Josie, but the time has come for you to tell me."

"I can't."

"I told you about Rock River. Is it asking too much for you to tell me something, just one thing?"

It wasn't, but she didn't answer.

"After what happened Saturday night, I thought you would, but you didn't."

"Why are you bringing that up?" she cried, pivoting to face him. "That man was horrible—"

"And just a minute ago, *when I was honest with you,* I hoped you'd confide in me, but no."

Everything inside her stilled. Guilt steadily chipped away at her. Davis Lee *had* been honest with her; he deserved nothing less. But she couldn't do the same.

Feeling as if the ground were crumbling beneath her, she

asked in a choked voice, "Why is it too much to ask that you let me tell you in my own time?"

"Because I don't think you plan to tell me," he said baldly. "All you've done is put me off."

"Well, all *you've* done is press me." She brushed past him and started for town. The thought of telling him she'd come here to kill Ian had her questioning her loyalty to her family. "I thought you had feelings for me."

"Don't play that card," he said tightly. He followed, snatching the burlap bag full of cans off the ground and catching up to her. He didn't touch her, but his body was very close. Too close. "You'd better change your mind about talking, and quick."

Her temper sparked by his demanding tone, she snapped, "I won't."

She walked faster, but his long legs easily kept him apace with her. They reached the edge of town. She cut between two houses, angling for the steps at the end of the Whirlwind Hotel's veranda.

"I guess I'll just have to find out your reasons for myself."

"By doing what?" she asked hotly, alarm racing along her nerves. If she told him she had come here to kill Ian, he'd be able to stop her—either through persuasion or coercion. What had started out as a quest for the justice her family deserved had become more about Davis Lee. That was wrong, wasn't it?

"All you need to know is I plan to keep a real close eye on you."

She faltered on the bottom step and looked sharply at him, saw the determination in his narrowed eyes. All the panic and frustration and fear that had been building inside her exploded into anger, made her voice tight. "Why don't you leave me alone?"

"Clear the air and things will be fine."

"I'm going in." She managed to get the words out, feeling cornered, suffocated.

"You're making this a lot harder than it has to be."

"Go away," she said through gritted teeth.

"If you change your mind, you know how to find me."

"I want you to leave me alone!"

"Your call, sweetheart."

She stomped up the steps and to the hotel's front door. From the corner of her eye, she saw Davis Lee stalk down the street toward the jail.

Josie made it to her room on anger alone, but as soon as she got inside, it drained out of her. She leaned back against the closed door. She stood in the deepening shadows for a long time, trembling and fighting a sense of drowning as she stared at the wedge of hazy light coming through the window. If he really cared about her, he would trust her. *Why should he?* argued a more rational part of her mind. *You haven't told him anything about the pain Ian and his brothers had caused, the justice they had escaped.*

But she didn't want to tell him because now she knew she would have to be the one to kill Ian. Pushing away from the door, she walked over to light the lamp on the bedside table and sank down on the mattress. Unable to stop her tears, she buried her face in her hands.

Her visit to the newspaper this morning had yielded plenty of information about the gang of outlaws, but no other names of people who might try to kill the surviving McDougal other than the ones she'd unearthed earlier— Catherine or Andrew Donnelly, Cora Wilkes, Susannah or Riley Holt.

Josie wasn't convinced any of those people had made— or would make—an attempt on the outlaw's life.

Because of her feelings for Davis Lee, her purpose was waning by the hour. How could she not fall for a man who was so careful of her feelings? Who worried so much about protecting her?

She didn't want to think about the way he had cared for her after the snakebite, how he had saved her from being raped and possibly killed. He had opened up to her, not once but twice, and asked her to do the same. He deserved no less, and she hadn't been able to give him the same honesty.

If she told Davis Lee everything, he could very well want her out of town, certainly out of his life. That thought stabbed cold fear into her. But the idea that Ian McDougal might escape justice again and never pay for all the murders he'd committed, all the lives he'd shattered, was horrifying. Her choice should've been easy.

Chapter Fifteen

No man needed killin' more than Ian McDougal. It was supposed to have been easy for Josie to get rid of the man who had destroyed her world. But then she'd met Davis Lee. And fallen in love with him.

She had realized that sometime after midnight. The giddy, fluttery sensation inside her was overwhelmed by anxiety. It was just like her to figure out something like love after she'd argued with the man.

When the pink-gray light of dawn crept into her bedroom, she hadn't gotten a wink of sleep, but she had made a decision. She would tell Davis Lee everything and after that... Well, she couldn't even think about what would happen after that.

She took a quick, cold bath then dressed quickly and put up her hair as apprehension fisted in her stomach. Refusing to put it off any longer, Josie made her way to the jail with Davis Lee's mended clothes. The garments were an excuse to see him in case he was still too angry to talk to her. But he wasn't there.

Cody Tillman, a sturdy young man about her age who looked as tough as rawhide, was filling in as deputy. He told her that Davis Lee had taken a prisoner to the jail in Abi lene, and would be gone for the day, possibly overnight. She knew which prisoner, knew Davis Lee was moving her attacker out of Whirlwind so she would feel safe. He'd promised to get rid of the man, but Josie wondered why he hadn't asked Cody to take the man. Had Davis Lee chosen to transport the prisoner himself so he could stay away from her?

Her heart ached. She *had* to see him.

That day passed so slowly that Josie could've waltzed across Texas and back. She kept constant watch out her window, but she didn't see him return. After a late supper, her way lit by moonlight and the lamps from the hotel and jail, she returned to Davis Lee's office. Perhaps he had slipped in while she was eating supper in the hotel's dining room. But he hadn't.

She was on her last nerve. Though she dreaded the coming conversation, she was ready to have it done. She wanted to tell him the truth, all of it, the minute he got back to town. She was too wound up to go back to her room. Even knowing Davis Lee might not return until tomorrow, she decided to wait outside his house for a bit, just in case. That wouldn't harm anything.

Woodsmoke drifted from the hotel and a couple of small homes behind. She moved across the street toward Haskell's, noting the store's darkened windows. The light from the jail shone weakly down the alley as Josie walked behind the mercantile. She drew up short. A candle glowed in Davis Lee's front window.

He was home. Her heart thundered. Sweat slicked her palms. Holding the bundle of his clothes tightly to her chest, she made her way slowly to the porch.

She wanted him to know that she had come here to get justice for her family, wanted to tell him why she'd kept the information from him for so long. She wanted him to understand, but would he? Nerves jumping, she blew out a breath. There was only one way to find out. Besides, if she thought on it further, she'd hightail it back to the hotel faster than a scorched cat.

She stepped quietly up to the door and stood there for a long minute, listening past the chirp of insects and the soft push of the wind for any sound from inside. The oilskin shade was down on his front window, but she saw a shadow pass in front of it. Determined to be as honest with him as he'd been with her, she knocked.

"Coming." The door opened and Davis Lee stood there, bare-chested, hair damp, bathed in the glow of a lamp in the corner behind him.

Her greeting slid back down her throat.

"Josie." His voice was flat.

"Davis Lee." She should've said more, had plenty to say, but her tongue wouldn't work.

The sight of his tautly muscled, golden flesh had desire pulsing through her in a wild rush. Denim trousers hugged his lean waist. Moisture glistened on his brawny shoulders. Her gaze helplessly traced over the dark hair on his chest, the well-hewn plane of his stomach, down his long legs. His feet were bare and behind him she saw a set of evaporating footprints.

A shiver worked through her as her gaze lifted to his. She read the steel in his eyes, the anvil-hard firming of his jaw. "I...needed to see you."

"I got that jackass to Abilene." His words were clipped. "He won't hurt you again. Or anyone else."

"Thank you." He filled the doorway, huge and intimidating. He clearly wasn't going to invite her in, but she wasn't leaving until she'd had her say. "I brought your clothes."

His gaze flicked to the bundle in her arms. "I told you I'd come get them."

"I thought you might need them. I stopped by the jail, but you weren't there." Taking the only chance she might have, she squeezed past him, catching a faint whiff of alcohol and the flesh-warmed scent of soap. She walked several feet to his dining table, noting the damp towel hung over the back of a chair he'd moved in front of the fireplace. He'd told her before that he had a bathing tub in a separate room at the back of the house.

She glanced over her shoulder, inwardly wincing at his sharp scrutiny. The door still stood open behind him, making it clear that he wasn't planning for her to stay. She swallowed hard. "All the mending is finished. You should be fixed up for a while."

"Thanks."

She squirmed at his impassive voice. There would never be any easy way to do this. "I didn't come to ask about your trip to Abilene."

"Then why are you here?" He folded his arms over his wide, solid chest and waited.

She couldn't bear him looking at her that way, so unapproachable, so put out. Wood shavings from his whittling littered the floor in front of the fireplace. His bottle of whiskey and a glass containing traces of amber liquid sat on the corner of the table. Whittling and drinking meant he was bothered about something. Maybe what had happened between them.

She carefully laid his clothes on the table next to the liquor bottle. "I wanted to talk to you about last night, the things I said. I told you to leave me alone, but that isn't what I want."

"Josie—"

"I didn't sleep a wink. It upsets me that you're angry."

He shut the door, but he stayed in front of it.

"This is a lot harder than I thought it would be." The crackle of the fire, the scent of pine shavings, the smell of his skin, had her remembering how he'd cared for her the other night, recalling in exquisite agony his mouth on hers, his hands on her body.

He watched her, looking grim and immovable. Fine, if he wouldn't talk, she would. Not sure where to start, she plunged in. "When I came to Whirlwind, I didn't intend to live here."

"Even though that's what you told me?"

"Yes." She held his gaze, clasped her shaking hands together. "But now I don't want to leave."

"Is there some reason you have to?"

"I didn't think you'd still be this mad," she murmured.

"Does that mean you're catchin' the next stage out?"

Pain sliced through her. "Is that what you want?"

"Does it matter what I want?" he asked archly.

His reference to last night and her refusal to tell him anything was unmistakable. Had she ruined what was growing between them? "It matters a great deal to me." She turned, paced to the other end of the table then back. "I care about you, Davis Lee."

"Is that right?"

"Yes." He held himself stiffly aloof from her. "Do you not want me to say that?"

He looked away, scrubbing a hand down his face. It was a long minute before he spoke. "Thanks for mending those clothes. If you'll wait a minute, I'll finish dressing and walk you back to the hotel."

"I really did come here to talk to you. Please?"

Feet spread wide, hands on his hips, he leveled his gaze into hers. "I need more time to cool off."

She knew if she didn't speak now, she might lose her chance. She would definitely lose her nerve. Walking the length of the table, her words poured out. "My family is dead, and sometimes I miss them so much, sometimes I'm so lonely that I can't breathe." He frowned so fiercely that her voice cracked; she battled back tears as she paced the other direction. "The only time I feel all right is when I'm with you."

"You're with me now," he said evenly, narrowing his eyes. "You don't look all right."

"You don't want me here, and I don't blame you. But please hear me out." Her boots clicked hollowly as she moved back and forth across his wooden floor. "I want to tell you about my family."

Her palms were clammy. She pulled off her gloves, stuffed them into her pocket. Her skin felt too small, her nerves laid bare. Turning jerkily in a whirl of skirts to go back the other direction, her thigh hit the edge of the table. The glass fell, hit the corner of a chair and shattered. "Oh, no!"

"Leave it," Davis Lee said tersely as she knelt to clean up the mess.

"Clumsy," she muttered as she picked up the biggest shard. "My parents— Ow!"

At the stinging prick, she dropped the broken glass. Blood welled from a small cut on her index finger.

Muttering under his breath, Davis Lee reached her in two strides and went down on his haunches several inches away, careful to keep his feet from the sharp pieces. "Let me see."

"It's not bad. Get the broom and I'll clean this up. I want to tell you—"

"You're bleeding. I'm not getting the broom." He rose, bent over and picked her up under the arms as if she were a little girl.

When his hands slid down to her waist, she held on to his hard shoulders. "Watch out. You're barefoot."

"I'll go around this side." He stepped backward then walked around to the opposite end of the table, setting her down on the edge closest to the stove. He moved away to retrieve the lamp from the shelf in the corner behind her. "Let me look at it."

"It's barely anything."

"It's still bleeding," he said pointedly. Placing the lamp on top of the nearby cupboard, he took her hand in his and shifted so that the light fell between them. He reached to the left and opened the small cabinet, pulled out a cloth and gently pressed it to her finger. "I don't think there's any glass left in it."

No one had ever made her feel so precious. Despite being mad at her, he was still taking care of her. He frowned in fierce concentration as he held the cloth to the wound for a few seconds. Her gaze traced the play of light in his dark hair, the edge of his cheekbone, his stubble-shadowed jaw. "You're always taking care of me."

"That's my job," he said dismissively. "To help people."

"No." She curled her left hand into her skirts so she wouldn't reach for him. "It's the kind of man you are."

He peered at her finger. "I think it's stopped bleeding."

"You're the best man I know."

"Why?" He raised his head, not looking angry now, but wary. "Because I don't like to see you hurt?" he asked gruffly.

This man calmed a part of her deep inside that had been a teeming crush of bitterness and sadness and loss for the past two years. Her heart squeezed. "My father was the only other man I've known with such a big heart, who cared so much about people." She lifted her hand to his face, her fingers skimming his bristly jaw as she murmured, "About me."

His gaze searched hers. "Not even William?"

"No. I've never known anyone like you." It was as if some buried instinct drove her to confess her feelings. "I've never wanted anyone the way I want you. Ever since the other night,'' she whispered, ''all I can think about is…belonging to you in that way.''

He stared at her in arrested silence, the heat and hunger in his gaze sending a thrill through here. ''Josie, when you say things like that, do you think I can turn away? Do you think I can ignore what you're saying, what you're offering—''

''I don't want you to ignore it or turn away.'' If he rejected her, she didn't know what she would do. Swallowing hard, she said, ''I don't want you to turn *me* away.''

''Dammit.'' His broad, warm hands cupped her shoulders as if to keep her at a distance.

She stayed very still. ''Cody said you might spend the night in Abilene. I'm glad you didn't.''

''I wanted to,'' he said roughly. His nostrils flared slightly as his hold tightened on her. ''But I couldn't stop thinking about you. Or this.''

His mouth came down on hers. Hard at first, then gentling as he kneed her legs apart and stepped between them, pulling her close in one fluid movement. Her skirts frothed around him; the scent of honeysuckle rose between them.

''I have wanted you for so damn long,'' he said hoarsely when he lifted his head. Careful of her bruises, he framed her face with his hands and brushed his lips across her mouth, her cheek, her forehead. ''You're the first woman in over two years I've cared about this much. When I thought you were leaving Whirlwind for good, I felt like I'd been walloped.''

''You did?'' she breathed, daring to hope that perhaps she hadn't ruined everything between them.

He nodded. ''I'm glad you're still here.'' He kissed her again, slow and deep and increasingly intense.

She slid one arm up the solid length of his, her palm curving around his nape. Her other hand flattened on his chest, over the heavy thud of his heart. She couldn't get close enough to his heat, the sleek angles of his chest, so different from hers. The feel of his arousal against her sent a jolt of need through her. One part of her desire-hazed mind still functioned, reminded her why she'd come. She knew she had to tell him *now.*

Struggling against the dark sweet draw of growing need, she flattened both hands on his chest, trying to slow him for a moment. But it wasn't until she touched his face and held it that he broke the kiss.

He lifted his head, breathing hard, his eyes burning with blue fire. "What is it?" he rasped. His gaze riveted on her mouth, he skimmed his thumb across her bottom lip, wet from his.

He stared at her as if she were the first woman he'd ever seen and a consuming swell of heat spread from her heart to her toes. She could barely catch her breath. "I want to tell you about my family. About William."

"I want you to tell me, too. Later." He took her mouth again.

She might never have more than this with him. There was no protecting her heart now, no resisting this man who touched the core of her in a way no other ever had. His kisses turned her entire body boneless, numbed her mind. Her reason began to splinter. "Davis Lee."

"Let me love you, Josie," he breathed against her lips.

She was lost. "Yes," she said on a ragged moan. "Yes."

Her agreement unlocked something desperate inside both of them. She crushed her mouth to his, locked her arms around his neck. He slid an arm beneath her legs and lifted her, making his way past the stove. Heat from the fireplace drifted around them then ebbed away.

As he shouldered open his bedroom door, his hand found her breast. By the time they tumbled onto his bed, he had her bodice half-unbuttoned. "No blade?" he asked against her lips.

"Can't with this blouse…in my skirt pocket." She helped him with the rest of her top, fighting her way out of the garment while his hand moved to her ankles.

He made quick work of the buttons on her boots. She toed them off as she reached behind her and unhooked her skirt, glad she'd again gone without a corset. Her fingers tangled with his as he unfastened her petticoat. He dragged it off along with her skirt, his hand going between her legs to cup her through the slit in her underwear.

Sliding her arms around his hard shoulders, she pressed into his touch, whispering his name. He pulled away, his features sharp with desire as he looked down at her, reaching for the buttons at the top of her undergarment. "I want this thing off. I want to touch you *right now* and I don't want to rip it."

Her breathing was as labored as his. "I have another one."

His wicked grin sent her pulse cartwheeling as his fingers moved nimbly down her front.

He was freeing the last couple of buttons when her hand slid down his taut stomach into his trousers. His muscles clenched; his mouth found hers. She undid the top button of his pants then the next, nipping at his jaw, lightly biting his ear.

The finespun fabric of her combination parted. His callused hands were on her breasts, his thumbs teasing the hard nubs of her nipples. As his mouth closed over the taut flesh, she arched into the wet, velvet heat, moving her hand to push her undergarment off.

He helped, lifting her against him and stripping off the combination suit along with her stockings. His eyes were hot with a raw need she'd never seen in another man. The same need that burned in her blood. She wanted to be part of him, wanted him to be part of her. The only thing that mattered was this man. Right here, right now.

He swept a hand over her hip as their mouths fused. She released the last button on his pants as his work-roughened palm slid to her stomach then between her legs, delving two fingers into her silky heat. When he pushed deep, she nearly came off the bed.

The flat of his thumb massaged the knot of nerves between her legs and she broke apart. Seconds, minutes later, she reached down and stroked him hard, urging him to her. The feel of his hot rigid flesh against her slick softness destroyed her last coherent thought.

He rose over her. "I don't want to hurt you. Is this your first time?"

"Second," she whispered, waiting for his reaction.

"Still sure?"

"Yes." She urged him forward. "Are you?"

"Yes." He slid inside her then paused, his muscles quivering with restraint.

He didn't seem bothered that she'd been with William once before. His hair-dusted chest heaved against her smooth one; his skin was sheened with sweat and shadow. Even in the dusky light, she could see his eyes blazing with such naked emotion that her heart ached. Her legs tightened around him. "Don't wait, Davis Lee," she begged. "Don't wait."

He moved deep and sure, steadily driving her up a dizzying peak; her hips met every stroke of his body. He laced his fingers with hers and brought their arms over her head, kissing her, possessing her, coaxing her to surrender every bit of herself. When she felt the tiny urgent pulses inside her, his muscles bunched and he went over the edge with her.

When his whole weight pressed her into the mattress, she held him tight, stroking the supple skin of his shoulders, the long line of his back. Moonlight washed over them. His breathing was ragged, his flesh slick on hers. He pressed hot, openmouthed kisses down the side of her neck. One hand curled possessively around her breast.

He smiled against her temple. "I didn't even get to see your hair down."

She laughed softly, still trying to catch her breath. "I can take it down now."

"Let me." He rose up on one elbow and worked her hairpins out then placed them at the bottom of the mattress. Undoing her chignon, he threaded his fingers through the chestnut strands and brought the mass to his face, inhaling deeply. He shifted to give her a soft kiss then, as if he couldn't help himself, another one.

She moved her hands over the tough sinew of his shoulders, the lean tautness of his hips, his rock-hard arms, touching and learning him the way he was her. He rolled to his side, taking her with him, holding her tight.

They lay like that for a long time. Lulled by the musky scent of their loving, Josie savored the feel of his arms around her, knowing this night might be only a memory, not the beginning of a future. Pale light filtered into the room and she drowsily made out a tall closet against the opposite wall. A pitcher and basin gleamed white on the washstand at the foot of the bed. The tangy scent of shaving soap teased the air. Far away, a cow bawled. Through the window she could hear the chirp of crickets.

She loved him. She knew he cared about her. Hopeful now, she knew there could be no more secrets between them. "Davis Lee?"

When he didn't answer, she lifted her head. He was asleep. She pressed a soft kiss to his lips and snuggled into him. When he woke, she would tell him everything.

Voices woke her, low and definitely masculine. Josie opened her eyes, saw the tall closet fronted by a pair of dusty black boots. She recognized the room as Davis Lee's.

Memory flooded back and heat flushed her body. She rolled to her back, pulling up the sheet and quilt. Without his warmth, the bed was chilly.

She wished she'd woken before him. That would've given her a little time to deal with the anxiety knotting her stomach. The uncertainty of how he would respond was as unsettling as finally talking about something she'd kept to herself for two years.

Not knowing who was in Davis Lee's front room, she wondered if she should get dressed then decided she should wait, for discretion's sake. She lay still and quiet in the bed. The voices stopped and she heard the front door creak shut.

She sat up, keeping the sheet over her breasts as she shoved the tangled mass of her hair over her shoulder. After a long minute, she heard the soft thud of footsteps, but Davis Lee didn't appear in the doorway. Curious, Josie slid out of bed, holding the sheet wrapped around her. She tiptoed to the door and peered around the frame to make sure he was alone.

He was. Wearing only his trousers, he stood in the middle of the room. His back was to her and he stared down at something he held. He lifted a hand to the nape of his neck, the muscles in his arms and shoulders rippling. She stepped out of the bedroom. "Good morning," she said softly.

He turned. There was a piece of paper in his hand, but it was the rigidness of his body, the guarded look on his face that held her attention. Concerned, she took a step toward him. "What is it? What's happened?"

He stared at her, his eyes dark with something she couldn't define. His words were measured, controlled. "Ian McDougal murdered your parents."

Her heart skipped a beat. How had he guessed? It didn't matter. She was going to tell him anyway. She pulled the sheet tighter around her nakedness. "Yes."

"And William."

"Yes." She nodded, suddenly immobilized by an icy, invading sense of suffocation. "I was going to tell you last night—"

"Tell me what? Why you came to Whirlwind?"

There was no missing the hurt, the accusation in his silky, razor-edged words. What was on that piece of paper? Where had he gotten it? "Yes."

"Let *me* tell *you.* You came for Ian's trial."

She nodded cautiously. "To see that he gets justice."

"And I'll make sure he does, one way or another." Davis Lee stepped closer, his eyes flinty with suspicion. "Since you know I want him punished as badly as you do, I have to wonder why you wouldn't tell me that's your reason for being here. Unless there's more, which I assume there is."

"Davis Lee—"

"So I asked myself, 'Why would Josie not want me to know that her parents and fiancé were murdered by the worthless sonovabitch sitting in my jail?'" His voice was as hard as the hubs of hell. "Because you came to kill him."

"Yes."

"And you were gonna use me to do it."

"No!"

Chapter Sixteen

"I'm not using you." Josie's heart slammed into her chest as she stared into eyes that were flat and remote. "I mean, it may have started out that way, but it's not like that now."

"That's rich. I don't know why I didn't see it." The black fury in his face sent a quiver through her. "When I confronted you in the alley, you'd been watching the jail for four days so you could figure out my comings and goings."

"Yes."

"The day I caught you in my jail, were you there to kill him?"

She wanted to look away, turn away, but she didn't. "Yes."

"Well, you sold me a bill of goods, didn't you? Made me believe you wanted shooting lessons."

"You were suspicious of me every moment," she cried.

"For good reason."

"I really did want the shooting lessons."

"Not really," he said, his voice hard-edged and sharp.

"I did. I wanted to learn how to use a gun," she said firmly.

"To kill McDougal in case you couldn't use your scalpel."

She hesitated then nodded.

"I started putting it together after you asked Jake to take over your shooting lessons. It didn't slip past me that, of all the men you could've asked for help, the one you asked was my deputy. The one other man who had access to Ian almost as frequently as I did."

"I admit that." Wary of the seething anger that he barely restrained, she asked quietly, "How did you learn all this?"

"I haven't had both eyes closed. I wired the sheriff in Galveston about you," he said savagely. "After that snake-bite. You'd already gotten my attention by moving into the hotel room that looks right down on my jail."

"That was a long time ago." She knew she had no right to feel betrayed, but that didn't stop the hurt she felt at his mistrust. "Why didn't you say anything?"

"Isn't that what I should be asking you? I sent more than one telegram, waiting for Galveston's telegraph machine to start operating again after the hurricane. I still haven't heard from Sheriff Locke."

"But you have a telegram in your hand. How—"

"This is from my cousin. I wired Jericho in Houston and asked him to ride to Galveston. He talked to Sheriff Locke there, who knew you. Not just because your father was well respected, but because you frequented his office every week asking for news of the McDougal gang."

Her head spun, her thoughts raced. She had wanted to tell Davis Lee the truth, but now that he knew there was no relief in it for her. Only a low drum of apprehension.

"And when you heard that three of the McDougals had been killed, and Ian was awaiting trial here, you came to Whirlwind. How am I doing so far?"

"All of that is true." When she had arrived, using Davis Lee's access to the prisoner had been her plan, but not any longer.

"Every minute you've spent with me has been for the

purpose of getting information about or access to that low-lifer.''

"No. Not for a long time, Davis Lee."

"Yeah? How long?"

"I'm…not sure." She tried to recall when her feelings had changed, when he had become more important than justice for her murdered family. "I think it was the first time you kissed me."

"Really? Maybe it was the night I told you about one of the worst things that's happened in my life? Or what about last night? You can say your feelings for me changed then," he said bitterly. "That you didn't sleep with me for any other reason than you wanted to."

"That *is* the only reason! I wanted to be with you. I still do. I—" *Love you.* She snapped her mouth shut, angry at herself for not telling him everything last night, at him for turning what they'd shared last night into something calculated and base. "What happened between us had nothing to do with McDougal and you know it. Don't try to say it didn't mean anything."

"It didn't."

She flinched. "I know you're hurt and angry. Yes, I should've told you why I came to Whirlwind. Ian murdered my family—"

"You don't have to tell me now. I already know."

"I'm telling you anyway." The past crashed over her, heavy and dark. The words spilled out; she hoped they made sense. "He killed my parents and William, who was there for dinner, and he would've killed me, but I wasn't home yet. But then I came home."

"Ian acted alone in this?" Davis Lee gave her a look that said she might as well try to convince him that roosters laid eggs. "The McDougals never did anything by themselves."

"Well, Ian did! My father was considered one of the most knowledgeable doctors in Texas about tuberculosis. I think that's why Ian came to see him that night. There were posters about the McDougals in Sheriff Locke's office, all over town. The whole state knew about those outlaws and what they'd done. I think Papa recognized Ian and either tried to get rid of him so he could contact the law or tried to send my mother or William for Sheriff Locke. That's when Ian killed them.

"I saw him, I saw his face. He ran out of my house and full-bore into me. We both fell. His gun flew out of his hand, but it was dark and he couldn't find it. I screamed and screamed until he ran away. When I got into the house, I found them. Mama, Papa, William. All dead. Blood everywhere." She wiped angrily at the tears coursing down her cheeks. "I identified Ian and he was arrested. The sheriff put him in jail. I thought he'd pay for what he did, but there was this judge—I told you about him—Judge Horn. He had a grudge because my mother rejected him more than twenty years ago. And out of pure spite, he let Ian go, let him walk away."

She pressed a hand to her trembling mouth, trying to stop from crying. Why couldn't he understand?

"It's not that I don't think he needs killin'."

"Then why are you so angry?"

"You know why," he said flatly. "The only thing you've cared about since you got here is Ian McDougal. You wanted information. You wanted to keep a close eye on him. I understand *that*. What I don't understand is how you could use me to get what you wanted. How you could go to my bed last night and believe keeping that from me was all right."

"I *didn't* think it was all right. It was wrong. *I* was wrong." She didn't know how to convince him or even if she could. "At first, I kept it from you because I didn't want you to talk me out of it."

"Or arrest you," he muttered.

She moved closer. He backed away and she felt it like a blow. Fisting both hands in the sheet, she wrapped her arms tight around her middle. "Then I kept quiet because I didn't want it to look like you were involved. And then I wasn't sure that I was going to kill him. I thought if I could figure out who else might want him dead, I wouldn't have to do it. I went to the newspaper and read back as far as I could, trying to learn everyone the McDougals had hurt, trying to find a way to make Ian pay without killing him myself. But there is no one else. This is what I was going to tell you last night. I tried. Remember? I said I wanted you to know about my family, about William. And then—"

"Ah, yes, you cut yourself. Did you do *that* on purpose? So you could play on my sympathy?"

"No."

"And sleeping with me before you told me the truth was what? An accident?" His lips twisted. "Oh, let me guess. You slept with me because you couldn't resist me."

"I couldn't," she acceded sadly. "Things happened so fast between us. I was wrong not to say something, but that doesn't mean that I…did *that* with you for any reason other than wanting to be with you. The night I was attacked, I was out walking so late because I was thinking about you, about us. I was trying to figure out a way not to kill Ian. I thought about telling you then."

"But that wasn't a good time either, was it?" he scoffed.

"I didn't tell you because I was afraid you wouldn't understand."

"You didn't tell me because it would've eliminated your access to him. The only reason you got close to me is so you could get information about McDougal." He cursed. "Did you think one night with you would make me let down my guard? Did you come here last night to seduce me, Josie? You did a damn fine job of it. I was so crazy for you I couldn't see straight."

"Don't believe that, Davis Lee. Please," she whispered hoarsely. She didn't remember moving, but she stood inches from him. One hand curved over his forearm. "You know it wasn't like that."

He shook her off. "If you weren't using me, then why not tell me everything about your family? What did you hope to accomplish by crawling into my bed? Freer access to McDougal? Maybe you thought I'd kill him for you. Or that I'd fall so hard for you that I'd escort you to the jail and watch you put a bullet in him."

"Last night, I came to tell you the truth." Anger slid into her blood and spread. She said evenly, "I should have done it, and I'm sorry I didn't. I'm sorry I hurt you, but I didn't *plan* on falling into bed with you. You have to believe that."

"No. I don't." His eyes were bleak and hard, unyielding. "Sounds like you didn't plan on a lot of things."

"I didn't plan on you at all." *I certainly didn't plan on you being the first man since William's death to make me feel something besides regret or pain.* Her voice shook, but she forced herself to continue, to keep her gaze on his. "I was going to come here and make sure Ian McDougal paid for at least three of the murders he's committed, but I met you. When I was bitten by that snake, you took care of me. And you were patient when you taught me to shoot. Then the other night, in the alley, I know you saved my life. I didn't plan on your kindness or your compassion or liking you so much."

"And now you're going to say you have feelings for me?"

"I do!" She inched closer, desperate to make him understand. "Do you think it was easy for me to accept that I was growing to care for you? I owe my family what the law wouldn't give them." Temper spiking, her voice rose. "Getting involved with you made me question what I'd come to do. Question my loyalty to the people who loved

me. How do you think it made me feel to know I was willing to turn my back on them in order to have something
with you? Would you have handled things so much better?"

"We're not talkin' about me." The words cracked the air
like gunshots. His eyes were vicious with anger and hurt.
"Put on your clothes and go."

He wasn't going to budge. Hope drained out of her. "I
deeply regret not getting all of this out in the open last night,
but I'm not sorry about what we shared."

"All right, I'll be the one to go." He stalked past her and
into his bedroom.

Her chest tight with pain, she followed.

He snatched his boots from in front of the wardrobe,
yanked open its door and pulled out a shirt, dropping it over
his head. Stone-faced, he pushed by her and went back into
the front room where he grabbed a pair of the freshly darned
socks she'd brought then sat down hard in the nearest dining
chair. Quick as lightning, he had on his socks and boots,
then rose, skirted the broken glass still on the floor and
strode toward the door.

Alarmed, she took a step toward him. "Are you really
leaving?"

The look he threw over his shoulder was brutal enough
to buckle her knees. His gaze raked her. "It would be best
if you were gone when I get back."

He walked out, leaving her standing in his front room
wrapped in a sheet.

"Do I have rocks in my head?" Davis Lee asked his
brother an hour later at the jail. Just thinking about Josie
made him mad enough to bite a bullet plumb in two.

With a vicious flick of his wrist, he skinned his blade
down the bark of the sixth stick of pine he'd whittled since
leaving his house. "Am I as dumb as a bucket of dirt? I
knew she was hiding something. I *knew* it, but I got involved

with her anyway. You'd think I didn't have the sense to spit downwind.''

Riley had settled into the chair behind Davis Lee's desk and put his feet up on the edge. "Seems there's a fine line here, brother. I mean, you really can't know for sure that she's lying about wanting to tell you the truth and when she planned to do it.''

"Oh, I know it, all right.''

"You must care a lot about her if you're this het up.''

Davis Lee pointed his knife at his brother. "You sound like an old maid. What I care about is that the woman lied to me.''

"All I know is when I got *this* mad at a woman, it meant I had feelings for her.''

From his perch on the corner of his desk, Davis Lee stared him down. Riley held up a hand in mock surrender. "Hey, I'm just makin' an observation. Should I remind you of how you got in my face when Susannah and I had a fallin'-out?''

"That was different. You were married. You knew you loved her.''

His brother eyed him shrewdly. "I didn't, but it took me nearly losin' her to figure that out. Don't be as chuckle-headed as I was.''

Davis Lee shaved off another curl of wood with a particularly vicious downstroke of his knife. "This is nowhere near the same. I don't love Josie. And Susannah didn't lie to you, didn't…use you to get something.''

Davis Lee had told Riley that Josie had used him to get information about McDougal, but not that she had slept with him for the same reason. Though he could tell by the steadiness in his brother's blue eyes that Riley knew. "You know what really burns me? I gave her more than one chance to come clean. I even told her about Rock River.''

"*What?*'' Riley's boots hit the floor with a sharp thud

and he sat straight up. "That means something even if you don't want to admit it."

"It *means* I'm an idiot." Davis Lee sliced the blade in a furious slide down the stick that was dwindling into a toothpick with each pass.

"Listen, I know you're mad as a hornet. I would be, too, but if you don't come to some kind of terms with her, I think you'll regret it. You look like you're ready to burn some powder."

"Don't worry, I don't plan to shoot her, but even finding out about how Betsy hornswoggled me didn't get me this lathered up. If I don't see Josie Webster till the Judgment Day, it'll be too soon."

"From what you've said, it doesn't sound like she came here to deliberately hurt anyone except that piece of human garbage back there in that cell."

"No, I just happened to be lucky enough to be useful to her." He was a fool. He'd thought he was being so smart, so careful, but she'd gotten to him anyway, burrowed someplace deep inside that Betsy had never even touched.

"Can't say I blame her for wanting to kill Ian McDougal." Riley's face hardened. "I'd like to hurt him myself just for the way he and his brothers endangered Susannah and Catherine, not to mention killing Ollie."

Davis Lee nodded. "I don't take issue with *why* Josie came. The bastard killed her folks, the man she was going to marry. It does bother me that she used me to get information about him. That she kept things from me when we…were past that. Or I thought we were."

He actually did believe she cared about him. Her feelings had been plain in her eyes when he'd taken her last night. Maybe it was his vanity, but he didn't think she could've faked that. Still, just because she felt something for him didn't mean she hadn't used him.

Riley studied him soberly. "What are you going to do?"

"Stay the hell away from her and watch my back."

He thought back over how often she'd come around, her constant post at the hotel window, how she always seemed to be watching, waiting for someone besides him. *How she'd slept with him while there was a secret between them.* Just the idea that he thought he might have loved her twisted his gut into a vicious knot.

He'd seen the hurt in her eyes, hurt that had nothing to do with what Ian McDougal had done to her and everything to do with Davis Lee's words to her. He thought of the times he'd seen pain in her eyes and wondered if he had caused it, when all the time it had nothing to do with him. Had her feelings *ever* had anything to do with him?

What if she really had thought that sleeping with him would lower his guard so much that he'd tell her he understood why she'd come and would do whatever she wanted regarding McDougal? He wouldn't say that out loud; it sounded ridiculous. Paranoid. But it didn't stop him wondering if maybe Josie was hoping Davis Lee would take her right to the outlaw then look the other way while she finished him.

He had started to believe that whatever her secret, it didn't affect him—*them.* Plain and simple, he'd let his guard down. Just like with Betsy, he'd been overcome by lust. Last night, the need to have Josie under him had burned away every ounce of common sense.

If she really had feelings for him, she would've told him the whole story sometime back. Wouldn't she?

Thinking about the way she'd looked at him while he was deep inside her, how devastated she'd seemed when he confronted her this morning, dimmed the anger inside him. He didn't want to feel anything *except* anger. If he did, he would never be able to stay away from her.

Oh, yeah, he'd come close to going under, but he knew

where things stood now. Those deep green eyes and sweet little body weren't going to snare him again.

Josie purposely stayed away from her hotel window. She hadn't seen him in four days. Four days of anger and hurt and frustration that had her doing sloppy work and ripping out stitches right and left. He hadn't believed her. It didn't appear he ever would. He needed time to cool off; Josie had thought maybe after a couple of days she could go to him. But just one look at his face, even from two stories up, had her keeping her distance.

She was in love with him. Thankfully she hadn't confessed *that*.

Sunday after church, she welcomed the distraction of Catherine's last fitting for her wedding gown. The dark-haired woman stopped by after the service. Josie hadn't had the courage to go and risk coming face-to-face with Davis Lee.

The wedding was scheduled for Wednesday, and though Josie had seen no sign of the groom, Catherine didn't appear anxious in the least. After pinning one final tuck in the bodice, Josie walked her friend downstairs. "Your dress will be ready tomorrow. I'll bring it by."

"Thank you. I've never had anything so lovely. You're very talented."

Josie smiled, feeling as if only half of her were there.

Catherine put a hand on her arm. "I know it's none of my business, but you look like you could use someone to talk to."

Josie did need someone, but Catherine? The woman was a dear friend of Davis Lee's and Josie didn't want her to think for a minute that she would try to come between that friendship.

"It's about you and Davis Lee, isn't it?"

Josie's eyes widened.

"We've seen you two together. Susannah and I. Cora. It's obvious there's something between you."

"Not anymore." Josie folded her arms tight against her middle. "We had words."

"I wondered. He's been like a bear and I've never seen him like that. Isn't there a chance you can work it out?"

"I don't know. I don't think he wants to and I can't say I blame him."

Catherine stared at her for a long minute then a slow smile broke over her face. "There was a time when Jericho wanted me to stay away from him."

Josie's jaw dropped. "From what I've heard, the man's head over heels for you."

"We had some things to resolve first." She told Josie how Jericho had arrived at her house, shot and bleeding. How she had nursed him back to health only to learn he had come there to arrest her brother.

Josie shook her head. "And you forgave him for keeping that from you?"

"He had good reason, but it took me a while to accept it."

The situation sounded like hers and Davis Lee's in reverse.

Catherine patted her hand. "Don't give up. Go to him."

Had he cooled off enough to listen to her? To believe her? And so what if he had? The memory of his harsh words had her spine going to steel. He had accused her of an awful thing. Maybe *she* wasn't ready to forgive *him*. "I'll think about it."

"He's a good man, Josie. And I think you're good for him."

Behind Catherine, the hotel's front door opened and Josie's heart quickened. But it wasn't Davis Lee. The man who stepped inside sweeping off his hat was taller, the tallest man she'd ever seen. Dressed all in black, with a gun belt slung low on his hips, he looked dangerous. His dark hair was ragged, his rugged features lined with fatigue and dust, but it was his light-colored eyes that caught her attention.

And the adoring smile that spread across his face, completely transforming him. "Catherine?"

Josie's friend let out a cry as she whirled and flew across the floor straight into his arms. He caught her to him, kissing her as he lifted her off the floor, his hat crushed against her back.

So this was the fiancé, the Ranger. The one who'd told Davis Lee all about her. She didn't blame Jericho Blue for doing what she should've done herself. But she didn't imagine the Ranger would be too eager to make her acquaintance.

Watching Catherine with her soon-to-be-husband magnified the hollowness Josie had felt since the awful morning when Davis Lee had gotten so angry at her. Thinking to give the couple some privacy, she quietly started for the stairs.

"Oh, Josie, don't go!" Catherine was breathless and flushed as she pulled Jericho forward.

He had looked rough when he first walked in. Now he looked besotted and handsome. "Catherine," he murmured. "I smell like horses and dirt."

"This is my fiancé." She glanced up at him, hugged his arm to her. "Jericho, this is Josie Webster. She's new in town. She's making my dress for the wedding."

"Nice to meet you." He shook her hand, a mild curiosity in eyes that she could now see were a stunning silver. "I'm glad to hear Catherine is actually having the dress made and not using that money for someone else."

Giving him a look, his fiancée said, "Trusting the money to Andrew rather than me was probably a good idea."

Josie smiled. How could she help it? "It's nice to meet you, too. Congratulations on your upcoming wedding."

"Thank you." His gaze shifted to Catherine, so tender that Josie felt she was interfering in a private moment. "Sweetheart, I don't want to interrupt, but Ma and the girls are outside—"

"Jericho!"

Josie froze at the sound of Davis Lee's voice and her throat closed up. His cousin must've been blocking her from his view because she heard him approach, his boots tapping on the wood floor. If he'd seen her, he wouldn't be coming this direction.

"I just saw Aunt Jess and your sisters. They said you were—" he saw her, faltered "—back."

For the space of a heartbeat, their gazes met and the air turned stifling. She thought she saw an inkling of pleasure in his eyes, but knew it must be wishful thinking.

He jerked his gaze away, trying to fix his attention square on Jericho. It was all he could do not to haul her to him and kiss her right out of her drawers. But that was his body talking, not his brain. He had tried not to think about Josie, but no matter how long he worked or how much he drank, he couldn't get her out of his mind. He'd finally given up. "Your ma said you did it. Resigned from the Texas Rangers."

"You did?" Catherine looked uncertain.

"It's all right." Jericho slid one arm around her waist and pulled her close. "It's practically expected that we leave service after getting married."

"So you'll be here all the time?" At his nod, Catherine beamed.

Davis Lee was pleased, too. Would've been more pleased if Miss Josie Webster weren't standing less than a foot away, looking all soft and pretty, teasing him with her honeysuckle scent. Since that night they'd spent together, he'd washed his sheets twice. Lye soap was strong enough to strip the stink out of a skunk, but he was still tortured by the faintest whiff of her fragrance.

He clapped Jericho on the shoulder. "Hey, I could use some help. I could swear you in as a full-time deputy."

With a smile, the other man shook his head. "I'll be happy to help you sometimes, but my hand's never gonna mend all the way, at least not enough to make me worth more than about four good shots. A deputy needs a more dependable gun hand."

Davis Lee saw Catherine slip her hand into Jericho's lame one. His cousin smiled down at her. "I thought I'd talk to Jed Doyle about partnering up in his gunsmith shop. Nobody stands to lose their life if my hand gives out while I'm building a gun."

Davis Lee slapped his cousin on the back, wondering for the hundredth time if Josie had really wanted him only for information on McDougal? What else could he think? "That's a good idea."

His gaze shifted to Josie. The square-necked bodice of her dress was cut just below her collarbone and he had a good view of that little mole he'd kissed plenty the other night. Since that morning at his house, his anger toward her had lessened, but it hadn't changed his mind. Watching her closely, he said, "I got a wire from the circuit judge who's coming for McDougal's trial. He should be here by Friday."

For a moment, she seemed stunned that he'd told her. And wary, as if she expected him to tell all to Catherine and Jericho. He kept remembering her face when she'd told him about her family, about William. Davis Lee fully understood her need to avenge their deaths, but would he have used someone the way she had? Would he have handled things any differently than Josie had? He admitted he wasn't sure, which didn't sit well at all.

Josie smiled at Catherine. "Is the circuit judge the one who will marry the two of you?"

"No. We asked Reverend Scoggins."

"It's good that you won't have to wait on the judge."

Davis Lee glanced at her. Was her voice shaking? "I figure McDougal's trial will bring in a wave of people from all over."

Jericho agreed.

Davis Lee looked at Josie. "I don't know Judge Satterly, but I've heard he's fair. I look for McDougal to be found guilty and strung up."

She nodded, the color draining from her face. He wondered what she was thinking. About leaving? Once McDougal was dead, she would likely get out of town. Davis Lee hated that thought, but if she stayed it would slowly kill him.

Jericho glanced at Catherine. "Davis Lee is gonna help us get Ma and the girls out to Riley's place."

She nodded. "I'll be right out."

After saying goodbye to Josie, the Ranger brushed a kiss against Catherine's temple then started across the lobby with Davis Lee.

"You'll still come to the wedding, won't you?" Davis Lee heard Catherine ask Josie.

"Of course. I wouldn't miss it."

Davis Lee opened the door and waited for his cousin to precede him. He glanced back, his gaze crashing into Josie's.

If she stayed, he'd have to be the one to go. Marshal Clinton had twice offered him a job in Abilene. Davis Lee would prefer to have more distance from the woman who'd gotten under his skin, but he didn't want to move any farther away from his family. If he lived in Abilene, avoiding Josie when he visited Whirlwind probably wouldn't take much effort.

Josie tore her gaze from his, exhaling a ragged breath when he walked out. She couldn't believe her legs hadn't folded the second she'd seen him.

Catherine shot her a sympathetic look. "I'm so sorry," she murmured.

"Nonsense." She forced the words out of her aching throat. "We do live in the same town. We're bound to run into each other now and again."

"If it helps, he looks as miserable as you do."

Josie didn't think so. She felt her smile tremble. "You'd better go catch your Ranger. I know you missed him."

Catherine nodded, smoothing her gray wool skirt self-consciously. "This is the first time I've met his mother," she said shyly. "And his sisters."

Josie reached out and squeezed her hand. "When Mrs. Blue sees how much her son loves you, she'll love you, too. I know it."

The other woman smiled.

"Now go." Josie fluttered her hand toward the door. "I'll bring your dress in the morning. I know you have a lot to do, especially with all of Jericho's family arriving."

"Thank you."

"You're welcome. I'll see you tomorrow." She waited until her friend had left before starting for the stairs, not so much because she was hoping for another glimpse of Davis Lee, but because her legs wouldn't work.

That was the closest she'd been to him since that awful morning at his house. And seeing him brought all the hurt welling back. There had been no forgiveness in his eyes today. The pleasure she'd thought she had seen there had never existed. After his initial surprise at seeing her, there had been only emptiness except for when he'd told her about the circuit judge.

Things between them were over. Avenging her family was all she had left. She owed Davis Lee nothing. She would attend Ian's trial, but if he weren't sentenced to die, Josie would kill him. And then she would leave Whirlwind, get far away from Davis Lee.

She knew it didn't matter how far she went or where. Her heart would stay here, with him.

Chapter Seventeen

Josie didn't see Davis Lee again until the wedding three days later. She had gone because Catherine had invited her, and if she were honest, because she wanted a look at Jericho's best man. Davis Lee was darkly handsome in a black suit and white shirt. Just seeing him made Josie's chest ache with regret.

The bride's young brother had walked her down the aisle, and Josie thought Catherine was the prettiest bride she'd ever seen. Evidently, Jericho did, too, because he couldn't find his voice for a moment when asked to repeat his vows.

After the ceremony, held at four o'clock in the afternoon for those who had a long drive home, Josie joined the rest of the guests at the Pearl Restaurant for refreshments and dancing. She danced with Mitchell Orr and all three of the Baldwins. Davis Lee didn't even look in her direction.

She wished she could follow suit. Her attention strayed to him more than she liked. She wanted desperately to talk to him, but his demeanor clearly told her not to.

One time, after a dance with Matt Baldwin, Davis Lee fixed his gaze on her. She could read nothing on his face, but was afraid he could plainly see her feelings for him. She could not spend one more minute in such close quarters with

Davis Lee. That he was clear on the other side of the room didn't matter.

She left, going outside and into the street, her shadow stretching in front of her as she headed slowly back to the hotel. During a slight pause in the music, Josie heard the sound of thundering hooves. She looked back over her shoulder and caught a blur of movement out behind the livery stable.

Turning full around, she saw a man stumble out of the jail and fall to his knees on the landing. Jake Ross!

With the lively music from the Pearl playing behind her, Josie gathered her skirts and ran. As she reached the bottom step of the jailhouse, Jake slumped back against the wall, his features creased in agony.

She raced to the top of the stairs. "Jake! What happened?"

The deputy leaned his head back against the wall, staring at her, his black eyes dazed and glittering with pain. She saw a dark stain on the shoulder of his shirt and sank to her knees beside him. "You're hurt."

"McDougal. He's gone. Get Davis Lee."

McDougal had escaped? She felt her heart stop then start with a painful kick. She struggled to keep her mind on the injured man in front of her. "Let me help you get to Pearl's. Dr. Butler's there with the other wedding guests."

"I don't think I can make it that far."

"Will you be all right if I go for him?" She could scream for help, but no one had heard her that night in the alley. She didn't imagine anyone would hear her now over the music from inside the restaurant. "I don't want to leave you alone."

"If you're worried about McDougal, he won't come back this way." His voice was labored.

No, Josie supposed the outlaw would get as far away as he could. "How long ago did this happen?"

"Minutes."

"You should lie down."

"If I do, my head will explode. I'll stay real still next to this wall."

"Okay, I'm going." She hurried down the stairs. "Don't move!"

Heart pounding in her chest, she burst through the open door of the restaurant. The dance floor was still crowded. Her gaze shot around the room and she saw Matt Baldwin first, standing against the wall while he spoke to Charlie Haskell. Matt saw her and frowned.

She rushed over and quickly explained about the deputy and the escaped prisoner. "Could you bring Dr. Butler? I think I should get back to Jake. Ian hit him really hard."

"It's done. I'll be right behind you."

She could feel Davis Lee's gaze on her as she whirled and rushed outside. He would know something was wrong and most likely come, too.

She reached Jake and sank down beside him, holding her aching side.

"That was fast." The smile he gave her was wobbly, his eyes unfocused.

"Let me…look at your head." She dragged in deep lungfuls of air. "Matt's bringing…the doctor."

The shy man gingerly bent forward and Josie winced at the gash just behind his ear. Blood matted his dark hair and stained the collar of his gray shirt. There was a smear of red on the side of his neck.

She heard the rush of approaching footsteps and glanced over her shoulder. Davis Lee and his brother were in the front. They were followed by Dr. Butler and all three of the Baldwins. Josie rose, making room for the doctor.

The slender man knelt and examined the patient's head. "You're gonna need stitches, son."

Davis Lee crouched in front of the deputy. "What happened, Jake?"

"McDougal was coughing up a storm. Seemed like it wouldn't stop. Then he started screaming that he was hacking up blood. By the time I got in there, he was on the floor." Jake carefully touched the cut on his head, his words labored. "I saw blood on his shirt and some on the cot mattress. He sounded like he was strangling on it. I was afraid he would choke to death so I unlocked the cell and went in. As soon as I knelt down, he shoved me. When I lost my balance and fell, he grabbed my gun and hit me twice. He took my revolver, and one of the rifles is missing."

Davis Lee muttered a curse.

"I'm sorry," Jake began.

"It's not your fault. I would've gone in there, too, if I thought he was about to choke to death."

"I should've been more suspicious since he tried something like that with Cody a while back. McDougal hasn't been gone long." The injured man inhaled sharply when Dr. Butler touched his head again. "Saw him tear out behind the livery. For what it's worth, he headed north."

For Indian Territory. As the doctor cleaned Jake's wound, Davis Lee stood and stepped over to Josie. "Were you the one who found him?"

"Yes." This close to him she could smell his soap-and-leather scent. Almost feel the arousing sweep of his hands over her body.

A muscle worked in his jaw. "What were you doing outside?"

"I was walking back to the hotel." The same distrust that had been in his voice the morning he'd found out about her plan for Ian was back. Her temper spiked. "And yes, I know the hotel is in the opposite direction from the jail. I heard a galloping horse and turned. That's when I saw Jake and ran to check on him.''

He stared at her. ''You better not have had anything to do with this.''

She felt the blood drain from her face; she swayed. ''How can you say that to me?''

His gaze moved over her and she thought perhaps she saw regret in his eyes. A minute later she was convinced it was a trick of the glaring sunlight. His face hardened and he moved away, saying to his brother. ''I'm going after McDougal.''

''Want me to come?'' Riley offered.

''We'll come, too.'' J. T. Baldwin gestured to himself and both his sons.

Davis Lee shook his head. ''I can travel faster if I'm alone. If I need help, I'll send word. I don't expect a man with consumption to get far.''

''Especially if his condition is worsening,'' the doctor agreed. ''From what Jake saw, I'd say Ian is one sick man.''

J. T. Baldwin offered the use of his fastest horse.

Davis Lee thanked him. ''My buckskin's fast. I'll take her.''

Josie stood behind him, her nerves throbbing with hurt. Now that Jake was in good hands, she had no reason to stay. Trying to slip away unnoticed, she eased around Davis Lee. He turned his head and leveled a long, unreadable look at her. Woodenly, she started down the stairs.

''Thanks, Josie,'' Jake called in a faint voice.

''You're welcome.'' Her gaze swept the small group that had gathered around the jail.

Cora Wilkes and her brother stood behind J. T. Baldwin. Seeing the pinched look on the other woman's face, Josie wondered how her friend felt about her husband's murderer escaping.

At the bottom of the steps, Matt Baldwin offered her his

arm. "Would you let me walk you back, Miz Josie? You look a little wobbly."

"Thank you." She took his arm and they started toward the hotel.

Matt's presence kept her from bursting into tears. How could Davis Lee have said such a thing unless he were well and truly done with her?

Well, fine. She'd let her heart rule her emotions for too long. Her need for a man—for Davis Lee—had made her forget the vow she'd made to her parents. To William. She wouldn't forget again.

She managed to thank Matt and make it to her room before a sob broke from her. Trying to see through her tears, she went to the window. Davis Lee was still at the jail, but he wouldn't be for long.

Drying her eyes, she pushed away thoughts of everything except Ian McDougal and what he'd done to her family. Let the anger and loss strengthen her determination. Along with a box of matches, her hairbrush and tooth powder, she rolled a clean undergarment up in an extra bodice. She exchanged her plum alpaca silk for a blouse and her split skirt, then put on her sturdiest traveling boots and brown wool traveling coat.

When Davis Lee rode out, she would be right behind him.

Why had he said that to Josie? Davis Lee wondered. After what McDougal had done to her and her family, she wouldn't help the outlaw *escape*. Kill him maybe, but not let him go free.

Davis Lee watched her walk away, regret making him want to call back the words. If he were honest with himself, what he felt was more than regret over what he'd just said to her.

Watching her dance with those men at the Pearl had made him want to plow through the crowd and carry her out of there, but she had every right to dance with whom she wanted. *He* was the one who had ended things between them. The one who'd been betrayed. So why couldn't he stop thinking about her, *wanting* her?

After making sure Jake was going to be all right, Davis Lee locked up the now-empty jail and took off for the livery. The sun hung in a fiery ball just on the edge of the horizon. About an hour's worth of light remained.

After grabbing his bedroll and a couple of canteens, he was on his way. With the ground too hard to hold more than the faintest track, Davis Lee positioned himself so that the sun would cast a shadow over any patterns in the grass. He saw one. A flattened patch with pieces of grass and dirt scooped out of the earth, crescent-shaped like the curved top of a horseshoe.

McDougal was pushing his animal hard, still in the direction of Indian Territory. Davis Lee had no doubt that was the killer's planned destination since the McDougal gang had hidden in various places there over the years.

As Davis Lee rode, he tried to keep his mind off Josie. He wanted to stop wondering what she did every minute, wanted to forget how she'd felt beneath him, wanted to stop feeling the hurt she'd caused. He hadn't forgiven her for sleeping with him before telling him her secret, but he knew he couldn't walk away from her yet, either.

His brother was right, Davis Lee finally admitted. He loved Josie. He'd hurt her, and right now it didn't seem to matter that she'd hurt him, too. After he brought McDougal back to Whirlwind, he would talk to her and try to make amends.

Having settled that in his mind, he swept his gaze across the prairie. The setting sun turned the grass gold, tipped the scattered trees in red. A faint path of trampled grass was still visible. Davis Lee reined up and dismounted, running his hands over the broken grass. He gave a curt nod, sure that the tracks had been made by the same horse he'd been following.

He walked forward several feet; the tracks veered off to the right, then the left. Had more riders come this way? Or was McDougal trying to throw him off? These tracks wouldn't lead him much farther, and since it was nearly dark, he'd need to stop for the night.

Davis Lee started to swing back into the saddle when he saw something in the distance behind him. A speck of black against the horizon on top of a hill he'd crested some time ago. He couldn't tell for sure, but his instincts hammered that it was another rider.

McDougal? It was possible the outlaw had backtracked, either to change direction or to come up on Davis Lee from the rear. Needing to make sure who that rider was, he climbed back in the saddle.

She'd lost him. In more ways than one, Josie thought sadly as she reined up the gelding she'd rented from the livery and squinted through the settling darkness. Night spread over the gently sloping hills, making it look even more endless. They were headed north; she knew that and not much else.

She'd managed to leave town within minutes of Davis Lee and keep him in sight without alerting him to her presence. But a while back, the crest of one hill had given way to level ground on the other side. For as far as she could see, there was only grass and scrub brush, randomly scattered lines of mesquite, pine and oak trees. No doubt Davis Lee would've run his horse flat-out on this stretch of ground. She might never catch sight of him.

She would have to stop for the night. She had passed a creek about fifteen minutes ago. Though she didn't want to backtrack, she had to think of her horse. Frustration swirled inside her. Losing sight of Davis Lee could destroy any chance of her finding McDougal. But she couldn't see in the dark, and it would be foolish to risk injuring either herself or her mount.

Holding desperately to the hope that in the morning she would be able to recognize a sign that would lead her to the sheriff or McDougal, Josie turned the gelding around. When they reached the small stand of trees close to the creek she'd seen, she dismounted.

While the gelding drank his fill, she gathered up twigs and broke off what slender pine branches she could to use for a fire. She had filled her canteens earlier and could do so again in the morning.

The wind sweeping across the prairie had turned chilly once the sun set. Slipping into her traveling coat, she briefly considered going back to Whirlwind, but she kept picturing that night two years ago. The bloody images of her parents and William. Blinking back tears, she knew she wasn't going back, not when she finally had a chance to kill McDougal.

Having never spent the night outside, Josie looked around uneasily. Pulling out her pocket revolver, she quickly loaded it. The light was fading fast so she turned her energy to building a fire. Stacking the kindling inside the circle, she lit it with one of the matches she'd brought.

By the low-burning flames of her small fire, she unsaddled her horse, dumping the saddle onto the ground behind her and rubbing the gelding down with a handful of grass. The faraway howl of a coyote had her edging closer to her horse. Undoubtedly all manner of animals came out at night. That was one thing Josie hadn't given any thought. Sitting on the ground, much less sleeping there, seemed an invitation for anything to crawl over her. She'd heard cowboys slept on their saddled horses; she would try that.

With the gun a comforting weight in her coat pocket, she went in search of more kindling. The firelight cast a weak circle so she didn't wander far. As she started back with an armful of wood, her horse blew out a heavy breath. He stomped one foot, then blew again. She carefully put down the wood, then edged her way behind the nearest tree and pulled the revolver out of her pocket.

She peeked out to see what had disturbed the gelding. The wind strummed across the darkened prairie, teasing her skirt. In the shadows, Josie made out her horse, his head down as he grazed.

He seemed fine now. She started out from behind the tree and saw something move in the shadows beyond her gelding. Her breath jammed hard under her ribs. Another horse, saddled but riderless, grazed its way toward Josie's animal.

Where was the horse's rider? Was it McDougal? Would he come back this way? Trying not to panic, she carefully and quietly thumbed down the hammer on her revolver. In the next breath, a hand clapped over her mouth, another locked around her gun.

Her scream muffled, she was yanked back against an iron-hard chest. She tried to bite the rough palm on her face. Her gun was ripped out of her hand and tossed away before she could do more than land an elbow to a stomach that was as solid as stone. A grunt sounded as a powerful arm locked around her middle, squeezing her breath out.

"Don't scream." The harsh voice was male. And familiar. "It's me. All right?"

Davis Lee! She stiffened, then nodded. As soon as he released her, she whirled, pushing at him and whispering roughly, "You scared me to death!"

"I meant to!" He grabbed her by the shoulders, towering over her like a black shadow. "What are you doing out here?"

"How did you find me?" Still breathing hard, she nudged a loose strand of hair out of her eyes. "You were ahead of me."

He released her, his expression furious in the fire's yellow glow. "We don't have to whisper. I circled the whole area and we're the only people around."

"I lost sight of you sometime ago."

"I knew someone was behind me. I doubled back, hoping to come across McDougal, but instead I find you."

Josie didn't care how mad he was. She was relieved at no longer being alone. He picked up her gun and handed it to her. She slid it into her coat pocket while he strode through the grass to his horse and untied his bedroll. Carrying his blanket and his saddlebags, Davis Lee stalked back toward her.

"Are you staying?"

"Of course. I can't go any farther in the dark. And you can't—"

"I'm going to find McDougal," she said hotly. "I got this far, Davis Lee. You can say what you want, order me around all you want, but I'm not turning back."

"I know better than to expect you to go back and I don't have time to make sure you actually do it. The only choice I have is to take you with me. In case there's any question, I'm not happy about it."

"That's obvious."

He pinched the bridge of his nose, his voice strained with patience. "Josie, I know you want this guy. So do I. But what were you thinking to come out here?"

"I was thinking I could keep up with you, which I did." At his flat stare, she added, "Until a while ago."

He dragged a hand over his face, then pulled off his hat and dropped it onto his saddle. "Are you willing to go so far in your revenge against Ian that you'll risk your own life?"

"I don't think I'm risking my life any more than you are."

"I can hit where I aim."

"Well, so can I." Most of the time. She was glad he couldn't see her face burning. "I have my gun and ammunition. Matches and an extra canteen of water, a bedroll, a coat. I think I've done just fine."

He glared at her.

"It's my life to risk." Because of the shadows, she couldn't be sure, but she thought he paled at her words.

In the next instant, fury tightened his features and he clamped one hand around her upper arm, pulling her to him. "And what about my life? Has it occurred to you that what you're doing puts me at risk? Makes me have to divide my attention between you and him, makes me less likely to anticipate something he might do. Did you think about that?"

"No," she said, suddenly feeling selfish.

"Your being out here alone isn't smart, Josie. What if your horse went lame? Or you ran out of water? Or you were hurt?"

"You don't need to worry about me." She tried to pull away from him. "I didn't come here to make things harder for you. I came because I had to."

"What if McDougal had been the one to find you?" he roared. "Josie, I couldn't—" He broke off, grabbed her face in his hands.

For an instant, she thought he would kiss her.

Moving his hands back to grip her upper arms, he stared at her, his face dark, his eyes glittering. "I don't like you being here."

She was bone-tired and sick of the friction between them. "You don't have to stay with me. I got this far. I'll get where I need to without you."

"Stop."

"You stop! It will be better if we separate. You can't concentrate with me around and I…can't, either."

His hands tightened on her. "I'm sure as hell not leaving you alone."

"I don't want you to stay."

"Well, I am."

"Why? So you can remind me over and over of how I hurt you, how I ruined things, how I betrayed you? Believe me, I know. I know it every single minute." The words felt choked out of her. "Please, let's don't say any more. When this is over, I'll go away. You won't have to see me ever again."

"Go away?" He went utterly still, his eyes hot with emotion. "You mean after you kill McDougal?"

"I owe it to my family."

"You owe them justice. And you can get that with Judge Satterly."

"We don't know that. Look what happened the last time Ian was supposed to be tried."

"Do you know what you're saying? Do you know what that means?" He released her and took a step back. "I'm the law. If you kill him in cold blood—if you even *try*— I'll have to do something about it."

"Like what? Arrest me?"

"Yes. I can't turn a blind eye, Josie. I won't. I'll haul you back to Whirlwind and lock you in the cell next to McDougal's."

She studied him, bitterness warring with understanding. "You've sworn an oath to do what you have to do, Davis Lee. So have I."

Hands clenched, he stalked to the other side of the fire and spread out his bedroll.

"What are you doing?"

"Getting some sleep. I suggest you do the same. We're going to need it."

She hated this distance between them. Numbly, she

picked up her bedroll and stepped on the saddle to mount the gelding.

Davis Lee put his hands on his hips. "Where are you going?"

"Nowhere. I'm sleeping up here."

"You'll fall off."

"No, I won't." She probably would.

"Dammit, bring your bedroll over here by the fire."

"I don't want to sleep next to you when you're so mad."

He looked up at the sky, a muscle working in his jaw. "It's safer if we're together."

"Doesn't feel like it."

"Have it your way." Muttering under his breath, he eased down to his blanket, turning his head to look at her. "If you're really going to sleep on your horse, don't put him under a tree. Snakes fall out of the branches sometimes."

Snakes? She immediately stepped off the saddle, considering the space he'd left for her between him and the fire. Irritated as all get-out, she stomped over and spread her bedroll.

She lay down and drew her blanket over her shoulders. It was nice and warm here. And though she wouldn't admit it to Davis Lee, she felt safer with him at her back.

"The fire will keep away the bugs," he mumbled sleepily. "The horses will keep anything bigger at bay."

Josie watched the fire slowly die. Despite Davis Lee's even breathing, she knew he wasn't asleep. Would he ever forgive her for using him to get information on McDougal? For sleeping with him with a huge secret between them?

She rolled to her back, looking up at the black velvet sky. Beside her she could feel Davis Lee's body heat. "The sky's really clear tonight. There must be a million stars up there."

He didn't speak.

"I can't stop seeing my parents' bloody bodies, and William's.'' Her voice cracked. ''I can't let Ian get away again. I just *can't.*''

Again Davis Lee said nothing. Her throat grew tight. ''I hope someday you'll believe that I truly care for you. And that you'll forgive me.''

She turned her head and looked at him. The firelight played across the lean angles of his face, tipped his eyelashes with gold. She wanted to reach over and touch him. Instead, she rolled to her side away from him and went to sleep.

The next morning at first light, Josie felt Davis Lee stir. She woke, tucked warmly against him. Neither of them spoke as they ate a few of the biscuits Davis Lee had brought, some of her cheese. After drinking their fill from the canteens, they refilled them from the creek. They were soon on their way.

Josie rode slightly behind him so as not to disturb any tracks he might see on either side of the horses. Her heart aching, she let her gaze trace the strong line of his back, the broad shoulders, his big hands.

She loved him, but she had also sworn a vow to others she loved. Now, all she had left was that vow.

Chapter Eighteen

Though he wasn't thrilled that Josie was tagging along, Davis Lee couldn't find fault with her efforts. She quietly kept up with his pace, didn't become impatient when he stopped to check the tracks.

They'd ridden ahead for an hour and found more than one set of tracks. The ones that looked freshest were headed in the direction from where they'd come. He and Josie turned their horses around and rode back. He kept a careful eye on the ground; Josie stayed slightly behind so as not to compromise anything new he might find.

They were past their campsite and about an hour or so from Whirlwind when he stopped and dismounted near a line of trees. He knelt, studied the ground then walked back to her. "There are some specks on the grass. I think they're blood."

"Blood!"

"Jake said McDougal was coughing up blood last night. Maybe he still is."

"Do you think we might be close to finding him?"

"I don't know. I want to walk ahead a bit and see if I come across any more."

She nodded.

He motioned her down. "You need to stay with me."

"Afraid I'll get to him first?" she asked coolly.

He looked right at her. "I don't want him getting to you."

"Oh." That shut her up.

"We need to be prepared if we find him," he said quietly. "Since he's sickly, he always has his gun at the ready. Aimed. Cocked. Understand?"

"Yes."

"That's why I'm letting you keep your weapon. If McDougal shoots first, you have a right to defend yourself. Understand?"

"Yes."

They hadn't walked more than ten feet when he paused next to a mesquite tree and held up his hand. She stopped behind him. Someone coughed repeatedly, sharp and hard. Davis Lee's gaze swerved to hers.

The noise came from their left, behind a screen of pines and a few half-grown juniper trees. Josie followed Davis Lee, trying to move as quietly as he did, her hand going to the revolver in her pocket.

They heard more coughing, then a strangled "Who are you?"

Davis Lee eased around the first tree, his gun drawn. To her left, Josie heard the crackle of dried leaves and twigs. She turned and saw someone run out of the stand of trees into a small clearing. Automatically, she took off after them.

Davis Lee hissed her name, but she didn't stop. If the person she'd seen was McDougal, he couldn't get away. Not again.

She dodged a few trees and came out in a small clearing. About thirty feet away, Ian stood with his back to her. A few yards in front of the outlaw, a man held a gun on him. Loren Barnes!

"Josie!" He sounded pained. "I know you followed Davis Lee to chase this piece of filth, but why?"

"He killed my family."

"Then you understand."

She heard the thud of boots as Davis Lee rushed up behind her. Loren thumbed down the hammer on his revolver.

Josie cried out, "Loren, don't! Think about Cora!"

"I am! You know how she's suffered. All because of this murdering bastard."

"If something happens to you, it will be worse for her."

"I have to do this." His voice was cold, clear.

"Put the gun down, Barnes," Davis Lee ordered, cocking his revolver.

Loren's face went blank, but his eyes burned with purpose. Josie cried out as he shot at McDougal, who threw himself on the ground then scrambled to a half-sitting position.

Davis Lee fired at Cora's brother. McDougal squeezed off two more shots. In her direction! Josie ducked. Out of the corner of her eye, she saw Davis Lee do the same.

Loren bolted, disappearing behind a pine tree. Ian now lay on the ground, his shirt stained with blood. She didn't know if it was from his lung condition, a bullet wound or both. She stepped toward him and saw more blood at the top of his shirtsleeve.

He grabbed his arm, squinted up at her. "Hey, I know you."

"Yes." Josie stared at him. Finally, the man who'd killed her parents was in front of her. And he couldn't escape, not this time. She brought her own gun up, snared in a vacuum of memory.

All she could see were her mother's sightless eyes, her father's hand reaching for his wife. William's hand clenched around a handkerchief she'd given him just after he'd proposed. Josie leveled her gun at the outlaw, pleased when she saw fear flare in his eyes. Maybe the same kind of fear that her parents and William had felt. She felt a strange sense of power that she could do that to him.

She was close enough that she couldn't miss. She wouldn't. "I've been waiting for you a long time, Ian."

"Lady, I'm already shot. Don't fill me full of lead."

It was quiet behind her. Too quiet. And she realized, as if coming out of a fog, that Davis Lee hadn't tried to stop her. He hadn't said anything for a long time.

She turned and saw him lying motionless on his back, eyes closed. Blood seeped from his side. "No!"

She rushed to him, falling on her knees.

Setting her gun aside, she found a pulse in his neck and shook his shoulder, trying to rouse him. She jerked off her coat, then her bodice and pressed it to his side. It was blood-soaked within seconds. "Davis Lee, please wake up."

His eyes stayed closed. He didn't move.

"Please don't die," she cried. "Please talk to me."

He stirred, his eyes opening to slits. "Josie?"

"I'm here." She took a breath, trying to steady herself. "You're hurt and I don't know how badly. I need to get you to a doctor, but I can't get you up."

"I think...I can do it."

"How?"

He pushed himself to one elbow, a groan tearing from his throat.

Josie bit her lip.

"Bring my horse."

She didn't want to leave him, but it was his only chance for help. Scooping up her coat, she pulled it on over her underwear as she ran back the way they'd come. She led Davis Lee's buckskin over. "What do I do?"

"Bring her here. Stand her with her left side to me, like I would normally mount."

She did it.

"I need something to grab on to once I stand up. I'm pretty woozy."

"You can hang on to me."

Balancing his weight on his right arm, he pushed himself to his feet, teetered. He clutched at the saddle as Josie braced one shoulder under his right arm. She didn't see any fresh blood coming from his wound. Maybe she'd stopped the bleeding for now. She held tight to his arm as he grabbed the saddle horn with his right hand and after a moment hoisted himself up, muscles straining in his arms and shoulders, his neck.

Cursing, he dragged his right leg over. Breathing hard, he slumped forward, his head resting against the horse's neck.

Josie picked up her gun and turned to see Ian scrambling away. Her finger went to the trigger and she started after him. There was nothing and no one to stop her from killing him.

Except the feelings she had for the man who leaned in the saddle, bleeding. Her head urged her to go after McDougal, but her heart… She looked back at Davis Lee. Her love for Davis Lee burned stronger than her need to go after the outlaw who'd murdered her family.

Decision made, Josie ran back to her own horse, mounted, then returned to take Davis Lee's horse's reins and lead him to Whirlwind.

"Davis Lee, hold on. You have to hold on." The words pounded through her brain.

She kept talking to him, checking to make sure he was still breathing. He couldn't die. She couldn't lose another person to McDougal.

McDougal. She could've easily killed him and she hadn't. She waited for the swell of anger that she always felt when thinking of Ian, the loathing that had dogged her for the past two years, but neither came. She looked back at Davis Lee, offering up a silent prayer that she could get help in time.

Ian had escaped. Again. And she found she didn't care. All that mattered was that Davis Lee lived.

A couple of hours later, Davis Lee was in his own bed being tended by Catherine. Josie paced in and out of his bedroom. He'd been unconscious for a while now. Jericho and Riley had met up with her just outside of town, on their way to help look for McDougal.

While Charlie Haskell went for Catherine, Jericho and Riley got Davis Lee into bed. A few minutes later, the nurse asked both men to hold the patient down while she removed the bullet in his side.

Josie stood in the kitchen with her eyes squeezed shut. When she heard a raw moan of pain tear out of his throat, her knees buckled. Charlie caught her and settled her in a chair. She was still trying to take in all that had happened. Cora's brother, Loren, had been the one to try and kill McDougal in the jail that night. He'd found Ian today because last night, Loren, like the others there, had heard Jake tell Davis Lee which direction the outlaw was headed. And now Cora's brother had vanished like McDougal. She didn't care what happened to Ian, but she worried about Loren.

Catherine stepped out of Davis Lee's bedroom, interrupting Josie's thoughts. The dark-haired woman's white apron was streaked with blood as were the rolled-up sleeves of her blue wool dress.

Josie stood, her hands trembling. "Is he—"

"He's going to be all right," the other woman said.

"Thank you," she breathed.

"But he's lost a lot of blood and will be weak for a while. He needs rest and food."

"I'll make sure he gets it."

Jericho and Riley stepped out of the room. Riley jerked a thumb over his shoulder. "He's asking for you, Josie."

"Thank you." She rushed past them and went to the right side of his bed to avoid jostling his wound. "Davis Lee?"

"Come here," he said in a guttural voice.

She sat down carefully, taking the hand he held out to her. "Catherine said you're going to be all right."

"You didn't kill him." His blue eyes were bleak with pain. "You had McDougal in your sights and you didn't take a shot. Why not?"

She didn't want any more lies between them, but would he believe her?

"Josie?" he asked hoarsely.

She stroked his hand. "The reason I didn't shoot Ian is because I love you. Even if we don't see each other after this, I want you to know that."

"I'm fadin'." His eyes closed, but his fingers tightened on hers. "Promise you won't leave."

"I promise."

He slept and she did, too. When she woke, he was sitting up in bed, still holding her hand. "Do you need anything?"

"Just you." He tugged her over into his lap and rested his head against hers.

He was warm and solid beneath her. For the first time since she'd seen him bleeding on the ground, she truly felt he would be all right. "I shouldn't be in your lap. You're going to hurt yourself."

"I wasn't shot there."

She smiled into his eyes, wanting to remember every second with him. No matter where she went, he would be part of her.

"Before I passed out, you said you loved me," he said huskily.

She kept her gaze on his, her stomach knotting. "Yes."

"You said you told me that in case we never saw each other again. Are you planning to leave?"

"I thought I should."

For a long minute, he didn't speak. She studied her hands. She should get up, end things cleanly, but she couldn't make herself move. Not yet.

"I have regrets in my life, Josie." He slid a knuckle under her chin and tilted her face up. "If I let you walk away from me, I'll regret that for the rest of my days."

"Really?"

"I can't let you go. Don't leave. I love you."

She stilled, half-afraid she was hearing things. "Even though I lied?"

"That went deep," he admitted. "But it doesn't change the way I feel."

"Have you forgiven me? *Can* you? Will you be sorry someday for loving me?"

"You showed me what's in your heart, Josie. You turned away from revenge, from murder. What would make me sorry is if I lost you."

"You won't." She lifted a hand and stroked his whisker-stubbled jaw. "I won't go. I won't ever go."

He kissed her, soft and slow and so thoroughly that when he lifted his head, she melted against him, feeling as if she were floating in a dream.

"You know…" Careful of the bruise on her jaw, he nudged her head back and nuzzled her throat. "Everyone saw you come into my house, an unmarried woman alone with an unmarried man. And—" he lowered his voice to a deep velvet whisper "—people have seen you in my bedroom. All sorts of rumors will fly now."

"The only ones who saw me in here were your brother, Catherine and Jericho. They won't say anything."

"Well, I have a reputation to think of," he said. "You have to make an honest man of me."

She laughed. "What do you mean?"

"You know what I mean. You're gonna have to marry me."

She sat straight up, staring into his eyes. "Davis Lee!"

"Is that a yes?"

"Have you thought this through?"

He nodded, his gaze hot on her.

"Are you sure?"

"Yes."

She looked down at herself, grimacing. "My hair is a mess and my dress—"

"Josie," he groaned. "Answer me before I expire."

"Yes." She laughed. "Yes, I'll—"

He took her mouth in a sweet, hot kiss.

Long seconds or minutes later, the front door burst open. They jerked apart at his brother came into the bedroom.

"Riley," Davis Lee growled. "This better be good."

"You're never gonna believe this!"

The grin on his brother's face was infectious and Josie found herself smiling, too.

"Loren Barnes just rode into town with Ian McDougal hog-tied and slung over his saddle. Jericho's putting them both in jail right now."

"Loren *and* Ian?" Davis Lee's jaw dropped. "That beats all."

"Just thought you'd want to know." With a knowing twinkle in his eye, Riley's gaze shifted from Josie to his brother. "Carry on."

As soon as the door shut, Josie turned to Davis Lee. "I guess Ian's trial can go on as scheduled."

His gaze was soft on her face. "I want to get married right now."

"Right now?" Josie about fell out of his lap. "No."

"What do you mean no?" he demanded. "You said you would."

"Davis Lee, you've just been shot."

"When then? Don't make me wait. Do you want a wedding like Catherine's? I don't think I can wait as long as Jericho did."

"No, I don't want a wedding like Catherine's, but I would like you to be able to stand up when we get married."

"Tomorrow."

"I'm not going anywhere. We can wait until you're healed."

"Tomorrow." He kissed his way along her jaw, down the side of her neck then gently sank his teeth into the curve where her shoulder began.

"All right," she murmured. "Tomorrow."

He chuckled. "You didn't even try to bargain with me."

She brought his head back to hers. "That's because I already have what I want."

He folded her hand in his and placed them both over her heart. "Me, too."

"Now, about that wedding—"

Eyes laughing, he kissed the starch right out of her.

*   *   *   *   *

Harlequin Historicals®
Historical Romantic Adventure!

TRAVEL BACK TO THE FUTURE
FOR ROMANCE—WESTERN-STYLE!
ONLY WITH HARLEQUIN HISTORICALS.

ON SALE JANUARY 2005

TEXAS LAWMAN by Carolyn Davidson

Sarah Murphy will do whatever it takes to save her nephew
from dangerous fortune seekers—including marrying lawman
Blake Caulfield. Can the Lone Star lawman keep them
safe—without losing his heart to the feisty lady?

WHIRLWIND GROOM by Debra Cowan

Desperate to avenge the murder of her parents, all trails lead
Josie Webster to Whirlwind, Texas, much to the chagrin of
charming sheriff Davis Lee Holt. Let the games begin as
Davis Lee tries to ignore the beautiful seamstress who stirs
both his suspicions and his desires....

ON SALE FEBRUARY 2005

PRAIRIE WIFE by Cheryl St.John

Jesse and Amy Shelby find themselves drifting apart after
the devastating death of their young son. Can they put
their grief behind them and renew their deep and abiding
love—before it's too late?

THE UNLIKELY GROOM by Wendy Douglas

Stranded by her brother in a rough-and-rugged Alaskan
gold town, Ashlynne Mackenzie is forced to rely on the
kindness of saloon owner Lucas Templeton. But kindness
has nothing to do with Lucas's urges to both protect the
innocent woman and to claim her for his own.

Harlequin Romance®

Contract Brides

From paper marriage...to wedded bliss?

A wedding dilemma:

What should a sexy, successful bachelor do if he's too busy
making millions to find a wife? Or if he finds the perfect
woman, and just has to strike a bridal bargain...?

The perfect proposal:

The solution? For better, for worse, these grooms in a hurry
have decided to sign, seal and deliver the ultimate
marriage contract...to buy a bride!

Coming Soon to

HARLEQUIN®
Romance®

featuring the favorite miniseries Contract Brides:

THE LAST-MINUTE MARRIAGE
by Marion Lennox, #3832
on sale February 2005

A WIFE ON PAPER
by award-winning author Liz Fielding, #3837
on sale March 2005

VACANCY: WIFE OF CONVENIENCE
by Jessica Steele, #3839
on sale April 2005

Available wherever Harlequin books are sold.

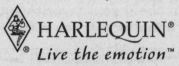

HARLEQUIN®
Live the emotion™

www.eHarlequin.com

If you enjoyed what you just read,
then we've got an offer you can't resist!

Take 2 bestselling love stories FREE!

Plus get a FREE surprise gift!

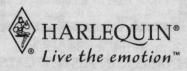